Sworn Loyalty

A Medieval Romance

The Sword of Glastonbury Series

Book 7

Lisa Shea

First Printing: September 2013

- 9 -

Print version ISBN-13 978-0-9855564-3-3

Listen to the wisdom of elders –
Then forge your own path.

Sworn Loyalty

Chapter 1

England, 1196

It is not death that a man should fear,
But he should fear never beginning to live.
-- Marcus Aurelius

Mary paused for a long moment before the pockmarked door of the Mangy Cur Tavern. Raucous shouts and harsh laughter made the dilapidated building shudder as if it were groaning in pain. She glanced around in the deepening twilight, her breath puffing crystalline in the biting air. There were no other travelers visible as the meager dirt road twisted into gloomy forest on either side. It was as if this one isolated clearing, with its scum-coated pond, shuttered tavern, and tumbled-down stables, was all that existed in the world.

She took in a deep breath, let it out, then pushed open the door.

A rough cheer of welcome rang in her ears, and it took all her willpower not to tug up on the low-cut bodice of her scarlet dress. She drew her worn tambourine from her hip with a gloved hand and waved it high overhead, sending a shimmer of sound into the crowd. The room was layered with dense, fragrant wood smoke. On all sides burly, scarred men sprawled at tables cluttered with half-empty mugs.

A stumpy, dark-haired man stood at the back of the tavern, his eyes sharp on her. "I knew you'd be back!" he crowed with satisfaction. "Barkeep, a mead for our songbird."

A path cleared for Mary. Her emotions roiled as she approached the stocky man. She was well aware that Caradoc's marked attentions afforded her protection from the rest of the gang. At the same time, the *wolf's head* was dangerous. He had well earned his outlaw status, the designation that he could be slain on sight like a rabid dog. His keen knife had found its way into countless backs throughout the county. His fiery temper could turn on the point of a pin. If she were to survive the next few weeks, and accomplish her mission, she would have to walk a delicate line.

The grimy stool at his side was vacated by one of his many bull-sized henchmen. She took it with a wave of her tambourine, then nodded gratefully to the flame-haired bartender who handed over a mug.

Caradoc thunked his substantial weight back down onto his own stool, then glared at the two other men at the table. "I told you she'd return, so pay up. Even though you're my brothers, you'll hand over what you owe."

Espan and Arbert were cut from the same cloth as their older brother – stocky, dark-haired, sporting heavy brows over brutish faces. They might have been twins, but for the twisted nose Arbert featured and the pair of hairy moles on Espan's left cheek. The men reluctantly dug into the leather pouches at their sides, handing over the coins to the delighted winner.

Mary took a long drink of her mead, her eyes scanning the rough crowd in the guttering torchlight. How long had she been out on her task? Three weeks? Four? The days and nights were running together in one endless, grime-smeared blur. She longed for the solid walls of her keep, the strict but predictable routine she had followed since she was eleven.

She gave a sharp shake of her head. She had known, all those years, that her privileged lifestyle came with an unshakable obligation. She was honor-bound to serve as guardian angel for Erik, whether he wanted it or not; whether he even knew of it or not.

From all reports it seemed she'd finally be able to fulfill her duty.

Caradoc's spittle spewed across the deeply veined table as he laughed, tucking the last coin into the bulging pouch at his side. He drew down a long pull on his ale, then turned to smile at Mary. "They said you might have gone south, to London," he growled, "but I knew better." His eyes took on a crafty look. "You know, if you joined our band, you wouldn't have to go from tavern to tavern to keep your tips fresh. I could take care of *all* your needs."

Mary forced her smile to stay bright. "I like to be my own master," she stated, holding his gaze. "Just like you. I am sure you understand."

His eyes grew smoky. "Indeed I do," he murmured, leaning forward. "Kindred spirits."

Mary downed the rest of her mead, grabbed up her tambourine with her left hand, and gave it a shimmering rattle as she stood. It had the desired effect – Caradoc sat back, a pleased smile spreading on his lips. The room's roar eased off as well, and a circle of attentive eyes focused on her. She felt uncomfortably like a doe in the center of a pack of wolves, and the image wasn't far off from the truth. Nearly every man here was a member of Caradoc's band; they would follow him without question. She could only hope that the news from her contacts was wrong, that Erik was not being drawn in as a sacrifice to this bloodthirsty crew.

The front door creaked open, and Mary's blood ran cold.

She had only seen Erik in person that one time, a full decade ago, but there was no mistaking the man who stepped across the threshold. He was tall, lean, with short-cropped blond hair and the controlled grace of a stalking panther. He wore a chestnut-colored leather jerkin over matching leggings, and a long sword hung at his hip. She knew through personal experience what the rigorous training regimen at the keep entailed. Michael, the Master at Arms, still spoke of Erik's skill at every turn. Erik's exploits in the Holy Land in the intervening years were nothing short of legendary.

Erik's eyes swept around the room, judging, calculating, and she held in a flinch as his gaze momentarily connected with hers. She needn't have bothered – he was scanning for dangers, nothing more. There was no way for him to connect the lithe, raven-haired gypsy woman in this den of thieves with the young, shy girl he'd once met in a quiet farming village.

Satisfied, he turned, putting a hand behind him to draw in a stunning blonde woman in an elegant forest-green dress. This time Mary knew she did not quite hold back the tremor of anger which coursed through her, but it did not matter. All eyes were focused on the newcomer, on the long, curled ringlets of gold which cascaded down her back and the sensuous curve of her ruby-red lips.

Erik's voice was a low mutter, but in the silence of the tavern Mary had no trouble hearing every word. "Lynessa, are you sure you wish to take your rest here?"

The woman's eyes grew bright, almost predatory, and she nodded, taking a step forward. "Absolutely. My cook said they had the worst mead here she had ever tasted, and I have five pounds on a bet. I can't believe it's more disgusting than that hell-hole in Augustine, but there's only one way to be sure."

A rumbling growl circled around the edges of the room, and Erik's hand eased to the hilt of his sword. His mouth set into a thin line.

"Lynessa, I think –"

She took a step forward, giving a delicate sniff. "Although, judging by the odor here, perhaps my cook was right after all."

Mary shook herself free of the shock which had nearly frozen her. After so long, after the years of training and the weeks of waiting, it was still hard for her to accept just how mercenary Lynessa was, how ruthlessly she was willing to discard Erik now that he no longer served her purposes. Lynessa had even neatly arranged it so Caradoc and his men would be drawn into the chaos, and they themselves would be brought down.

Mary did not mind the latter one bit, but she absolutely had to prevent the former.

There was a movement at her side, and she glanced over. Caradoc rose menacingly to his feet, by all looks a dominant bull preparing to stomp an intruder into a bloody pulp.

She knew she had only seconds in which to act. Mary took a dancing step in front of Caradoc, whirling her tambourine up with a glint of shimmering gold, drawing all eyes to her. Lynessa blinked in astonishment, her mouth hanging open.

Mary's smile grew into an authentic grin. Lynessa hadn't planned for *this* in her intricate schemes and machinations.

Mary pitched her voice to be condescending but patient. "Oh, Lynessa, my dear, is this really the limit of your planning skills? I had hoped for something a little more elegant."

It was another moment before Lynessa was able to close her mouth and pull herself up in an affronted huff. "What in the world are you talking about?"

Mary gave a wave in the air with her tambourine hand, releasing a delicate trill of sound. "I was telling Caradoc just the other day that I'd seen the sheriff's men in the area. Now here you are, and you just happen to þe stirring up trouble." She draped Erik with a dismissive glance. His fingers were wrapped around his sword hilt, his eyes carefully sweeping the antagonized group of men. "Let me guess," she continued. "You draw Caradoc's fine band of men into attacking your pet, and when they heroically defend their home, you send the sheriff and his team after them?"

Caradoc was at her side, his greasy hair nearly bristling with anger. His two brothers were close behind. "Maybe it's time we taught that damned Sheriff a lesson," he growled. "Starting with this whelp here."

The mood in the room crackled with energy, and Mary clung desperately to her path. If she could not divert the thieves now, Erik would be slain. All she had worked for would be lost.

Lost forever.

She pitched her voice low, low enough that Caradoc would think it meant for him alone, but she held her body pointed at Erik. She hoped with every ounce of her being that the man contained a shred of instinct for self-preservation.

"Dear Caradoc, you are no man's master," she insisted in a seductive purr. "Least of all that arrogant sheriff. Yes, you want to make them pay. But do it on your *own* terms, on your own schedule. Choose your own location." Her voice became husky.

"Create an epic tale which will ring in the great halls for centuries to come."

Caradoc's eyes lit up at that, and Mary warmed with the slightest kindle of hope. She had studied him carefully for weeks now, preparing for this eventuality, and her research might just pay off. If there was one thing Caradoc craved, it was to build a legacy for his name.

Caradoc puffed up his shoulders, tossing his hair back as he strode forward to stand before Erik. His head only came up to Erik's chin, but with his barrel chest and muscled hands … Mary held in a shiver. It would be an even enough contest just between those two, never mind the twenty rabid men who ringed them.

Caradoc's voice was the soft growl of a wolf. "*I am* the master here," he stated, "and I will not have our sanctuary disturbed by the likes of you. Go, and take that pale trollop along with you." Lynessa gave a soft cry of outrage, but bit it back when Caradoc's amber gleam swung around to pin her. After a moment Caradoc returned his gaze back to Erik. "Do not think this is the end," he warned, his voice deceptively quiet. "No matter where you hide, no matter who you hide behind, we are everywhere. We will find you, and we will have our fun. On our own terms. In a place of our own choosing."

Mary had no doubt that any other man would have been running for the door, pleading for his life, scampering from the palpable threat which pulsed in the smoky air. But Erik took his time, his eyes making a slow circuit of the men in the room, drawing around to –

His gaze settled on hers, and Mary gasped as if an electric shock had coursed through her. For so long there had only been that one painting over the keep's fireplace, the eyes dead and stagnant. But this Erik was vibrantly alive, full of passionate energy, and the corners of his eyes creased with dawning understanding. She was not sure what he thought he knew, but she prayed to God that he would turn and leave before all Hell broke loose.

He nodded, and then he was taking Lynessa by the arm, stepping back toward the door, and ushering her through. He gave one last look to the room before closing the door behind them.

Mary leapt into the center of the room, shimmering her tambourine in triumph and raising her voice high. "Caradoc!" she cried out, hoping with all her heart to distract the men - to give Erik the cover he needed to safely get away. "Caradoc!"

The cries were taken up on all sides, tankards of ale were raised in toasts, and at long last Mary's breaths came in full, even draws.

Caradoc's eyes glazed in fury. "When I find him, I will kill him myself," he vowed. "I will break every bone in his body!"

"I know you will," encouraged Mary, taking the mug of mead that the barkeep pressed into her hand. "But make sure he is brought to you unharmed! You want to savor every moment of his punishment for yourself."

Flames of delight blossomed in Caradoc's eyes, and he climbed onto a nearby table. The surface groaned under his weight, but held steady.

"You men!" he cried out to the roiling masses. "Tomorrow we will go out to hunt down this Erik. But I want to make it clear – he is *mine*. He is to be brought to me without one scratch on him. And then we shall have an arena!"

Cries of delight and anticipation thundered around her, ringing in her ears. She hoped by all that was Holy that she could get to Erik before Caradoc's clan put into motion their plans for revenge.

Chapter 2

Mary drew in a deep breath, wrapping her heavy, black cloak close against the late afternoon chill. The tambourine hooked at her hip dug into her flesh, and she adjusted it to the left. She carefully stepped across the courtyard, watching for the pushed-up stones which protruded in dense constellations before the central tower. As she had hoped, Espan and Arbert had been more than happy to open the main gates to her and send her through. She could see three other men on the walls, but no more, and she mouthed a prayer in thanks. Success tonight would be a miracle of the highest degree. She would light candles at the chapel every blessed day without fail if she and Erik survived this.

She shook her head as she approached the door. She had not in a million years thought Caradoc would act so quickly against Erik. She had assumed she would be granted two or three days in which to plan her next move. Instead, less than a full day had passed before news came that Erik had been captured and was being held in the abandoned watchtower.

Mary shuddered. Caradoc was, at this very minute, out gathering up every last member of his clan of wolves' heads for a gathering of massive proportions. By tomorrow night a full fifty men would be present for drinking, gambling, and the Grand Arena.

She could only hope that her guidance last night in the tavern had been successful. If Erik was truly unhurt, she might have a chance. If not ...

She pushed open the door with a gloved hand, stepping into the small anteroom and shouldering the door shut behind her to hold out the sharp breeze. An unkempt, lanky man with mouse-brown hair glanced up from his chair in the corner where he sat by a small fire.

His eyes sharpened with delight as he took her in. "Caradoc ain't here," he snapped. "He's out with the men. Be back tomorrow morning."

She drew her lips into a smile. "Ah, Wymon. I am not here for Caradoc," she assured him. "I am here for you and for the guards below."

His beady eyes widened at that, and a lecherous grin grew on his face. "That is the best news I've heard all day," he murmured, drawing to his feet. "I claim first dibs on you then."

She gave a regretful shake to her head. "I am afraid I go down and take care of the others first," she sighed.

Wymon took a step forward with a surly frown, and she put her hands out to forestall him. "This way you get me all night long," she pointed out. "As soon as I am done with them, I am all yours."

A wolfish grin spread across his face, and he waved a hand toward the sturdy door at the side of the room. "Better get started, then."

Mary took a step toward the door, then turned to look at him over her shoulder. "No fair peeking, now," she advised him. "No matter what you hear, you just wait up here for me. That way it will be all fresh and new to you when I return."

He gave a sharp laugh at that, sitting back down on the worn stool. "That won't be a problem," he promised. "They sunk those dungeons deep, so the screams of the victims wouldn't disrupt the feasting of the delicate highborn." He rubbed his hands toward the fire. "Make all the noise you want."

Mary smiled at that, then turned to the door.

Wymon hadn't been exaggerating about the depth of the structure. As she continued to descend the spiral staircase past guttering torches and skittering rats, Mary began to believe all the tales she'd heard about the torture that went on here.

By the time she reached the small landing at the staircase's foot a visceral force was pressing in against her chest, restricting her breathing. She took a moment to settle herself - to focus on the task at hand. The door before her was banded with iron and featured a small grate at eye level.

She peered in.

Thank God, he seemed unhurt.

Erik wore the same dark leather from the tavern. His arms were tied with rope to metal rings high on the wall, out at forty-five degree angles from his head. There was a dark smudge on one cheek, but overall it looked like Caradoc's men had heeded her suggestion and brought him in unharmed.

Now all she had to do was get him back out again.

She let her breath out, the tambourine gave the softest of chimes, and to her surprise his eyes flashed up to hold hers. The blue-grey gaze swept with confusion, then melded with understanding and alarm.

He gave his head the smallest of shakes.

She gave a wry smile. She was certainly not going to back down now.

She gave a sharp rap to the door, and there was a scrambling noise from the left. In short order five men were striding toward the door. She looked them over as they approached the window, counting her blessings. Caradoc had left his weaker men to guard the shackled prisoner, leaving the better fighters up on the wall. It would serve her well.

The taller one, with a shock of flame-red hair, stepped up to the window. Mary recognized him as Geoff, brother to the barkeep at the tavern. His voice was thin and reedy. "Mary, is that you?"

She slid a welcoming purr into her voice. "In the flesh," she agreed. She unhooked her tambourine, drawing it up to give it a shimmer of sound. "I have come to keep you lads company for a while."

Geoff had the door open before she finished speaking, his eyes roaming her with heated pleasure. "Come in, come in," he welcomed. "We were just having some ale and discussing how Caradoc would bloody Erik first. You know, for the pre-fight entertainment. What do you think – wild dogs, perhaps?"

They piled back onto their stools, and Geoff had a mug before her in a flash, filling it to the brim with ale. "Stan here thinks it'll be a boar," he added. "But I think Caradoc wouldn't want to hurt the man *too* much before the main attraction began."

Mary gave a hearty laugh. "Whatever it starts with, it'll end with his death!" she cried out with rich pleasure. "To the fight!" She raised her mug in a toast. The men clunked their own mugs against hers, and then she brought the ale to her lips, drinking it down in one long swallow.

The men looked at her with delight, then promptly did the same, wiping their mouths off on their sleeves when they were done.

Mary flashed a brilliant smile at them. "Another round!" There was a cheer as the ale was poured out, and once again she raised her mug. "Here's to Geoff – I bet five pounds on Geoff's brilliant gamble. The first challenge Erik will take on will be a pack of wild dogs."

Geoff's eyes lit up with pleasure. "To wild dogs!" Mary brought the mug to her lips, and the men raced to drink down their ale before she did. She paused, as if contemplating something, then absently put her mug down. She stood and walked toward Erik.

She drew the front of her cloak open as she approached him, revealing the long sword she wore at her left hip. She fingered it with warmth. Storm had brought this fine blade to her three long years ago. It had been three years since the death of Lady Cartwright. Mary had wondered, all that time, when she would finally be able to put the sword to its proper use. When she would be called on to protect the man she had vowed to keep safe.

Now she knew.

She had been careful never to draw the sword in the bandits' presence. The scabbard itself was nondescript. No mark on her clothing or outer gear could alert them to her ties to the keep Erik had grown up in.

The keep that had been her home these past ten years.

His eyes flashed from the sword back to her face, his gaze haggard. "You need to leave," he insisted. "What you are planning to do –"

The men behind her laughed in raucous delight. Geoff's voice was rich with pleasure. "You will be witness to exactly what you will be giving up, Erik. First you turned your back on your family; now you will lose your hold on mortality as well. Seems fair that we celebrate life as you tick out your remaining minutes toward a brutal, tortured death."

Mary held Erik's gaze with serious intent. The man was a master swordsman. If ever she could use advice, now would be the time. "What would you recommend?"

"You should turn around and go –"

She gave a sharp shake of her head, interrupting him. She dropped her hand to the dagger at her side; her voice was a low murmur. "I will do this with or without your help."

He held her eyes for a long moment, then blew out his breath. He nodded, his gaze firming in resolution. He briefly scanned the five men behind her, then drew his attention back to her. "Start with Geoff," he instructed, his eyes glancing to the dagger. "Short and swift. Then you'll have to take the other four on together."

Geoff's voice was an outraged shriek. "Short and swift?"

Mary turned, drawing the dagger at the same time, and launched it toward his throat. The surprise was complete – he didn't even put his hands up in defense as the sharp blade buried itself into his carotid artery, creating a fountain of blood that sprayed across his friends.

Mary drew her sword in her right hand. She swirled off the cloak with her left, sending it snapping into the eyes of the stocky man to her left. He threw his hand up to his face with a cry, and she spun hard to her left, drawing her blade down into the cleft of his neck and shoulder. He dropped with a gurgle as she turned to face her remaining three opponents, putting herself between them and Erik.

The wolves' heads now had their swords drawn and were staring at her with fury in their eyes. The man on her left shook his head as he looked her over. "We thought you were one of us," he spat.

She raised an eyebrow. "I was in your bar maybe five times at the most," she pointed out. "Surely you need a little more than that to join your den of thieves."

The corner of his mouth turned up. "Maybe a blood oath," he growled, and then he was in motion.

He swung at her left hip, and she spun her sword counter-clockwise, slamming her blade down on top of his, driving both into the ground. A sword came in toward her right bicep, and she rotated her right foot back, whirling her sword clockwise, deflecting the blade across the front of her body.

Erik's voice was sharp behind her. "Duck!"

She snapped her head down, and the whistling sound of a blade stirred the hair on the back of her neck. She drove her sword in a forward thrust, catching the center man in the abdomen. He screamed in agony, falling back to the ground.

"Right!"

She drove hard right, a fiery snake burned up her left leg, and she spun with focus, driving the flat of the blade against his ribs, then pulling up hard. The blade cut into his under-arm, and he fell like a stone.

There was one man left, but the world was coming in and out of focus, and heaviness descended on her body. She feinted left, then swung toward his right thigh, but his sword slammed down on top of hers. She leapt back to open up some distance between them. Her body slammed into Erik's.

The aroma of leather and anise enveloped her, his chest was strong and sturdy, and for a moment she simply wanted to close her eyes. She could lean against him for an eternity; slip serenely into the darkness which waited patiently for her.

His voice was steady in her ear; calm, quiet, and firm. "Reverse J."

She gave the tip of her blade a quick clockwise turn, then drove it straight up with every last ounce of her energy. The sword slammed into resistance, there was a scream of pain, and then the world shivered into ebony stillness.

* * *

Someone was calling her name, low, urgent, but it seemed an eon before she could blink her eyes open. She was sprawled on her side in a dusty room, staring at a moisture-slick stone wall. Her sword hilt was still in her right hand, and she wrapped her fingers around it, the texture of the leather comfortable in her gloved grip.

"Mary. Reach up to your right. Find the belt buckle."

The words swirled in her head. After a long minute she released the sword, forced her arm to move, and sure enough the shape of a buckle came under her fingers. With careful attention she undid the latch and tugged the leather free.

His voice wrapped around her, supporting her. "Put the belt around your upper left leg. Pull it tight."

It took longer than she thought, and her hand was slick by the time she finished, but finally the belt was cinched. She fell back, exhausted.

Erik's voice eased into her thoughts. "Now fling your sword as far from you as you can. When Caradoc shows up, tell him the men fought over you." There was a pause, and his voice added a note of respect. "He will believe that in a heartbeat."

Alarm sounded in Mary's head, and she pushed herself up to a sitting position. Her head throbbed, but she forced herself to turn and look up to him. He seemed miles above her, his arms stretched up in a letter Y, his wrists tied with thick, coarse rope. She rolled onto her side, wriggling her way over to Geoff's corpse. Her leg was beginning to throb with pain, and she knew she didn't have much time.

Geoff's eyes stared blankly at the ceiling.

She wrapped her fingers firmly around her dagger's hilt before yanking it from his throat. She put the blade between her teeth, then turned her attention to a nearby stool. It seemed to carry the weight of the universe, but inch by inch she managed to drag it over to rest beneath Erik's right arm.

His voice was rough. "Mary, once you do this, there's little chance of turning back."

She gave him a wry smile, speaking through the dagger's metal. "That was never an option."

She took in a deep breath, gritted her teeth, then pushed herself up onto her knees. Staggering pain seared through her, and she nearly lost consciousness again.

Erik's voice swirled around her. "Mary –"

She shook herself back to awareness, put her hands on the stool, and forced herself to stand. Sweat beaded on her forehead and she drew in long breaths. She balanced herself carefully on her injured leg, then, closing her eyes for a moment, pushed hard to step up onto the stool.

The pain nearly sent her collapsing to the floor. She flailed out and grabbed hold of Erik's shoulder, her full weight slamming down against him. She knew the strain on his shoulder joint must be immense, but he did not make a sound. He remained stock still and steady beneath her. Slowly she was able to right herself. She worked her way up to hold onto his wrist with both hands.

She carefully removed the knife from her teeth and began sawing. The rope was thick, and she pushed hard to work her way through the layers.

Her knife slipped.

Suddenly there was a gash on his palm, blood slipping from it in a thin curtain.

Mary gasped. "Oh, Erik, I'm –"

"I am fine," he reassured her. "Just keep going."

She nodded, struggling to focus, and bit by bit the strands unraveled. The world was fading from her, and she could almost see the energy draining from her arms. Just another inch, just –

The world spun, she was falling, and then Erik had ripped his arm through the remaining rope and pulled her tight against him, holding her. She hung limp, her energy spent.

After a long moment his hand slid down her arm and gently took the dagger from her grasp. "Hold onto my waist," he murmured.

She dutifully slid her arms around his torso, drawing even closer to him. He moved his free hand up to his other wrist, making quick work of the tie there. The ropes fell. His arms came around her, supporting her. He held her close as he drew in several long breaths.

At last he stood back, turning to sit her on the stool. He dropped to one knee at her side, examining the tourniquet at her leg, then made quick work of Geoff's shirt to create a bandage. He swaddled her injury, using the belt to hold it in place, then eased her sword and dagger back into their places. His eyes lit on the tambourine, now spattered with blood, and he hooked it on her waist.

His voice was a low murmur. "If we are lucky, none who arrive later will ever know you were here."

He then strode to the side of the room, where he picked up his own sword and dagger. The sword stayed in his hand as he returned to Mary, wrapped her cloak around her, and drew her up cradled in his arms.

He glanced at the closed door. "What do we have waiting for us?"

Mary's throat was tight with growing pain. "One man in the chamber upstairs. Then five on the wall."

Erik glanced at the bodies on the floor, giving a wry grin. "Sounds fair to me."

She shook her head. "These men were half-drunk and were the dregs of the band," she countered. "You have both Espan and Arbert waiting for you up there. Plus three of Caradoc's trusted lieutenants."

His eyes shadowed, but he nodded. "Then I will have to get through them."

He pulled open the door and began the ascent. The slow, careful climb up seemed to be even longer than her descent had been, but Erik showed no sign of weariness as they finally arrived at the dimly lit landing area.

She turned to put her mouth near his ear. "Let me go in first," she murmured. "I can distract him."

He nodded, carefully placing her down on her feet. She swayed, but forced herself to take a step forward, hobbling, pulling the door open.

Wymon's eyes lit up as she stepped into the room, then darkened in frustration as he took in the blood caked on her leg. "God's teeth, look what they did to you," he snapped. "Surely they knew I was next."

Mary nodded. "Yes, you are," she agreed without inflection.

She took a staggering step to the right, and Erik moved like a panther, thrusting at Wymon, taking him through the ribs before he could call out. The man slid down to the ground, his head falling back.

Erik nodded toward the guttering fire. "You stay here; stay warm. I will come back for you."

It was tempting, so tempting, but Mary gave her head a sharp shake. "No."

Erik's eyes snapped to hers. "Surely you know you cannot fight, Mary. You can barely stand."

"I cannot fight, but I will not have you face them alone," she insisted. "Even if all I can do is sit on the stairs and be a witness, I will be there for you."

A note of respect came into his gaze, and he put his left hand out to her. She pushed the main door open for them, stepping out into the late afternoon sunshine, the frosty air causing her breath to billow in soft clouds. Erik was right at her side, his eyes sweeping the empty courtyard. His gaze drew up to the surrounding walls - to the men who lounged along its length, watching the forest beyond.

He eased Mary down to sit on the rough stone stair, his eyes holding hers for a long moment. "However this turns out, you have my heartfelt thanks for all you have done."

His eyes were blue-grey, the misty color of a distant sea, and she was lost in their far horizons. She wanted to fold herself into his arms, to immerse herself in his warmth, and leave the rest of the world behind.

A furious shout came from the wall.

Erik ran his hand along her cheek before turning, standing, and striding down the few stairs to stand at the end of the unevenly stoned courtyard. The few out-buildings around the shadowed edges were run down with gaps in their timbers and sagging beams. Mary saw the skittering of a badger in what was once the stables, but it was the five men scrambling down the narrow stairs from the wall who clearly had Erik's attention. The men formed a line before the gate, with Espan and Arbert in the center.

Espan spoke up first, his face mottled deep crimson. "What have you done with the others?"

Erik gave a smooth spin to his sword, loosening up his wrist. Mary wondered if the wound on his hand was giving him any difficulties with his grip. She cursed her clumsiness; it could easily lead to the death of them both.

Erik's voice was smooth and even. "You five will find out soon enough where your friends have gone," he promised.

Espan pointed his sword at Erik's chest. "Get him!"

The three lieutenants hollered in unison, charging Erik with swords raised high. Erik brought his sword over his head, parallel to the ground and edge facing forward. The first attacker's blade slid along its length, releasing off to his left. Erik whipped the tip around to the right, driving it hard into the attacker's kidney, and the man went down with a groan.

Erik swept his blade diagonally across, tip down and left. He blocked the second man's swing, lunging forward and right to continue his sword's up-thrust motion. He caught the second man in the groin, turning to rip his blade through the attacker's thigh.

The third man dove with a thrust straight for Erik's heart. Erik smashed his sword left to right, knocking the blade off-center so it barely missed his right arm by inches. He spun in place, his momentum carrying his blade tip around at blinding speeds toward the man's stomach, ripping it open in one long, crimson gash.

Erik glanced down at the three men writhing before him, then back up at Espan and Arbert. The two had lost their bantering arrogance and carefully contemplated Erik. They spread apart, stalking toward Erik, flanking him on either side.

Mary leant forward, her hands clenched together. Erik's sword skill was better than she had expected, better than even the glowing reports of the men at the keep had made him out to be. After all, they had last seen him as a lad of sixteen, only beginning to realize his potential. He had been away for ten long years, deep in the harshest conflicts of the Holy Land. That the time there had honed him was an understatement.

But the two men in front of him also carried a reputation for their skill with a blade – and their ruthlessness in battle. They were the core strength of Caradoc's band. Their entire focus was now on the blond man before them.

The men pounced, and it was all Mary could do to remain on the stair, to not dive in and offer Erik some relief from that maelstrom. It was as if three alpha wolves fought for control of a pack. The spinning blades, the thunder of a fist landing against a skull, the stomp of a boot against an exposed knee, spun in her mind faster than her eyes could follow. None could survive in that whirlwind of violence and razor-edged swords.

Erik's sword drew high and right, slicing diagonally across Espan's face. A pair of deep groans echoed as Espan collapsed and Erik's abdomen simultaneously flowered with a ribbon of red. Mary's breath froze. If Erik had a stomach wound, all was lost. His digestive juices would burn him away from within. It was a truly agonizing way to die.

Arbert was staring down at his fallen brother with unbelieving shock, and then he bellowed in rage, charging hard at Erik.

Erik did not move.

Mary's heart stopped cold. Erik seemed to have gone beyond himself with the pain of his injury. He would be mown down, defenseless, like a lamb trussed and trusting on a pagan's solstice altar.

Then, at the last moment, Erik leapt to the left, dodging the whistling blade by mere inches. He spun clockwise, whipping his sword around, and drove the edge hard into the back of Arbert's neck.

The decapitation was instant.

Arbert's corpse fell like a rag doll.

Erik sagged to one knee, the welling of blood from his stomach darkening the front of his tunic. Mary raced across the courtyard to his side, ignoring the excruciating pain echoing from her injured leg. She pulled up his jerkin to examine the wound.

After a moment, she sighed in relief. "It didn't make it through your muscle, thank God," she murmured. "A deluge of blood, but once we staunch that the wound should heal, given time." She pulled her dagger from her belt, reaching over to cut a long strip of cloth from Espan's cloak. In short order she had fashioned a thick bandage around Erik's waist.

He wearily pushed himself to his feet, then drew her up beside him. His eyes moved to the run-down stables, but she shook her head. "I have a steed in the forest," she informed him. "I trust him far more than any of the beasts you would find in there."

He gave a wry smile. "You seem to have thought of everything." He glanced around at the fallen bodies. "We will have to move fast, though, to stay ahead of the rest of the pack. Lead on."

He looped his arm around her waist and they made their way through the lengthening shadows, pulling open the front gate and crossing the short distance into the woods. The oak-brown horse was right where she had left him, tied to a speckled birch, and she gave him a fond pat before untying his reins.

Erik climbed up into the saddle, putting down a hand, and in a moment he had drawn her up before him. She settled into place, his warmth and security drawing around her like a cocoon.

She turned her head to the side so he could better hear her. "Head toward the old mill in Sibsey; I have a relay horse there. Our only chance lies in outrunning our pursuers before darkness hits."

He glanced down at her leg; a fresh sheen of blood glimmered through the bandage. "How many relays?"

"Three," she responded. "We ride hard until nightfall, and then we lay low for a week. We'll be far enough that they are unlikely to find us. By staying quiet for the week they will think we got clear away to Wales or Scotland."

He nodded, pressed in on the horse's sides with his thighs, and they were in flight.

Mary faded in and out of consciousness as the world thundered around her. Erik's arm was steady around her waist, holding her in the saddle. She knew the ride must be sending just as much pain through his body as it did hers, but she could not tell from his even breathing or focused attention on the road ahead. He stayed off the main roads, sticking with forest paths and farmer's ways. She knew it had only been an hour or so, but by the time the mill drew into sight she was exhausted, her body drenched in sweat despite the frosty air biting her nose.

A roan horse waited for them at the side of the abandoned mill, his ears twitching forward at their approach. Erik slid down first, putting his arms up for her, catching her as she nearly collapsed against him.

Mary's voice sounded weak even to her own ears. "Two more legs," she murmured. She didn't know if she was reassuring him or herself.

Erik's eyes went to the oak-brown horse, which stood with his neck down, his sides heaving. Mary took a step forward and gave a gentle pat on the horse's withers. The steed gave a sharp snort of air, nickering as if in protest, but then headed off at a trot into the forest.

Erik climbed up into the saddle of the fresh steed, and Mary could see by his movements that he was wearying. His stomach wound was giving him more trouble than he let on. But his smile was encouraging as he put a hand down to her. "Round two," he offered.

"The cobblestone bridge at Stickney," she responded.

He drew her up more than she climbed. After a moment she was settled in place in his warmth, nestling herself against him, and they were in motion again.

* * *

She blinked her eyes and realized she was standing, supported by Erik, his arms around her. She shook her head; the whooshing of frigid water echoed in her ears. The roan was nowhere to be seen. A dappled grey horse stood before them, shifting his weight, his hooves making soft clinking noises as they came down on the stone of the bridge.

Erik's voice was soft in her ear. "I know you are exhausted," he apologized, "but I need to know the final leg."

Her thoughts were still sluggish, but a trace of nervousness whispered into her mind. He had followed her lead without question up until now, with the pressure of the Caradoc clan overwhelming all else. Now they were two hours' hard ride from the threat. They were alone in the gathering dusk. He might balk at where she planned to take them.

She drew in a breath, steeling herself. There was only one way to find out.

Her voice was a mere whisper. "Avoca's Folly."

There was a long pause. Mary could feel the tension slide into Erik, the chill in his pose. Then he was carefully turning her around, bringing his eyes to meet hers. His gaze edged with a sharpness she had not seen before.

His voice was rough. "You know who I am."

She nodded, struggling through the weariness. "You are Erik of Cartwright."

His lips pressed into a thin line. "And you know that my Aunt Avoca threw herself to her death from that tower some fifteen years ago. It is a cursed location; my mother closed it off ever since."

Mary kept her voice even. "And now your mother is dead."

Erik flinched, his gaze chilling further. "She died when I was at the Crusades," he agreed. "She willed the entire property, including the eastern corner with Avoca's Folly, to a distant relative I had neither met nor heard of. There is a new Lady Cartwright; one who would not welcome us."

Mary flushed. She hoped he would attribute her discomfort to the searing pain coursing through her leg and not to his words. There was indeed a new Lady Cartwright, had been for three years now, ever since that week of torment during which Erik's mother had succumbed, in growing agony, to an infection of the stomach. Mary had done everything she could, had tried every remedy and called for every healer within reach, but in the end it had been no use. The Lady had for so long been a domineering, powerful, almost invincible force in her life. In the end she had been reduced first to a writhing, wailing woman, and at last to a moaning, pleading child. Her thin fingers had laced into Mary's own long after life had left her fragile shell.

"There is a new Lady," agreed Mary in a low voice. She looked to the ground. While she understood Erik's mother's instructions, it still pained her to follow them. It was Mary's nature to be forthright and simple - to state how things were and take what came. But the past Lady Cartwright had not trusted in Erik, or at least not trusted in his ability to hold off the influences of Lynessa.

From what Mary had seen these past few years, she could not say she blamed the Lady one whit.

She swallowed, running a hand wearily through her hair. "Given the split you had with your mother ten years ago, and that she did not reconcile even on her deathbed, the last place anybody would look for you would be on her property." She looked up at him. "And as for the Folly, it's even less likely that any searcher would want to go near that place. Rumor is that it's haunted."

His eyes were still, the grey-blue almost ice. "That is the rumor."

"So we head out?"

Mary held her breath. If he refused, she could hardly force him to this path. As it was, she could barely stand.

He paused for a long moment, his eyes moving from hers to stare toward the northwest. Pain seeped into his gaze, along with a hint of longing. At last he nodded. "I have trusted you so far, and you have been well worthy of that trust. We follow your plan."

He pulled himself up onto the grey, then drew her up before him. Mary wondered if she imagined it or if he left a bit of distance between them Perhaps his carriage was slightly stiffer and more careful in where he touched her. But then they were in motion, the world was blurring alongside her, and she once again faded from thought.

* * *

A moon was shining amongst a glittering of stars. Mary realized she was being carried. Erik's feet were making a crunch-crunch noise as they moved across the thin layer of snow that surrounded the tower's walls. He was working his way cautiously toward the main gates, picking his steps carefully amongst the tumble of rocks and weeds. The grey steed was nowhere to be seen.

Mary roused her energy, drawing herself up out of the stupor that called to her so strongly. "Not that way."

Erik glanced down at her in surprise, but his movement stopped. He swung his head from left to right along the length of the high wall. "I thought this was the only gate?"

"Continue along the wall to the right," she instructed. "About a quarter of the way around."

He obliged, making his way by the shimmering moonlight, holding her easily against him. She heard the soft siren song of sleep and fought it with effort. They were nearly there; she only had to hold on for a few more minutes.

Finally the swath of ivy was just ahead. She pointed at it with a shaking finger. "Over there. Pull that aside, but gently."

He snugged her up in his left arm, dropped to one knee to balance her, and then reached forward with his right. The ivy formed a thick curtain over a small hole made by tumbled down stones. If he crouched, there would be just enough space to make it through.

He carefully eased them both through the hole, taking care to rearrange the ivy once they had passed. Then he stood and looked across the small courtyard and the tall tower at its center. His eyes drew to the shuttered window at the top, and a shiver ran through his body.

Mary's vision blurred, and she focused on the moment. "Walk in the stream."

His eyes went first to the undisturbed dust that lay across the width of the cobblestone area, then to the thin trickle of water that meandered across one side. Nodding, he made his way carefully along the slick stones, each footfall erased by that rippling cascade.

At last they were at three short steps before the tower and the wooden door, banded in iron. He looked at it for a long moment, then gave a heft against it with his shoulder.

The door remained firmly in place.

He looked down at her, raising an eyebrow.

Mary wriggled out of his arms, leaning against the cold stone for a moment as she gained her feet. Three more minutes. She only had to last three more minutes, then she could sleep all night and day.

She found the loose stone to the right of the door, pulled it free, and handed it to Erik. Then she reached her hand into the hole, her fingers searching for the thick rope. *Ah, there it was.* She drew in a long breath, gathered her strength, and pulled.

There was a creaking noise from within, and then a soft thud.

She reached forward with her hand, gave a gentle push, and the door swung open.

Erik nodded in appreciation. He replaced the stone, then wrapped an arm around her waist as they moved into the circular room. It was coated in dust, housing only a broken table and an upended chair. Moonlight streamed in through one barred window, and a circular staircase headed up in the far corner.

Erik turned, closed the door behind them, and reset the bar in place. He looped the rope back over its pulley and laid the end in front of the hole. Then he turned to look at Mary.

"I assume we go up?"

"Up we go," agreed Mary with a weary smile. "And then we sleep."

His arms were around her, and she could sense the exhaustion which traced through every motion he made, but his steps were steady as he moved them up the long spiraling steps. Thin arrow slits let in glimmers of light, but the stairs were dark and dusty. He was careful to feel for each step with his foot, ensuring his stability before moving up another stair. It seemed hours later that they came to the shallow landing and a sturdy wooden door.

Mary's mouth quirked into a wry grin. "And here we are. Our home away from home for the next week."

Erik maneuvered her forward. He lifted the latch with his left hand while balancing her off to the right. Then he swung the door open.

He stopped, his eyes widening in surprise.

Mary's eyes followed his gaze, a sense of satisfaction warming her. She had done everything she could to prepare the room for an escape, and by Erik's reaction her efforts had not been in vain. The one full window overlooking the front courtyard was shuttered, but not solidly, so streams of moonlight lit the room in silvery streaks. To the right was a large, low bed, mounded with four thick royal-blue blankets. A pile of pillows stretched across its headboard.

A table with two chairs stood along another wall, and beside it shelves were stocked with apples, turnips, wheels of cheese, loaves of bread, and a wealth of other food stuffs. Large barrels were marked as ale, mead, and wine.

The third wall's shelves held the other supplies. There was a stretch of bandages, needles, herbs, and ointments. One shelf held clothing and a pair of folded cloaks. Another contained sword-sharpening stones, polishing cloths, as well as a collection of daggers.

Erik's voice held respect. "You really are prepared," he murmured.

Mary smiled despite her exhaustion. "I tried to be."

He moved over toward the bed, dropped to one knee, and used his left hand to pull back the blankets. She rolled gratefully onto the thick mattress. She sank into it, and when he lay the blankets back over her it was all she could do to remain conscious. It seemed a heaven on earth.

He glanced over at the cold fireplace, his brows creasing. "We cannot risk a fire."

"No, we cannot," she agreed. She put a hand out to him. "We will have to keep each other warm; these blankets should be more than enough."

He glanced again at the fireplace, then the closed shutter, and nodded. He stood, went to the door, closed it, and dropped the bar in place. He lay a hand on it for a long moment, as if willing it to provide the final layer of protection for them. Then he turned and came to the other side of the bed, easing beneath the covers.

He drew her in against his chest.

To Mary they were together on the horse again, his sturdiness protecting her, his careful attention aware of danger. She was safe.

In a blink she was gone.

Chapter 3

Mary couldn't breathe. The thick, billowing smoke filled her nose with its acrid stench. The scorching wooden walls of the grain box she hid in blistered her skin. All around her she could hear the agonized screams of her friends and family.

She slammed her hands over her ears, gasping for breath, and she was burning ... burning ...

A cool cloth was gently pressed to her forehead, and she struggled to open her eyes. It was late afternoon, judging by the streams of sunlight coming through the chinks in the shutters. Erik had a thick, dark brown cloak over his shoulders as he carefully patted down her face. The frosted edges of his breath made plain the chill of the day, but her skin flamed with crackling heat.

Erik's eyes creased with concern. "You have a fever," he murmured. "I need to take a look at that leg of yours, now that you are awake."

She nodded, and he helped her wriggle into a sitting position, handing over a mug of mead for her. She gratefully drank it down, the liquid tracing a silvery path down her throat and into her stomach. He waited for her to finish, then moved down to unwrap the bandage from her leg.

Blood was crusted all along the wrapping, and he used the mead on a cloth to dab away at it, working his way down to the wound itself. The tension in his brow eased.

"No infection that I see," he told her. "Still, you need to lie still for the day. Get as much sleep as you can. Are you up for some food?"

Her throat ached with rawness. "Maybe an apple."

He rebandaged the wound with fresh wrappings, then tucked the covers back around her. Soon he was at her side with an apple, cutting off slices for her and handing them over one by one.

When she was finished, he moved over to the shutters, peering out without touching them.

Mary followed his movements with her eyes. "Anything yet?"

He shook his head. "Some pilgrims passed early this morning, and a short while ago a farmer went through with his wagon. Our tracks outside the walls, at least, are now nicely covered. No sign of our pursuers yet."

"I give them two more days," mused Mary.

Erik looked over with a question in his eyes.

"They would have found our first horse's prints from where he waited for us," she explained. "So they would start by looking everywhere we could have gotten to on that horse. A relatively small radius."

"And when that fails, they will keep working their way outwards," agreed Erik. "Plus, as you mentioned, they will think it unlikely I would head in this particular direction."

His eyes shadowed, and he turned, looking at the thin arrow-slit which pointed west. He slowly moved across the room, hesitating a moment before leaning his head to look through the narrow gap. "You can just about make out the keep from here," he murmured. "That was my home, until ten years ago."

And for the past ten years, that keep has been my home.

Mary's heart filled with a longing to stand by his side, to wrap her arms around him, and to soothe his tormented soul. She ached to feel his hands twine into hers. She fought down the desire with effort. The emotion would interfere with her ability to do her duty.

If only she could tell him –

She pushed the thought away. She did not know how much longer she would have to hold back information from Erik, but Lady Cartwright had been clear on this point. Mary had to evaluate him for as long as she could, learn as much as possible about him, before revealing the truth.

She had to find out if he was free of Lynessa.

Mary's brow shadowed. It had been Lynessa who had created the schism, those ten long years ago. Lynessa had driven Erik from his mother's side - had made Lady Cartwright vow in fury that she would never take him back.

But surely he was no longer under the blonde's spell. Not after she'd led him to his certain death.

Waves of dense darkness descended on her. Her thoughts muddled and drifted away like sparks floating up from a dying campfire.

* * *

Mary wearily pushed the hair from her face, struggling up to a seated position. Gentle morning sunlight was streaming through the gaps in the shutters, and Erik was standing at them, attentively watching the forest beyond.

Mary drew her gaze along his profile. The painting in the keep had been of a young man. A lad on the cusp of maturity, preparing to set out into the world. The soldier before her was weathered and toned. He was someone who had seen what life held and had tested himself against it. There was a strength within him, a passion that she had never sensed in all the years of staring into the canvas eyes.

She remembered how he had looked at her, just before turning to fight the five wolves' heads in the crumbling courtyard. He had laid his fingers against her cheek, and her heart had flamed to life –

He suddenly turned, and she dropped her eyes to her lap. Her cheeks blazed with a heat she knew had nothing to do with any fever.

In a moment there were sounds of motion as he strode to the shelves, drawing out bread, butter, and a mug of ale. He brought them over to her with an attentive gaze.

He knelt at her side. "Feeling better?"

To Mary's surprise she was ravenous. She could barely wait for him to smear the butter on the bread before she devoured it, washing it down with the occasional draw on the mug. He smiled in appreciation as she tucked the last end of the crust into her mouth.

He turned to refill her ale. "I'm glad to see you've got a healthy appetite." His eyes drew down to the blanket. "How does your leg feel?"

She gave her toes an experimental wiggle. Her calf answered with a solid ache, but it was a far cry better than the searing pain of two days ago. "Healing."

"Good."

He paused for a moment, holding her gaze. "I know the leg was the worst of it, but sometimes in combat we end up with other injuries we don't notice. If they fester, they can cause serious trouble. You should check yourself over to make sure the leg is the only thing to keep an eye on."

She nodded in agreement. "You are right, of course."

He moved to the shelves, took down a fresh dress for her, and lay it across the end of the bed. Then he turned, walked to the arrow slit in the western wall, and put his back to her, giving her what privacy he could.

She pushed the blankets off and, starting with her toes, went carefully up her body. She drew off her dress as she went, glancing up at Erik, but he remained resolutely in place.

There were scrapes and bruises in a number of locations, but nothing serious beyond her leg wound. The rest would heal quickly and easily. The leg would take longer, and would leave a nasty scar, but the limb would remain fully functional.

She drew on the new dress, and then looked at her hands. The brown gloves were still in place, almost a part of her, and she hesitated before drawing them off.

Even after all these years it was still a shock to look at her hands. She had worn these gloves for so long – almost a decade – that the gloves seemed the natural state of her hands, not this twisted, scarred flesh beneath. The burns had been severe, and it was only through God's grace that the digits remained functional, that she could still wield a sword and manage a knife.

She turned her hands before her, fascinated by the mangled flesh. That she could have endured that pain …

Erik's voice came from across the room. "Everything look all right?"

Mary glanced up in panic, but he had not turned. He still stared out into the distance, to the keep he had abandoned ten years ago; the family he had left behind.

She quickly pulled her leather gloves back into place. "Yes, everything is as it should be," she informed him. "Only the leg needs tending to."

She pulled the blanket back over her. "You can turn around now, if you wish," she added. "I am decent again."

He turned, moved over to one of the chairs, sat on it, and picking up a whetting stone. He took the sword from the table and began sharpening its edge with long, steady strokes. Mary could see the slight hitch in his movements as he tried to do the action with his left hand when clearly he was used to doing it with the right.

Mary looked down for a moment. "How is your sword hand doing?" she quietly asked. "I am sorry to have wounded you in such a vital place."

He shook his head, not pausing in his motions. "You risked your life to come in to get me, when nobody else stirred a finger on my behalf," he pointed out. "A cut on my hand is a small price to pay."

Mary's gaze moved to his jerkin. The thickness of the bandage bulked it out around his abdomen, and she could see the fabric's whiteness through the slice in the leather. "And the other wound?"

"It lets me know it's there, like an angry wildcat, but I am cautious not to twist it open again. If I can be easy on it for another few days it should start to mend."

Mary pursed her lips. "The gash was long. Surely we should stitch it?"

Erik's voice was dry. "Already did."

Mary looked at him in shock. "What, you stitched your own stomach wound?"

He nodded. "You were both exhausted and feverish. The wound needed stitching to avoid infection. Not much other choice."

Mary paled at the thought of the pain he must have endured. "Next time, wake me. I can work through a fever."

He turned to look at her, raising his eyebrows. "Next time?"

She smiled despite herself.

When he smiled in return a flush of heat washed through her.

He turned away suddenly, his eyes moving to the shelves neatly stacked with loaves of bread and rosy apples. When he spoke his voice seemed rough. "Do you live here alone?"

Mary's cheeks burnished with warmth. She dropped her eyes to her gloved hands, pulling a cuff to settle one more firmly around her fingers. "I ask only one thing of you, while we heal up in this tower."

He stilled at that, and his gaze moved to the blade before him. "Anything."

A tendril of desire traced through her. This consummate swordsman, a man of honor who had defied his family for the love of a woman, had put himself fully in her hands. A wealth of longings cascaded through her thoughts, but she pushed them away with well-practiced discipline. She owed it to the Lady who had taken her in to follow her orders to the last.

Still, her voice was hoarse when she spoke. "I have my reasons for valuing my privacy. Please do not press me for more information. I will give it when I am able."

He glanced toward the arrow slit, and at last he nodded. "You ask very little, for what you have done. I doubt anyone at the keep even gave thought to sending out a full rescue party."

Mary flushed at that, looking down. She let her hair fall to shield her face. There had been heated discussion in the keep's central hall when Lynessa's plan had become known. It was only with the greatest of effort that her counter-scheme had been allowed to move forward.

She had presented her argument so many times that to summarize it to Erik took little thought. "The Caradocs have nearly fifty men, and no matter how they got their hands on you, they would have hunkered down in that tower," she pointed out. "If the keep's troops had tried to get to you with a full show of force, you would undoubtedly have been slain before they reached that final room."

Erik did not answer, but his draws of the stone against his sword became angular and hard.

* * *

Something drew Mary into wakefulness. She blinked her eyes against the soft light, gaining her bearings. It was barely dawn, judging by the soft shadows. Erik was peering through the shutters, his body at full alert, his sword in his hand.

Mary eased silently from the covers, drawing up the cloak by the bed and wrapping it around her shoulders. She carefully hobbled around to stand beside Erik, tilting her head to get a better view without touching the shutters.

Four men on horseback stood before the outer wall's gates, staring up at the tower.

She resisted the urge to draw back and lunge for her sword. Instead she held stock still. To them the shutters were a dark, impenetrable wall, with only shadows behind. As long as nothing moved suddenly or caught their attention, the tower would seem long abandoned.

One of the horsemen nudged his steed forward, pushing back his cloak's hood. The shock of orange-red hair caught Mary off guard. Surely Geoff could not have recovered from the dagger to the throat? She remembered him lying there, dead –

She shook her head. Of course. It was his brother, the bartender. Her mind searched for a name. Josiah, that was it. They must have called out every last man if he was on the road and not guarding the home base.

Josiah turned to the other men, his anger clear in his angular movements. "Come on, then," he called to them. "That bastard has got to be somewhere. We'll ferret him out, no matter what rat hole he has crawled into."

The men looked nervously amongst themselves, and finally a burly man with dark curls spoke up. "But that's *Avoca's Folly*," he stated almost in awe. "The place is cursed."

"God's teeth, Bronson are you nothing but a mewling infant?" growled Josiah, dismounting and striding toward the gates. "It is a building of stone and wood, and we *will* search it."

He gave a solid push to the gate. There was a wild, drawn-out shriek, somewhere between the cry of a banshee and the howl of the damned.

Bronson screamed in panic, the horses reared and bucked, and Josiah jumped back a few paces, fear lighting his eyes.

The noise stopped, and the men settled the horses. Josiah took in several deep breaths, then stepped forward again, cautiously poking at the door with his sword.

There was a flurry of motion, and a trio of warthogs streamed through the opening, racing for the safety of the nearby woods.

Josiah gave a relieved laugh, pushing at the gate with his shoulder and opening it further. He stepped around it, looking at its back side. "Just a warthog nest," he called out to the others. "Been here a long time, by the looks of it."

"See!" replied Bronson, his voice agitated. "Nobody could have gotten in or out. We can mark this place off our list."

Josiah turned, his eyes bright with fury. "You three get in here now, or I turn you over to Caradoc and explain to him how you shirked your duty to find his brothers' assassin."

The men half looked like they would be willing to face that judgment, but, reluctantly, they dismounted. They drew their swords and came in slowly after Josiah, looking in every direction at once.

Josiah moved across the dusty courtyard, kicking at a stone with his boot. "Doesn't look like this ground has been trod in years."

Bronson's movements were tight with fear. "Probably fifteen years," he muttered. "Since that crazy biddy flung herself out the window and smashed her brains open on this very ground."

Erik stiffened, and Mary put her hand out to his arm, feeling the tension that lined each curve. After a long moment he let out a breath, his gaze never leaving the men who crept toward them.

Josiah looked around the empty courtyard before coming up the three steps to the tower's main door. He gave it an experimental push. "Locked," he muttered.

He took a step back, sheathed his sword, and then took a running start at it. The shudder echoed throughout the tower, and a frisson of fear shot through Mary.

There were four of them, and if that door gave way ...

Josiah was stepping back, shaking his head. "Could be that rubble is blocking it from the other side," he mused.

"Of course it is," agreed Bronson. "The place has been abandoned for years and years." He waved his hand at the courtyard. "Clearly nobody has been near this place since that suicide. There's no way Erik would be in there. Right, Sander?"

Another man, flaxen haired with hollow eyes, stepped forward. "It was cursed by that unholy act," he agreed promptly. "Just like your brother Arth-"

Bronson spun to glare at him, and Sander quickly changed his phrase. "I mean, of course *any* corner of Lady Cartwright's land holdings would be the last place Erik would come," he expanded. "After Erik burned that village to the ground, if he showed his face his own landholders would be the ones to attack him. That new Lady Cartwright and her keep guards wouldn't even have to stir a finger."

A low growl emerged from Erik's throat, and Mary tightened her grip on his arm. They only had to last a few minutes and the danger would be past.

Just a few more precious minutes.

At last Josiah nodded, turning. "You are right, of course," he conceded. "My guess is that Erik turned tail and fled south, maybe even to get a ship back to France and the Holy Land. He had only been back to England for a year – I would bet that the hot deserts of Jerusalem feel more like home to him now."

The other three men were already striding toward the gate. "South it is," Bronson agreed. "I'm sure Caradoc will see the sense of that."

In a moment the four were mounted, riding hard toward the south.

Erik let out a long breath. He rested his head on the shutter for a moment before turning to Mary with hollow eyes.

"I did not burn down the village," he stated wearily, as if this had been a discussion he'd had many times in the past.

Mary knew she should soothe him. She should celebrate the departure of the threat. But his words lanced at a sore within her, ripped off the scar, and stirred into life the pain and grief which always seemed to boil so near the surface. She turned away from him, shielded her face, and sank down onto the bed.

"What did happen, then?" she asked, striving to keep her tone even.

His eyes flashed, but after a moment he nodded, moved to the barrel and poured out a mug of ale for each of them. He handed her one, then took the other and sat down at the table.

"With all you have done for me, you have the right to ask any question you wish."

He took a long pull on his mug. "I was sixteen, and I thought I knew everything." He sighed, looking off toward the west, toward the shadow of a keep through the narrow beam of light. "I could best any man in the region. I was the only child, in line to inherit the keep and its lands from my mother. I was young and arrogant."

He took another drink. "When rumors of bandits came to us, I laughed at them." He shook his head at the memory. "I insisted I be given command of the troops to assess the situation."

He ran his thumb along the edge of the mug's handle. "Cintersloe was the name of the town. It was a beautiful little farming village, nestled alongside a gentle stream, with a small church and even a cozy tavern. The people were friendly and warm. They were nervous about the threat, of course, but when I arrived it put their hearts at ease."

His brows drew together, and he looked down.

Mary waited, her ale untouched between her hands, her heart pounding. Lady Cartwright had refused to speak on the subject; had refused to speak one word about what had caused the rift between her and her son. Even the staff at the keep had been little help. The stormy fight had gone on behind closed doors, in the Lady's bedroom. Afterward, all they had seen was the boy storming out, saddling his horse, and thundering away into the night.

Erik ran a hand through his blond hair, riffling it. "Word arrived that Lynessa was traveling with a small entourage perhaps three miles to the south. The bandits had been seen in the same area. I did not hesitate. I gathered up the men, and we headed south."

Iron bands constricted Mary's chest. She remembered the stirring of the men, the wheeling of the horses, and the baffling confusion coursing through her as they streamed away south, toward miles of empty forest.

Her voice was a mere whisper. "You took all the men."

He sharply glanced at her, his eyes defensive, but after a long moment he nodded. "I thought Lynessa was in trouble," he stated in a low voice. "She was special to me. I had hoped that someday she would consent to be my bride." He paused for a moment. "I had pledged to protect her. I took that vow seriously."

He took another long draw on his ale. "But in the end I could not find her. It was pitch dark by then, moonless, so we made camp in a small clearing and waited until morning to return to the village."

Mary put her head down. The screams had lasted all night long. She could still hear the angry licking of the flames as they pulled down the houses; the sharp grunts of the bandits finishing off the survivors. She had huddled, alone, unable to breathe, in the bottom of the grain storage bin where her mother had hid her.

Erik's voice was flat. "They were all dead by the time I returned," he stated. "The buildings were smoldering ash heaps; the bodies were strewn everywhere. We went immediately back to the keep, to let them know what had happened and to make sure the rest of the villages were warned."

Mary's voice was tight. "And your mother had a talk with you."

He gave a low laugh, finished off his ale, and stood to pour himself a fresh one. He stared at the barrel for a long moment. "A talk," he repeated. "She was beyond furious. She had always been a hard woman, and perhaps the death of my father and my aunt had something to do with that. But I had never seen her in a rage like this. I could understand it, but when –"

He shook his head, returning to sit. "She accused Lynessa of being involved in the atrocities, and I snapped. I told her that Lynessa would soon be my wife and mistress of this keep. My mother swore she would disown me before she saw that happen."

He gave a harsh laugh. "I challenged her to do it."

He looked down at his hands as if the shock of the scene, ten years ago, was fresh in his vision. "And she did," he murmured, his voice resonating with surprise. "In one instant, all I held dear was gone. You should have seen the look in her eyes. It was absolute and final."

Mary laced her gloved fingers together. She knew well the look that Erik meant. She had seen it every day. She'd seen the sharp, angular motions of the woman; the thin lines which seemed to barely hold back fury. Up until the illness had taken hold of her, Lady Cartwright had been a force of nature.

Erik looked back out toward the west. "And so I left. I rode to Lynessa's family." He gave a wry smile. "While they were welcoming enough, they made it clear that a sixteen-year-old boy with few prospects in life was not an appropriate match for their daughter."

His gaze became distant. "I think they meant for me to go back and apologize to my mother, to regain my lands. But pride kept me from doing so. Instead, I signed up for the Crusades to earn my fortune and make my own name."

He took another pull on his ale. "Ten long years ago," he murmured. "It hardly seems like that much time has passed."

Mary nodded, finally bringing her own mug to her lips, her own thoughts lost in the distant past.

Chapter 4

Strong winds swirled the thick oak branches by the church into motion, the horses milled in agitation as the men clambered onto their backs, and Mary ran toward Erik, her heart thudding in her chest.

"Where are you going?" she cried out. "You can't leave!"

He looked down at her with a calm smile. "I will be back soon."

Agony ripped at her chest. "You won't!" she insisted. "You will leave, the bandits will come, and everything will be engulfed in flames. My friends will be killed. My parents will be slain!"

He climbed easily onto his horse, wheeling it around. "I will be back soon," he reassured her. He waved to his men, and the group thundered away toward the south.

She ran after them, racing as fast as she could, but he was drawing away from her, ever further, and she screamed at the top of her lungs.

"Erik! Don't leave me! The bandits are coming!"

She was sobbing, her entire body shaking, and Erik's arms were wrapped around her, holding her close against his chest. Pain lanced through every part of her body, and it was all she could do to suck in breath through the emotion that engulfed her.

His voice was a murmur in her ear. "I won't leave," he promised. "I won't leave you."

"But you *did*," she moaned, the past and present melding into one fiery ball of torment. "You left us! My village was a firestorm!" She could barely get the words from her throat.

"They ripped down the altar at the church. They ruthlessly slaughtered everyone I loved!"

Erik stiffened, then his breath blew out in surprise and he pulled her in.

Her sobs overwhelmed her.

Time seemed to be lost.

At last her crying slowed, and she slumped, drained, against him. Erik gently pressed her back to look her in the eyes. His voice was hoarse with shock. "I had thought no one was left alive. You survived that hell?"

She nodded, drawing her sleeve across her face. "My mother hid me in a grain bin and told me to stay within it, no matter what I heard. She told me to stay there for two days, in case they came back."

"Oh, Mary," he sighed, wrapping her in a comforting embrace. "I am so sorry." He ran a hand down her hair, soothing her. "Where did you go?"

She closed her eyes, beyond exhaustion. "A widow took me in."

* * *

Mary hobbled around the room, easing more weight onto her left leg, relaxing in satisfaction as it bore it without much complaint. They were five days into their stay at the tower, and she knew in two more that Erik would be ready to move on. She had to learn as much as she could in this time she had with him.

She looked over to where he sat at the table, undoing the bandage on his hand. He nodded at her with a wry smile, then went back to his task.

A shaft of pain pierced her heart, that she was holding back information from the man who had faced overwhelming odds at her side. She pushed the thought away. Her job was to keep Erik safe and to find out if he was still under Lynessa's influence. That is what she had been trained for these past ten years, and it was time to do her duty.

She pitched her tone to sound casual. "So, why did you return from the Crusades when you did?"

He scooped out a small amount of ivory ointment from the jar at his side, carefully dabbing it along the length of the scar across his palm. "Three years ago I received word that my mother had passed and that, true to her vow, she had left me nothing. I was bitter. For over a year I lost myself in battle and drink."

He put the lid back on the ointment jar, then carefully wound a fresh bandage into place. "Finally I grew to accept what life had given me, and I took stock of my situation. I had amassed a healthy sum of money over the past years. Lynessa's priest had sent messages from her every other month. She adored me, was thrilled to hear of my continuing success, and was waiting eagerly for me to return."

He gave a soft shrug. "It took another six months or so for me to finish my work in the Holy Lands, and then at last I set out for England."

Mary strove to keep her voice even. "And went to Lynessa?"

He gave a yank to the bandage, settling it in place. "And went to Lynessa," he agreed. "Her parents had passed away, and she welcomed me warmly into the family home. I thought life would be simple. We would at long last marry, begin our family, and enjoy a full, contented life."

"But ...?"

Erik flexed his hand, watching his fingers contract and expand in slow rhythm. "She wanted to take her time. She wanted to get to know me again, after I'd been gone so long. I understood, of course. I had been away for ten years. So I took things slowly. I courted her properly."

Mary pitched her voice to remain neutral. "That sounds reasonable."

He stood, walking over to stare out through the narrow arrow slit. "She had repairs she wanted to make to her family home; I gladly made them. There were banquets to throw, trips to take, and fresh horses to buy. I funded each one with contentment.

This was my new life I was building; my future family I was taking care of."

He was still for a long moment. "But finally, about a month ago, I sat down and had a talk with her. I felt we were ready to move forward with our wedding."

He shook his head. "A few days later, when we were out on a trip to see friends of hers, robbers struck the house. They knew where my gold was kept; they took every last coin. And even then I did not begin to suspect. When we worked with the sheriff to investigate who might have done it, Caradoc's name came up. Lynessa said she had the perfect plan for figuring out who the guilty party was. It involved her and me going, alone, to a certain tavern."

Mary nodded in understanding. "And you walked into her trap."

He gave a short laugh. "It was right there, before my face, and even so I could not believe it. Half of me believed I was lucky to have you there, my guardian angel, to deflect a dangerous situation. And the other half, precision-guided by Lynessa, believed her explanation – that her plan had been working perfectly until you meddled with it. That you were a harlot working to do me harm."

Mary tilted her head to one side, intrigued. "So, how did you end up in that dungeon?"

His lips pressed together. "She had waited for me for ten long years. I had abandoned my home and family for her. I had vowed to keep her safe. I still could not bring myself to believe that she had turned on me so thoroughly. I gave her one last chance. She promised, if I met her by the crossroads church the following afternoon, that she would prove her plan was worth pursuing. And so I went."

"And Caradoc was waiting?"

He nodded. "Caradoc was waiting, with twenty of his men, and Lynessa was nowhere to be found." He ran a hand through his hair. "Even then, some small part of me insisted that she was ambushed. That she had nothing to do with my capture. After all these years, it was hard to let go of that dream." His eyes shadowed. "It was hard to accept that I had lost everything for no reason."

Mary watched him stare out into the distance, knowing that there was nothing she could say to ease that burden.

* * *

Only the faintest glow frosted the edges of Erik's face as he gazed through the shutters. Mary wearily blinked into wakefulness. Dawn had not yet arrived, and her breath billowed in frosty clouds. The impression of his body in the blankets was still warm, and she knew he had just risen.

She could see the shadows beneath his eyes. "Come back to bed," she murmured. "It is too cold to be up yet."

He turned, holding her gaze. For a moment she saw a wave of longing, of rich desire, course through him. Then it had been shuttered as carefully as if he had eased closed the wooden slats before him. "You need your sleep; your wound is still raw," he stated. "The last thing you need right now is –"

He cut himself off, looking back out the window, his shoulders tight.

Mary burned with heat. Every ounce of her body called for him to come to her - to slip beneath the blankets and be hers. She had dreamt about him for so long. She had imagined and reimagined him by her side. And here, against all belief, he was standing.

He was all she had ever wished for.

That he would resist her out of concern for *her* health staggered her. After all, everyone knew that a man who abstained for too many days would damage his health. It was worse than going without food. He was the keep's unmarried lord - it was expected that the unattached females in the realm who had an interest would do their part to maintain his humors. To bolster his internal balance. She would be castigated if she allowed him to fail now, when he was so close to redemption.

And her own heart called to her so strongly -

She dampened down the flames with effort. She had to be objective. If they slept together, she would be unable to judge him clearly. She would be incapable of –

She blew out her breath, turned, and pulled the blankets over her head.

Who was she fooling?

Even now, when it had only been his body against her at night, the soft heat of his breath against her neck, she knew that she was enraptured by him. Ten long years of living in his home, of hearing his name, of waiting eagerly for the monthly letters from his commanding officer describing his latest ventures, had soaked him into her heart as surely as if they had lived together as man and wife.

At last she flung off her blanket, sure that sleep would never return. "All right then," she ordered. "If you are up anyway, let us take a look at that stomach wound of yours."

He glanced over in surprise. "You have some medical knowledge?"

Mary snorted. Lady Cartwright had certainly insisted on her learning all about broken bones, gaping wounds, and whatever other grisly injuries happened within the keep's radius. "Come on," she prodded. "Sit down and let me see."

He paused for a moment, then nodded, bringing one of the chairs over by the window where it caught the delicately growing golden streams. He carefully raised his arms up over his head. She stood behind him and drew off the jerkin with practiced ease. She had trained with the keep soldiers for enough years to know the ins and outs of a man's equipage.

A jagged scar coursed like a lightning bolt diagonally down his back, starting at his left shoulder, zigging over his spine before trailing away over his right hip. She stared at it in awe, and without realizing it her hand reached out to trace its path.

Erik's voice had a hint of amusement in it. "Forgot about that. A memento from the Holy Land. A minor action in Arsuf."

To Mary it was as if a Celtic legend, long thought to be a fairy tale, had suddenly sprung to life before her. She knew about the event, of course, knew every tiny detail of it from the letters the Commander had sent. Nine of Erik's men had been captured by the enemy and were set to be tortured as a warning to others. Erik had snuck through enemy lines, taken out countless guards, and gotten all nine men to safety. This grievous wound should have laid him low for months, but the commander had proudly stated that Erik was back in action after only a few weeks' rest.

Giving herself a shake, she knelt at his side and carefully unwrapped the bandage. She winced as she saw the long gash across his abdomen. The stitches were steady, neat, and she wondered how he had managed such a task on his own, especially with a wounded hand. He watched without comment as she drew two ointments down from the shelves and attentively cleaned the wound, then re-dressed the line. She looked with a critical eye along each side of the cut.

"No infection that I can see," she reported with relief. "You did a good job. But you will have to be quite careful in the coming days. If you tear any part of that open, an infection could kill you before you realized it had taken hold."

"Well do I know," he agreed. "We will have to hope the bandits give us that time."

She took down a fresh bandage, wrapped it around his stomach, and tucked in the loose end to hold it fast. Then she eased the jerkin back down over his body.

Her hands lingered on his shoulders as she finished settling it into place. For a long moment she wished they could just stay at the Folly, suspended in time. They'd be safe from vows, machinations, and duties. Her fingers strayed, just for a second, to gently brush against the side of his neck.

Then she stepped back, forcing herself to break the spell.

She had one more day.

Only one brief day remained for her to watch this man before her.

To strive to gaze into his very soul.

* * *

Oranges and crimsons were streaming across the floor when the sound of hoofbeat tickled at Mary's awareness. She glanced at Erik. In a moment both were at the shutters, straining their eyes across the lengthening shadows and seeking any sign of movement.

The rhythm came closer, and soon the four riders were in view. Josiah's red hair glowed in the sunset. His temper seemed even shorter than on his last visit.

The bartender pulled hard on his reins as the group neared the gate. "I swear, he seems to have vanished into the mist," he snapped, "It is ridiculous even to return here. Surely he is in Gaul by now."

He swung down off his horse, drew his sword, moved to the partially open gate, and gave it a vicious kick. There was a squeal from the warthogs. The animals streaked toward the tower, running to hide behind it.

"Damned beasts," snarled Josiah. "This place is cursed. Anybody would be a fool to stay here."

The three other men followed, leaving a cautious distance between them and their irate leader. Bronson made a wide circle around the gate, his dark curls bobbing nervously.

Josiah strode across the courtyard, came up to the door, and gave it a solid kick.

The tower shuddered.

Mary grabbed at Erik's hand, lacing her fingers into his. They had certainly healed some in the last six days, but they were nowhere near full strength. Erik's wound would be torn open with his first swing, and she doubted even he could last long after that.

If the men got in ...

Josiah kicked again, shouting out in anger. "You fiend, are you in there?" he bellowed. "Come out and face me, you coward!"

He spun on his men. "You – Sander - go around back and see if there's any other way in."

The flaxen haired man blanched, then nodded and headed off at a trot.

Mary glanced at Erik in concern. The bars on the other window were old and rusted. If the men made a concerted effort to pull them free …

There was a squeal, a scream, and Sander came running back toward the group, limping heavily. Blood spurted from a wound in his calf.

"Damn beast jumped me when I wasn't looking!" Sander cried out in fury. "Look what he's done!"

He plunked down on the steps, and Bronson cut some cloth from his cloak, tying it around Sander's leg.

Josiah shook his head. "Did you find anything?"

Sander lurched to his feet. "Give me a moment."

Mary's heart thudded against her chest. Erik glanced toward the door, his eyes settling for a moment on the bar which sat securely in its channel. His lips pressed into a thin line as he ran a hand along the bandage at his waist.

Sander stumbled his way to his horse, moved his hands to the saddle, and yanked off the crossbow that hung there on a loop. He slipped a bolt into its groove and cranked the winch back as he moved again toward the tower. He vanished from sight below them.

Mary found she was holding her breath.

There was a sharp pop, a whistling noise, and then a high pitched scream of pain which cut off into silence.

Sander came into view again, a satisfied look on his face.

Josiah growled in exasperation. "God's teeth, Sander. Was there another way into the tower?"

Sander shook his head. "Nah, just one tiny window. Barred. No way in."

Josiah turned to the door and slammed his fist hard into its center, causing the tower to shudder. "Cursed," he spat.

He stepped back, looking around the desolate courtyard. "I ain't wasting another drop of blood on this place. The man is in Gaul, and if Caradoc wants to seek him there, good luck to him." He turned on his heel, striding out through the gate. Bronson looped an arm under Sander's shoulder, helping him back to his horse. In only a few moments the foursome was streaming south.

Mary found her hand was still intertwined with Erik's, and she folded against him in relief as the hoofbeat faded from hearing. His arms came up around her, and nothing else mattered.

* * *

Mary blinked her eyes open, stretching in relaxed comfort. For the first time since the battle there wasn't a throbbing pain in her leg; she relished the peace. She rolled on to her side, unsurprised to find Erik standing by the shutters, his eyes watching the road.

She wondered how hard it was for him to climb out of bed each morning; if he felt the same hollowness she did when their warmth was separated. Every morning she woke to find him gone, and he would not join her at night until after she had fallen asleep. And yet she sensed the moment his body was there against her – and she ached the moment he left.

She pitched her voice to be gentle, but she heard the note of longing which traced through her words. "Are you sure you won't rest just a little while longer before we have to rise?"

He turned at that, eyes smoky, his gaze tracing along her hair which hung loose about her face. "Better not to," he murmured. He moved to the shelves, busying himself with gathering a loaf of bread, a small plate of butter, and a mug of ale.

He returned to sit cross-legged at her side. He waited patiently for her to prop herself up to sitting before handing over the items.

She leant back against the pillows, took a bite of the bread, and washed it down with the ale. A sense of loss swam through her. This was day seven.

Would he insist on going his separate way?

Erik was carefully watching her. "What is wrong?"

She gave a wry smile. "I was starting to enjoy our little retreat," she admitted.

He chuckled at that, leaning forward to brush a stray hair from her face. "You enjoy being waited on hand and foot?"

Her grin grew. "I definitely could get used to that," she agreed. "Although having access to a roaring fire would be quite a treat."

He raised an eyebrow in curiosity. "Oh? Tired of having to rely on my body heat to keep you warm?"

The thought of his lean length pressed against her coursed through her, creating a warmth wholly unrelated to skin temperature. "You were kind to turn yourself into a human heat rock," she murmured hoarsely. "A noble sacrifice in payment for my efforts."

His eyes grew serious at that. He took the mug from her, putting it to one side, before turning back to take her hand.

"There is nothing I could ever do which would repay you for your efforts," he stated, his eyes holding hers. "When I was hanging in that dungeon, knowing that days of torture stretched out before me, I lost all hope. I began planning ways of charging the group as soon as I was free, so I would go down quickly. I saw no other way out. I had fully accepted my death."

His eyes blazed with passion. "And then I looked through that grated window, and I saw your face. I had no doubt in my mind that you had come for me."

She nodded, caught in his gaze. "Of course I came for you."

He gave a low groan. "Even though I was not there for you when your village needed me?"

She ran her hand along the side of his face, and he trembled beneath her touch.

"The bandits were the guilty ones," she murmured, caressing her fingers along the side of his neck. "I never lost faith in you. You have filled my thoughts, my dreams, and I could want no other."

He groaned with desire, and it was as if some last internal dam had been breached. His lips lowered to meet hers.

Mary gasped. Electricity flooded through her body, rushing along every inch of skin. They had slept against each other every night, been in close proximity every day, and she had fought relentlessly against the longing which had called to her. Now an explosion had been unleashed.

It seemed they could not remove their clothing quickly enough, that the need to be cautious around their injuries only added to the heated torment.

And then they were free.

They tumbled and twined; cried out and reformed. For a long, glorious span of time all else was forgotten.

It was only when they were lying, exhausted, their limbs enmeshed, that he glanced down at her hands and chuckled. "We never even got your gloves off," he gently teased.

She flushed, looking away, trying to draw her hands down beneath the covers.

He stilled then, carefully raising himself on one elbow, looking down at her. "I thought it was just the cold you were concerned with. It is more than that?"

She nodded, still unable to meet his gaze.

He ran a hand tenderly along her hair, gently turning her head to his. "You should never feel embarrassed before me; not about anything," he murmured. "Not after what you have done for me." His eyes glanced at her gloves, then back into her eyes. "Take your time. You will know when you are ready."

He leant forward to kiss her on her forehead, then rolled to his feet. "But for now, we should get packed and ready to go."

Mary's heart thudded with an erratic beat. "Go?"

He gave her a wry smile. "You have been taking care of everything up until now, and have set quite a high bar for me. It is now my turn." His eyes were quiet for a moment. "Unless you did have a plan from here?"

Her throat went dry. Her plan became nebulous at this point. The only way to know what Erik was truly like was to see what he would do when given free rein.

She was proud that her voice held steady. "If you have somewhere to go, I will be fine here."

His gaze held hers. "Would you come with me?"

Her breath caught. "I would."

He smiled then, pulling on his leggings. He buckled on his scabbard, sliding the sword in place.

A nervous tremor ran through her, and she fought to rein it in. "Where are we going?"

He turned back to face her. His eyes held a mix of emotions, and she could not quite name them.

"I think it is time I headed home."

Chapter 5

Mary was impressed; clearly Erik's time in the Holy Land had taught him the value of efficiency. He had them packed and through the outer gates in less than a half hour. They would not be able to make it all the way to the keep before night fell, not with her injured leg, but they could at least get close. Then it would only be a short walk the following morning before they were safely behind the walls.

Mary gave her head a shake at the thought, drawing in a deep breath to forestall the rising tremor in her heart. She had planned for this as one possible outcome, and the keep's staff would know what to do. They would claim the lady of the house was ill and could not be seen. It would give Mary a window of time to observe Erik in his home - to see how he acted; how he treated the men around him.

Mary winced. The burden of lying would mount on her shoulders, pressing down on her, until she became unable to –

Erik pulled to a stop at her side, looking down at her with concern. "What is it, Mary? Is it your leg?"

Mary looked down, keeping her gaze away from his insightful stare. She ran a hand along the bandaging. The leg was throbbing, it was true, but it came nowhere close to the turmoil that was gnarling in her heart. It was not natural to her, this deceit. Every ounce of her being called on her to simply reveal the truth - to explain the situation and hope he would understand.

She let out a long breath. "I will be fine," she murmured.

He held his eyes on her for a long moment, as if trying to gauge her stamina, then he nodded. He slid an arm around her waist, gently supporting her, and they set in motion again along the narrow deer track. The woods were oak and maple, leafless in the winter chill, with dappled light sending golden streaks down between the bare branches. Her cloak was well crafted, keeping a layer of heat against her body, but the tip of her nose tingled with the cold.

They came up to a large, misshapen boulder of icy grey granite, and Erik turned left. "Ten years, and I know these woods as if I played in them yesterday," he mused, half to himself. "This was my world. I thought I would live here forever, would raise my children and my children's children ..."

Mary kept her gaze lowered, holding back a wry smile. At that same intersection she would have turned right, not left. Five years ago Erik's mother had built a wooden bridge across the stream, creating an easier route through this pass. Erik was heading the long way 'round, toward a natural ford. Erik had no way of knowing about the change, and given her current restrictions she had no choice but to follow silently at his side.

Her foot hooked on a root and she stumbled, cursing under her breath. Erik knelt at her side, his face creased with worry. "If there is somewhere you would rather go, I would do all in my power to get you there safely," he offered.

She gave a sharp shake of the head. "I have nowhere else to go," she stated. The truth of it pierced her to the core, just how much she was risking. If things went poorly, everything she had known and cared for could, once again, be ripped away from her.

Erik's eyes were steady on her, and he nodded, drawing her back to her feet. They moved along in silence for a while, through moss and fallen trunks, past birch trees stripped of their bark by hungry deer.

The sun was nearing the horizon before Erik called for a break, drawing them into a shallow cave. He looked regretfully at the mouth before shaking his head. "Still can't risk a fire," he murmured. "There's no guarantee that Josiah and his men aren't roaming around, looking for a trace of us." He gave an experimental twist of his torso, holding in a low groan. "And I am still not in any shape to properly defend us."

Mary looked down, her face flushing. All throughout the day Erik had not made one sound of complaint, not all the times he had to half carry her when her leg gave out. She had almost forgotten that his injury was just as serious as hers.

"I am sorry –"

"No," he said instantly, turning to face her. "Don't ever be sorry. If it weren't for you, I wouldn't be here. If I have to give my life to keep you safe, then I will do so gladly."

Mary's breath caught. For so long he had been a visceral presence in her life, a still center amidst a turmoil of emotion. Every day his honor had been disparaged as a source of anger and shame. She had tried to understand his mother's fury, understand her sense of betrayal and jealousy. And yet every time she had gazed at that painting over the fireplace, all she could imagine was what it would be like to have that fierce loyalty protecting her.

And here he was, kneeling before her, his eyes steadily on hers.

She wasn't sure if she leant forward, or if he did, but suddenly they were kissing, his lips firm and sure on hers, and her arms slid up around his back to pull him close. He put an arm out to lower her down onto the ground.

It was a long while before her breathing eased again.

She lay curled up against his chest, soaking in his warmth, when the thought came to her. He had said, even as he had been captured the final time by Caradoc's men, that he still held out hope that Lynessa was innocent in all of it.

A shiver ran through her core. Despite all Lynessa had done to him, a thread still connected the two. Mary wondered if he would ever be free.

Chapter 6

Mary forced herself to take long, deep breaths as they came around the final bend toward the keep's outer gates. It was only midday but she was already exhausted. Two days on the road had taxed her healing body more than she thought possible. She was grateful that only a short distance remained between her and the comfort of a warm fire. But it was the thought of the homecoming, and all it entailed, that tightened the muscles at her shoulders.

Erik's stride was slowing as well. She knew that this was just as difficult for him as it was for her, although for different reasons. To him, this was the home he had been exiled from. The family he had let down and deserted. He had turned his back on his mother's love, all for Lynessa.

Mary shook her head. If only he could have seen his mother during his decade of absence. The woman might have snapped in anger, but it was clear that her heart was with her son. Lady Cartwright's eyes had kindled with hope every time the main door of the hall swung open. The older woman would turn, seeking her son's remorseful gaze, hoping against hope to hear his vow that he would put her above the trollop who had caused so much harm.

That day had never come.

Erik and Mary walked steadily up the road side by side. Mary fought to keep herself from folding her hand into his and lending him her strength. She knew this homecoming was something he needed to face on his own.

By the time they reached the main gates the wall was solidly lined with guards. A burly man with salt-and-pepper hair stood at the center, his leather armor embossed with a pair of crossed swords. Mary knew the family crest as well as she knew the feel of her sword in her grasp. It was emblazoned on the banners in the great hall, on the blankets in each room, and on the carven back of the large oak chair at the center of the head table.

Erik's gaze drew to the man, and it was a moment before he spoke. His voice was steady and even. "Michael. It has been a long time."

Michael held his eyes, examining the man before him. Finally he nodded. "Ten years," he stated quietly. "You have filled out."

Erik drew his gaze down the line of men, each armed with crossbow or longbow, all weapons ready but undrawn. "Quite a contingent you have out today."

Michael's eyes stayed calmly on his. "Bandits have been in the area." He paused for a beat. "Perhaps you know something about that."

Erik's eyes shadowed. "Indeed I do," he murmured. He took in a deep breath, looking the older man in the eye. "Mary and I officially request sanctuary in the keep. Once she is safe, I will explain all I know of the situation and do whatever I can to help."

Michael's eyes moved to hers, a question held within them. She gave the slightest of nods.

Michael looked back to Erik. "My Lady Cartwright is currently indisposed, but I will grant temporary sanctuary to you and your friend until we receive full confirmation from her," he offered. He looked down below him. "Open the gates."

The thick, wooden gates swung wide.

Erik paused for a long moment, his gaze on the large courtyard before him. Then he strode forward, stepping deliberately across the threshold, returning home at last.

Michael moved down the steps to join them, reaching the ground as the gates were barred shut. He came around to stand before Erik, his eyes carefully assessing the man. Mary could see the tension in Michael's form. The warring between the fond Master of Arms who had been all but a father to him and the loyal servant of the keep who had dedicated his life to its protection these past ten years.

At last he put out an arm to Michael. His voice was gruff when he spoke. "I'm glad to see the Saracens weren't able to best you."

A glimmer of a smile came to Erik's face. "After the training you put me through, they were hard pressed to match me," he stated, clasping Michael's arm with warmth. "I gave thanks to you, after each battle, for the rigorous workouts you inflicted on me."

"You were always my best pupil," returned Michael, releasing his hand. "I was sore pressed when you left."

A silence fell between the two men, and after a moment Michael turned to Mary. Mary could see the warmth in his eyes, but he pitched his voice to be distant. "And who is your traveling companion? Mary, you say her name is?"

Erik gently laid a hand on her shoulder. "Yes, and I would ask that you treat Mary with the greatest of honor. She risked her life to save me. When that bandit carved up her leg –"

Michael's voice went hoarse. "You are injured?" He dropped to one knee before Mary and pulled back her cloak, revealing the bandage. He scanned it before looking up at her. "Have you checked for infection? You know that –"

She smiled fondly at him. "Erik has taken good care of me," she soothed him. "What I could use right now is a warm meal and a hot fire."

Michael drew up to his feet, nodding. "Of course." His eyes creased and he rounded on Erik. "Wait, are *you* injured?"

Erik gave a wry smile. "Just a minor wound across my stomach. A few stitches, nothing more."

Michael shook his head, running a hand through his hair. "I swear, you could get your leg hacked clean off and say it was a minor wound," he muttered, but there was a sparkle in his eye. "Let us get both of you in and seen to."

Erik slid his arm around Mary's waist, and Michael fell in at her other side. Mary could feel the tension easing out of Erik's stance with each passing step, the sense of comfort and relaxation he felt as he moved deeper into his home. Michael pushed open the main keep doors before them, and they walked through the narrow hallway before it opened into the great hall.

It seemed that the entire staff of the keep had found a reason to be present as Erik stepped into the room. Their faces were curious and cautious, but most held welcome as well. He had been their beloved young lord for so many years, and Mary knew they had missed him sorely while he was gone.

Erik's stride slowed, and Mary wondered how many times he had imagined this day - had envisioned his return home. His arm at her waist drew her in, holding her close, and she leant against him.

His step hitched, and Mary followed his gaze. He was looking at the empty grey fieldstone above the fireplace. A frown crossed his face, quickly erased again.

Mary knew what he had reacted to. From the day he had turned one, a painting of him had hung in that spot. Over the years the images had been updated. The day he had stormed out, the painting had shown him as a strong young man, dressed in a forest green tunic, his blue-grey eyes gazing resolutely out over the hall.

Now there was nothing to show he had ever been there.

They walked past the long, wooden tables, heading for the main table setting across the back end of the hall on a raised dais. Erik's mother had had a flair for the dramatic, and everything from her ornately carved chair to the elegant tapestry tablecloth and gold chased plateware spoke to her high station. Mary had often wondered what Erik's father had thought of all this, but the man had passed away only a year after his son's birth, gored by a stag on a Christmas day hunt. His wife had ruled with an iron fist, determined to pass a strong holding down to her son.

And then that son had abandoned her.

Erik's eyes were steady on the chair as they approached, then he lowered his eyes and moved to his seat at its right. He helped Mary into the smaller seat beside him, and Mary fell into it gratefully, a sigh escaping her as she relaxed into the familiar chair.

It was going to be all right. She was home.

Michael was at her right, Zelda poured her a glass of her favorite wine, and she smiled up at the buxom lady, giving her a toast before drinking down half of it in gratitude and relief. Tina, her tight red ringlets shining in the firelight, lay down a trencher with chicken stew and turnips, and Mary could have kissed her. The smell was nearly intoxicating.

She folded her gloved hands before her.

To her left, Erik's voice was hoarse. "May I say grace?"

Mary started, shaken out of her near dream state. For a moment it had all been so familiar, the fragrant smells, the presence of Michael at her side, the chair she had sat in for over ten years. Erik's voice zinged into that peace with the force of a lightning bolt out of a clear summer sky. He was here, now, present in the chair which had remained vacant for a decade. That empty chair had remained a stark reminder, throughout her time at the keep, that she was only second place in Lady Cartwright's heart. There had always been a spot between them, and it would only take Erik walking through that door to permanently keep them apart.

Her voice was shaky. "Of course," she murmured.

Erik clasped his fingers together, bowed his head, and Mary could hear the raw passion in his voice as he spoke. She wondered how many times he had recited these words when huddled around a tiny campfire in the deserts of Jerusalem or crouched over a small hunk of bread in the creaking hull of a merchant ship.

"Dear Lord, bless You in Your wisdom. I cannot fathom the plan You have for me or the twists my life must take to reach Your goal. I can only pray for the strength to meet the challenges You have set for me and the courage to do what must be done. Thank You for this nourishment, that I might live another day and move one step closer toward –"

There was a rough break in his voice, and Mary glanced sideways through shuttered lids. Erik had brought his forehead to his hands, and there was a glistening at his lashes. Mary looked down at her food again. She could only imagine how hard this must be on him.

At last he spoke again, his voice rough. "Thank You," he said simply. "Thank You."

Mary found her own throat was tight. "Amen."

They opened their eyes, and the feasting commenced. She had always loved Ygraine's cooking, and the woman had clearly outdone herself, knowing that the master might be returning home any day. The chicken was spiced to perfection, the rosemary and sage gravy brimming with love.

Zelda moved to Michael's side, whispering in his ear, casting a sidelong glance at Mary as she did so. Michael nodded, then leant forward, speaking to Mary and Erik.

"The Lady of the house wishes you welcome and bids you stay as long as you will. Erik, you can have your own room. Mary, she prefers that you stay with her, as there is not a room suitable for a woman currently made up."

Mary kept her face steady. "As she wishes."

Erik's gaze was still, and Mary wondered what emotions lurked behind that mask. "So she will not come out to greet us?"

Michael gave a short shake of the head. "She is currently indisposed," he informed Erik. "I am sure in time she will feel better and come out to welcome you properly."

It seemed only minutes before Mary was leaning back in her chair, comfortably full, the flickering heat of the hall seeping into her bones. For so long there had been an edge of cold in every motion; it was almost an unremembered luxury to feel this warm. Then Michael was rising to his feet, offering them both a short bow. "I must return to the walls," he murmured. His eyes went to Erik. "Perhaps later you can find me there, and we can discuss what we face with these bandits."

Erik rose to his feet. "Of course," he agreed. "I will share everything I know."

Michael held his gaze for a long moment, a look almost of contentment coming to his eyes. Then he turned and strode down the length of the great hall before vanishing from sight.

Erik watched him go, then at last turned to Mary. "I would like to take a walk around and determine how my home has changed since I left," he murmured. "If you would like, I could see you to your chambers first."

Mary gave a shake of her head. "I would prefer to go with you," she countered. "If you don't mind, of course."

He smiled at that, offering his arm. "I would be delighted to show you my home."

They walked together toward the courtyard. Mary was touched by how well he knew every person there - their relationships, their interests, and their dreams. It was as if he had never been gone. The staff glowed under his attention, came to life, and Mary realized just how cold and sterile the keep had become under his mother's harsh rule.

Erik's feet turned toward the stable, and a tremor of nervousness ran through Mary's heart. She hoped against hope that Michael had remembered to stable her own steed at the farmstead down the hill, not in her own stall. If Erik saw the horse …

A sigh of relief escaped her as they moved into the low building. The stall was empty; the halter missing from its peg.

They moved up to the wall, talking with the soldiers. Erik examined the chain of the gate and the readiness of the armory. His face grew still as he looked down the line of weapons, and a fresh nervousness built within Mary. What if he did not approve of how she had maintained the keep over the past few years? What if he was disappointed in this home he had returned to?

They were climbing the steps back toward the great hall before she ventured to put her thoughts into words. "You have been away for ten long years," she murmured. "You have seen great palaces and elaborate temples. Does your home now seem small in comparison?"

He looked over in surprise, shaking his head. "Far from it," he stated. "If anything, I am reluctantly impressed with this new Lady Cartwright. My mother had always been more interested in outer appearance than inner substance. For her it was about the embroidery on the guest linens and the presentation of the great hall." He turned and looked back up toward the line of guards on the wall. "The men are better equipped than I have ever seen, and seem more comfortable with their arms as well. I have to say I am impressed."

A glow eased through Mary, and she looked away. That he approved of her efforts meant more than she would have thought.

He was walking forward, his stride slowing, and she had no doubt where he was headed. He moved to the spiral staircase at the side of the hall, taking the flight with steady steps, then walked down the hallway. At last he stood before the wooden door of his room. He placed his hand on it for a long moment before pushing it open.

Mary knew exactly what he would see as the door swung open. The room had been frozen in time since he left. The maids had cleaned it daily, the linens were always kept fresh, and the surfaces dusted.

The forest-green curtains on the double windows were pulled to the side, letting in the streaming afternoon sunshine. To the left lay a low bed, with matching blankets, a trunk at its side. A dresser on the opposite wall displayed several knives and a pair of buckles. Shelves stored tunics, leggings, and a training sword.

Erik stood still for a long moment, as if disbelieving that it really was just as he had left it. Then he stepped in, moving from place to place, running a hand over a hilt, breathing in the fragrance of the place.

Mary closed her eyes. So many days she had sat here, in the center of the room, drawn in by the melding of leather and anise. She had wondered just who this young man had been and what had driven him to leave.

Her eyes flickered open, and he was there. He was standing there, before her, his eyes tinged with wonder.

He stepped forward to take her hands in his. "It is still so hard for me to grasp," he murmured in a rough voice. "That it is all here, just the way I left it. I saw so much destruction, so much desolation, in my years in Jerusalem. I half expected to return and find the keep in ruins."

"But it is whole," murmured Mary.

His eyes eased at that, and he drew her in against him. His voice was a sigh. "It is whole."

His presence sung to her; she found herself relinquishing all her weight to him. He gave a low chuckle, pressing a soft kiss at her forehead. "And you are exhausted," he added. "Let us get you to bed."

They left the room, and he closed the door gently behind him. Then they walked the short distance down the hall to the master bedroom. He gave a glance toward the door, then nodded. "I am sure the Lady will take good care of you," he murmured. "I shall leave you to the care of her maids." He ran a hand tenderly down the side of her face. "I will see you in the morning." His gaze stilled. "Now I need to speak with Michael and tell him everything I know of the bandit threat." He gave her a short bow, then turned and headed down the hallway.

Mary waited until he was gone before pushing open the door to her room.

The Lady's large, ornately carved canopy bed sat to the left, its dark wood dominating the room. It was topped with gold-chased tapestries and embroidered pillows. A fire blazed in the marble fireplace to the right. The heavy curtains were pulled shut, layering the room in shadows even at this hour.

Exhaustion seeped into every corner of her being, and she stumbled without thought to the foot of the bed, to the small trundle set up there, facing the fire. His eyes were there, above the fire, gazing down at her as they always did. She pushed aside her covers, rolled into bed, and instantly fell asleep.

* * *

There was an odd noise, and she bolted instantly awake. The room was flickering in darkness. Only the low embers of the fire sent stuttering shadows across the room. She strained to hear in the dark what had shaken her out of her chaotic dreams.

There. A soft thud, from just down the hall.

Her mind sorted and searched for its meaning.

Suddenly awareness flooded through her, filling her with a glowing, golden warmth.

Erik was home.

The sound was one she had never heard, not in all her long years of living in this keep. It had been one Lady Cartwright had dreamt about, had prayed for, had hoped for, and had cried for.

It was the sound of Erik closing his bedroom door.

Mary rolled to a sitting position, staring at the fire, straining to hear even the slightest noise. Would he go to stare out the window, taking in the view he had enjoyed throughout his childhood? Would he be resting on the bed? The sense of his presence loomed larger in her mind with each passing second. Every cell in her body craved his touch, craved his voice in her ear, his scent in her lungs.

She wanted him.

She knew she should resist.

In a blink she was on her feet, moving swiftly through her door. Perhaps she would just ask him how his talk with Michael had gone. She would gain his thoughts about his first day home. She would …

She was at his door, giving the softest of knocks, and the door pulled open before her fist could land a third time.

He was pulling her in, his arms were around her, and her lips found his in the shadowy darkness. She could think of nothing else but that he was here, he was finally here, and she belonged to him.

Chapter 7

The crispness of the dawn air in the courtyard tickled her nose, and Mary stretched her arms over her head, relishing the sensation. Before her, the men of the keep were practicing thrusts and blocks, following footwork that she knew by heart.

Michael was at her side, watching over his men with an attentive eye. "So after all of this, he is still not quite free of her?"

She nodded, a weight pulling her heart. It had been hard enough to draw herself free of Erik's embrace last night, the sweat of their lovemaking still fresh on her body. She had known she had to return to her own bed, to retain some small semblance of objectivity.

But to think of that woman …

Michael made a small motion of his head, and she glanced toward the keep. The front door was opening, and Erik was standing there, gazing out over the courtyard. To all appearances he was looking out over his home, assessing its readiness, and turmoil settled into her soul. What would he do when he realized she was the one who stood between him and all he held dear?

He came down the steps toward them, nodding his greeting as he approached. He wore his leather armor, and his sword was at his hip. His lips drew up into a smile as he joined them, looking out over the men.

"So many years, and yet the footwork is as familiar as my own breathing," he murmured.

Michael glanced over with a smile. "Perhaps you would be up for a round?"

Erik's grin was instant. "Absolutely."

Michael stepped with him toward the center of the courtyard. "I'll go easy on you, what with your injury and all."

Erik's eyes lit up. "Perhaps I should go easy on *you*," he countered. "What with you nearing old age and all."

Michael laughed out loud, drawing his sword and saluting. The men around him fell back at once, giving them room, and excited murmurs moved through the crowd. Stable boys and laborers emerged from the nearby outbuildings, drawn by the chatter.

Erik answered the salute, and the two men were circling. Mary leant forward, her heart pounding. She had trained with Michael for ten years, and knew every twist and turn of his attack. She had seen his imprint clearly on Erik's maneuvers against Caradoc's men. She was curious just how well the two men would be matched against each other. Michael had been the trainer – but Erik had faced the heat of battle for ten long years.

Her eyes went to his stomach, to where she knew the wound was healing. She wondered if it would hamper his efforts.

If it did, he didn't show it. He launched a high, twisting attack, bringing his sword down toward Michael's left shoulder. Michael dodged to his right, trailing his sword, deflecting the attack down and away. He spun his sword in a half-arc, aiming for Erik's side. Erik leapt back, leaving just enough space for the sword tip to whistle across his front, then thrusting straight into the gap. Michael leant to the side, the blade barely missing his ribs.

Mary could barely keep up with move and counter-move. Cheers rang out all around as the footwork resounded on the cobblestones, the clang of blade on steel echoed against the walls, and the flash of a smile accompanied a particularly challenging block.

Then suddenly both men were still. Erik's blade lay against Michael's neck. Michael's was pressed up into Erik's groin.

The men in the ring erupted into cheers and delighted conversation. Erik and Michael clasped arms, Michael adding a solid pat on Erik's back as the two approached Mary.

She smiled, shaking her head. "You weren't kidding, Michael," she commented as they drew to a stop before her. "You have done yourself proud, training this one."

Michael looked Erik up and down, chuckling. "He has mastered much since he left my care," he countered. "If he did not have that injury, I doubt I could last long against him."

Erik clapped the older man on the arm. "It is only due to your training that I lasted long enough to learn on the field at all," he pointed out. "Many good men died there."

A shout of alert came from the wall, and all three of their heads instantly turned to look. One of the men-at-arms was staring fixedly to the north. "Riders," he called out. "Twenty."

Michael sprinted toward the stairs, Erik close at his heels. It was all Mary could do to hobble at a frustratingly slow pace to catch up with them. Every step up the long stone flight sent her wound a fresh volley of pain. Finally she made it up to the main corridor of the wall – and froze.

Lord Paul was pulling up before the gates, his troops milling about him. He wore an elegant crimson cloak over his leather jerkin, and his greying hair framed a leathered face.

She pulled back away from the wall, hoping against hope he had not seen her. For all of her planning, she had not taken into account the fact that he might come by. He had been a family friend of Lady Cartwright's and had become something of a foster uncle to her. His lands lay on the northern front and his occasional visits had been wonderful breaks for Mary from the stark quiet of her daily routine.

But not now.

Not with Erik just returned home.

Lord Paul was calling up to Michael, his rough voice reflecting his love of mead. "Good morn, Michael. I'm here to lure your Lady out for a bandit hunt. I hear several have been spotted nearby, and I think a good day of scouting should get us clear of these vermin."

Michael's voice was tight. "I am afraid that Lady Cartwright is inconvenienced today, Lord Paul."

Lord Paul's booming laugh echoed across the courtyard. "You cannot be serious, man. That woman is as tough as my finest hunting dog. In the ten years I have known her, I have never once seen her laid low by injury or illness."

Erik took a step forward. "Where did you see the bandits?"

Lord Paul's head swiveled to take in this newcomer. His eyes focused for a long moment before a steely look came into his gaze. "So the prodigal son returns home."

Erik's voice stayed even. "It is good to see you, Lord Paul."

Lord Paul's eyes sharpened. "So suddenly you are home - and suddenly a woman whose strength rivals any man I know is unable to see me?"

Erik's gaze held his. "I have nothing to do with –"

Lord Paul stood in his stirrups, his gaze returning to Michael. "I insist Lady Cartwright be brought out to speak with me immediately."

Michael's jaw clenched. "Sir, you are in no position to –"

Lord Paul gave a wave of his hand, and his men lined up on either side of him, their hands dropping to the hilts of their swords. "Either you produce Lady Cartwright this very instant, or I swear –"

Michael swept down his hand, and as one the troops along the wall readied their bows.

Mary could not take any more. She ran to the edge of the crenelated wall, leaning over, calling down to Lord Paul. His greying curls, his sturdy strength, filled her with fondness, and she smiled at his loyal defense of her. "It is all right, Paul," she reassured him. "I am all right."

He settled back down into his saddle, his creased face easing. "What is all of this about, Mary?"

"I will tell you over dinner," she reassured him. "A minor leg wound, nothing serious. But for now, I'll send out ten of my patrol with you; they were about to head out for their rounds anyway. Hopefully you can catch up with the bandits before they leave the lands. Where were they spotted?"

"By the new bridge, down on the southern river," he explained. "Four of them, snooping around."

The main gates were pulled open, and the keep's troops streamed out, mingling easily with those of Lord Paul. He gave a look between Erik and Michael, then nodded to her. "I will definitely want to hear the full story at dinner," he prodded.

"I will have Ygraine make your favorite pheasant stew," she promised with a smile.

That eased the severity of his gaze, and he nodded, giving a short bow. Then he wheeled his mount, heading out toward the south. The men followed along behind. In a minute the hoofbeat was lost in the distance.

Iron bands began compressing Mary's lungs, and she was acutely aware of just how focused every soldier's gaze was on the forest, on the road beneath them, on anything but her and Erik.

If she had envisioned the hundred different ways she might break the news to him, that she was the new owner of the keep he adored, this was not one of them.

She turned without a word, made her way to the steps, slowly hobbled her way down them, then eased the short distance along the edge of the courtyard to the small stone chapel that stood to one side. There were two rows of five pews, divided by a slim aisle, and a simple circular window at the end that radiated with a hazy glow of light. The candles she had lit earlier in the morning still flickered along one wall.

She half fell as she reached the main altar, the weariness of the world pressing heavily on her shoulders.

There was the creak of a door closing behind her, and then a presence that she knew could only be one man.

His voice, when he spoke, was quiet and rough with emotion. "Why did you want to keep it a secret?"

Something about his tone caused her to blink and turn. She leant back against the altar, looking at him in surprise. "You knew?"

He gave a wry shake of his head, his blue-grey gaze steady on hers. "When I saw you fight the men in that hellhole of a dungeon, I could see Michael's imprint on you as clearly as if he had branded you," he stated. "The way you moved, the angle at which you held your blade, all glowed with his training. When you reacted instantly to my reverse J command, I knew it as surely as if you had shouted his name out loud."

He took a step forward. "The rest came gradually. Your survival of the massacre at Cintersloe brought sense to how you had arrived at the keep. Your explanation that a widow took you in connected your plight to my mother." His eyes held hers. "But there was still the mystery. Why would you have come after me yourself? What was your intention?"

Mary could barely breathe. "And what is my intention?"

He drew another step closer. "When I talked with the staff, I was not sure what I would find. Would they be fearful of my return? Hopeful for rescue from a harsh mistress?" He gave a soft shake of his head. "To my surprise, they seemed more content than I had ever seen them. The kitchens were well stocked and neatly maintained. The soldiers' gear was sharp and showed sign of regular use and care. They seemed pleased with their lot." His voice dropped down. "More than that, they seemed content with my return. I posed no threat to their way of life."

Mary's throat was dry. "What do *you* intend?"

He gave a ghost of a smile, looking her over. "For so long I assumed I would come home and somehow reclaim my possession of this keep," he admitted, his voice hoarse. "And yet now I find it run in exactly the way I might hope, by a woman who risked her own life to save mine." He gave a shake of his head. "I am not sure I could ever have dreamt for more."

Mary leant back against the altar. "You once would have dreamt of far more," she quietly pointed out.

He gave a wry grin. "I once had reached for many things," he agreed. "Life has taught me the folly of those ambitions. Now my goals are much simpler. My realization of human weakness is much more acute. If this is what lies in store for this keep, then I am content."

He dropped his eyes for a moment, and when he raised them again, they were steady and strong. "You asked me, in the tower, to respect your privacy. To let you reveal your personal tale in your own time. I pledged to do so, and I hold to that pledge."

He gave a nod to her, turned, and then he was gone.

Mary's breathing came back to her in long draws. In a moment, Michael strode into the room, glancing around before coming up to her side. "Are you all right? What did Erik say?"

She shook her head, giving a wry chuckle. "He knew already," she informed him. "Your training gave me away. Once he grasped the situation, it seems he accepted it."

He ran a hand through his hair. "The lad was always too smart by half," he sighed in chagrin. "I should have known he'd realize you were with the keep the moment you had to take on your first opponent." He looked back to Mary. "So, what do we do now?"

She gave a soft shrug. "We remain true to our plan. We see what we can determine about the hold Lynessa has over him."

Her eyes went to the door, to where Erik had turned and left her.

And what if Lynessa's hold over him could not be broken?

Chapter 8

Mary fiddled nervously with the broach at her breast, smoothing down the elegant forest-green dress for the tenth time. She knew it was nearly the hour for dinner, and yet she could not bring herself to pull open the door, to descend and face Erik in her new personae. She had hoped beyond hope that she would have more time to ease into this role, to learn more about him. But it was not meant to be.

Finally she took in a deep breath, pressed open the door, and headed down the empty hall. The spiral staircase, so familiar to her, wrapped her in safety, and her footsteps slowed as she neared the bottom. She walked around the corner and into the great hall.

Erik and Lord Paul were standing together by the head table, conferring in low voices, and both turned as she stepped into the room. Lord Paul's eyes held pride. Erik's gaze moved slowly down her form, soaking her in as if seeing her afresh. Lord Paul gave a low chuckle, leaning toward Erik. "First time you've seen her dressed properly?"

Erik only nodded, his eyes on hers. She slowly approached the pair, her heart pounding, and as she reached them Erik put out his hand. She laid hers in his, and he lowered his head to press the tenderest of kisses against her fingertips. Even through the gloves she felt the movement, and a flutter rippled throughout her body.

He stood, looking her over. At last he spoke, his voice rough. "You are stunning."

Her cheeks flushed, and she looked down. Only Lord Paul had ever commented on her looks. She had taken those words of praise with a smile, thinking he was being sweet but perhaps not overly accurate. The look in Erik's eyes was another thing altogether. The heat of it coursed down through her toes.

He turned, then, her hand still in his, and led her over to the central chair. Her feet came to a halt of their own accord, and he turned, his brow creasing in confusion.

His voice had a rough, forced quality to it when he spoke. "There is no need for deception any more," he pointed out. "You should take your proper place at the table."

Mary's throat closed tight. She could only stare at the chair, the chair that had previously been used by but one woman. A woman whose hard, black eyes she could see even now, staring at her in disapproval.

Lord Paul's voice eased into the tension. "Erik, your mother has been the only person to use that chair for over twenty years," he commented quietly. "Just as your own chair has been left empty since the day you departed, so has your mother's chair remained vacant. Mary has only ever sat at her own place." He nudged his head toward the low, simple chair.

Erik's eyes went between the large, carven throne and the humbler spot, and there was a softening of the tension at his shoulders. He gave a quiet nod, then guided Mary to her own chair, taking the seat beside her. Paul sat at her other side, and in a moment the servants were moving around them, pouring out the wine and delivering the food.

Lord Paul kept up a running conversation throughout dinner, talking of the elusive nature of the wolves' heads, how they had once again managed to escape the patrol, and the status of the various villages in the area. Mary was grateful for it. She could feel Erik's presence at her side as a glowing fire, drawing her to him, but she could not bring herself to turn or speak. Everything had changed so quickly. The danger of it, the potential to be burned, sounded strongly in her head.

The plates were cleared, mead was brought, and Lord Paul looked over toward the fireplace. "Maybe we should relocate?"

Mary gave a nod, standing. Lord Paul moved over to the chair he always took, a dark leather one with a low table alongside it. Mary eased down to sit at his feet, carefully tucking her injured leg beneath her. It was all so familiar. How many nights had she sat here like this, with Lady Cartwright on the low couch opposite, listening to Lord Paul share his tales as the wind whistled outside?

Erik stood to the side, his gaze on the empty stone above the fireplace, lost in thought.

Lord Paul looked between them for a moment before drawing his gaze up to Erik. "Tell us of your times in the Holy Land."

Erik gave himself a shake, turning. "You yourself served in the Crusades when you were young. You warned me it would be brutish, nothing like the stories told in bards' songs. I laughed at the time, but now I see the truth of it."

Lord Paul nodded. "And yet, even in the darkest night, there is often a glimmer of light."

Erik ran a hand through his hair. "Sometimes the black is absolute."

Mary leant forward. "But surely, for example, when you rescued those three nuns from –"

Erik stared at her as if she were speaking in tongues, cutting her off. "How could you know about that?"

Mary flushed, but there was no way to un-say what had been blurted out. "Your commander wrote us," she admitted.

Erik looked between them in baffled confusion. "What, Commander Bavent? He wrote you?"

She held his gaze. "Yes. Your mother had an arrangement with him. Every month she wrote him with a status of his daughter, who was lodged at the St. Francis convent a short distance to the north. And every month he wrote back, sharing details of your activities."

Erik took a moment to absorb the news. "I knew of the letters," he stated at last, "but I never had any idea that I was their subject, or that the incoming ones were from my mother."

Mary gave a wry smile. "She did not want you to know of it," she agreed. "But she lived for them." She glanced at Lord Paul. "The moment one arrived, she would send for Lord Paul, and we would gather right here. He would read it to us, over and over again, until we had memorized every word. And then it became almost a prayer for us, one we could recall at will, for the long month before the next one arrived."

Erik looked across to the empty table, to the throne that sat vacant at its center. "I had no idea."

Lord Paul gazed fondly down at Mary. "This lass could probably recite to you every action you have taken, every siege you withstood, every campaign you fought."

Erik's eyes drew down to her, and there was a tumult of emotions in his gaze – the surprise melding into respect and something stronger.

Lord Paul spread his arms. "If you are not interested in talking about your time in the Holy Land, maybe you have some questions about the keep or its lands? How it has fared since you have been gone?"

Erik looked over to Lord Paul at that, his gaze even. "The keep's people. Yes, I have a question."

Lord Paul arched an eyebrow. "Ask, and I shall answer."

Erik's gaze became steely. "I would like to hear how you allowed Mary to end up alone in the Mangy Cur tavern without support nor succor."

Lord Paul's shoulders tensed. "I had nothing to do with that decision," he stated firmly. "I myself would like to know how Michael thought –"

The main door pushed open, and Michael strode in, coming over to join them. "Night patrol is taking over," he reported to both Mary and Erik. "Nothing of concern. It's been quiet out there."

Erik held him with his gaze. "And what do you have to report about sending Mary alone into Caradoc's home base?"

Michael's stance sharpened, and he glanced down at Mary. His lips pressed into a thin line.

Mary sighed, running a hand through her hair. "It wasn't Michael's fault," she explained. "He argued long and hard for other options – for any other option. But in the end I overruled him. It was the only path I saw which might –"

She cut off, realizing that she had almost been drawn into revealing the core of Lady Cartwright's mission for her.

She flushed, looking down.

Erik's shoulders were drawn tight. "Which might *what*?"

Mary's eyes were pulled to the empty sofa, to where Lady Cartwright had glared down at her with those marble-cold eyes. Mary could still salvage part of her mission. She could still follow through with the task she had been ordered to fulfill.

Erik's gaze sharpened, and for a moment it was as if Lady Cartwright was looking down through his eyes, staring with that same focused determination. "God's teeth, Mary, I accept that you own the keep. I am not contesting your leadership here. I accept you have every right to sleep in the master suite, to sit in the family chair, to tear down my portrait –"

Lord Paul was on his feet, a pulsing vein bulging at his neck. "Now you have gone too far!"

Erik put up his hands in a move of surrender. "I was only saying –"

Lord Paul took a step forward. "I was here that night," he growled, his voice rough. "I was here the night the messenger came in with the news that you had left for the Holy Land. Your mother flew into a rage. Until then she had been absolutely convinced that you would return home any day - that your fleeting infatuation with Lynessa would come to an end. But when that messenger finished speaking –"

His eyes went to the bare wall above the fireplace. His voice dropped low. "She was like an enraged boar. She dashed her crystal goblet of wine against the floor, shattering it. Then she strode over to that painting on the wall, the one her eyes barely left any time she was in this room, and she ripped it down from its hook. She flung it into the fire."

Erik's eyes widened, and he turned to stare into the roaring flame.

Michael's voice was hoarse. "And then Mary dove in after it."

Erik's face went white with shock. He turned to Mary, his gaze moving down to her gloves.

He gave a low groan. "I thought you had been burnt during the destruction of Cintersloe."

Mary looked down at the leather gloves, then into the maw of the fireplace. She could remember the moment with vivid clarity. The painting of the man she both resented and craved with all her heart. The violent crack as the frame hit the back of the stone. The fierce crackling as the flame took hold. She had moved without conscious thought, a sheer rush of emotion, and she had grabbed the fiery image to drag it out. The shock had carried her through for a minute or two. And then the searing pain …

Erik was kneeling before her, holding her hands in his, looking into her eyes. "Why did you do it?"

She gave her head a shake, hardly knowing herself. But his eyes were steady on her, and she tried to put it into words. "You were always there," she murmured. "A part of the keep. I had seen too many people burnt. She couldn't burn you, too." She put her head down, wrapping her arms around her knees. "She couldn't burn you."

The room went quiet, and after a moment Erik had put his arms around her, drawing her up against him in a tender carry. He nodded to the other two men, then turned and headed for the stairs. Mary eased against his chest, the aroma of anise surrounding her, comforted by his steady stride. He moved down the hall to her room and pushed the door open with his shoulder.

The thick curtains were pulled shut, and the only light came from the low embers in the grate. He glanced around in the gloom, then took a step toward the large, canopied bed.

Mary tensed, her arms wrapping tightly around his chest. "No."

Erik froze, looking down at her. "I don't understand …?"

Mary nudged her head to the right. "By the fireplace," she murmured.

Erik took the few steps toward the fireplace and stopped in surprise. He took in the low bunk stretched across the foot of the bed - the small pillow and thin blanket which waited there.

He glanced back at the large, carved canopy bed. "But that bed is –"

"That is the bed Lady Cartwright died in," stated Mary, her throat tight. "I sat there with her, until her ghost left her, and for hours afterward. I kept hoping I could bring her back with sheer strength of will." Her voice dropped. "It was Michael who finally pried my fingers loose from hers. Michael who took me downstairs and held me while I sobbed."

Erik knelt by the small bed, carefully settling Mary into it. He stayed there at her side, his face contrite. "I am so sorry, Mary. I should have been here. I should have carried that burden."

Mary's voice was tight. "She would have liked that. She never gave up hope."

He shook his head, tenderly brushing her hair back from her face. "I was too stubborn to see it," he murmured in a low voice. "I thought she hated me."

The corners of Mary's mouth turned up. "She adored you with a passion that was stunning to see." She raised a hand to gently trace the planes of Erik's face. "One I understand well."

Erik groaned, his lips brushing across hers, first tenderly, then with growing heat, and she was lost.

Chapter 9

Mary blinked her eyes open. Her bedroom was in its perpetual gloom, but the thinnest traces of morning light eased around the edges of the curtains. The fire had all but died out, and she wearily rubbed at her eyes. She would have to get another log onto the fire and give it a chance to catch, before she began her morning routine.

She groaned, rolling to a sitting position.

There was someone in the room with her.

It was a moment before the panic eased, leaving behind the realization that Erik was standing there. He was clad only in his leggings, staring up at the remnants of the painting which hung over the fire. Her eyes followed his, coming to rest on the image she knew so well.

The fire had done its damage. Most of the image was blackened and beyond repair, soot and curling ash visible in fragmented layers. Only the face had survived, the blue-grey eyes staring from a mottled, brown surface.

Erik's voice was hoarse. "My mother had the image hung here?"

Mary nodded, looking down at her gloved hands. "She felt the guilt of her action keenly and wanted to always be reminded of what she had done." She let out a breath. "When I was first burned she tended to me herself, here, in this room. Three times a day she spread ointments of ivy and leek on each finger. She fed me wild beet soup. When she saw the scars would not heal, she had these gloves made for me." She turned her hands before her, looking at the embroidered design tracing along the cuff of each one. "I have worn them ever since."

Erik turned and knelt before her, taking her hands in his. He looked up into her eyes.

Her cheeks flushed and shame swept through her. But at long last she nodded her head.

Carefully, tenderly, he undid the button at the right cuff, then eased the glove off of her hand. She fought the instinct to curl her fingers, to hide the mangled flesh beneath her other gloved hand. Her throat grew tight as he brought his head down to her hand, gently kissing each finger in turn. The sensation was so raw, so tender against her flesh, and her body flushed with heat.

Then he was turning to her left hand, sliding the leather from her skin, and the softness of his lips against her hands melted her.

He took her hands in his, laying them against his face, and she marveled at the sensation of his skin beneath her touch. She saw the strength of will it took for him to resist the passion, to remain still as she slid her hands down along his throat, across the strength of his shoulders, curling around to slide across the muscles of his back.

His breathing was ragged, his eyes smoky with desire. And yet he remained in place, his body nearly trembling with the effort.

She brought her hands back up to the back of his neck, pulling his head down to hers, kissing him tenderly at first, and then with growing passion. He gave a growl, and at last his reserves broke, and he was pressing down full against her, all else forgotten.

* * *

Mary stood alongside Michael on the wall over the gate, staring out at the forest in the darkening twilight. Erik had gone out on patrol with Lord Paul, and the group was due back soon.

Michael crossed his arms on the stone block before him, leaning upon it, his gaze following the road to where it bent away through the trees. "You care for him."

Mary's cheeks flushed, but she knew it was both foolish and impossible to hide it. Undoubtedly the entire keep knew that Erik had spent the night in her room; had noticed the way her eyes trailed after him as he headed out with the patrol group.

Michael's voice held caution. "What has he said about Lynessa?"

Mary dropped her head, letting her dark hair fall like a curtain before her face. Lady Cartwright had trained her ruthlessly for this very task. Mary knew the danger she found herself in, and yet she found it nearly impossible to resist Erik's draw. She wanted with all her heart to believe in him.

Lady Cartwright had believed in him, and it had led her to die alone, in misery.

Mary's throat tightened. "Erik still holds out hope that Lynessa is innocent in all of this. Despite everything she has done."

Michael's grizzled face remained steady. "Where does that leave your vow?"

Mary struggled to inhale. It was as if her lungs had turned to stone, refusing to bring in more air for her.

Where did it leave her?

Lady Cartwright had been adamant on the subject. She would rather see the keep torn down, stone by stone, than turn it over to the woman who had caused the family so much pain. Mary had sworn on her life to only present Erik with his birthright if it was absolutely certain he was free of Lynessa's influence.

Her voice was a whisper. "I do not know."

Michael glanced at her, hesitance clear in his motions. "I have a suggestion, but I doubt you will like it."

Tension trickled along her neck, working its way to lace though her shoulders. "You want to lure Lynessa in."

He gave a nod. "The only way to see how he acts with her is to bring her to him." His lips drew into a line. "It could also give us the opportunity to draw more information from her, about her relationship with the Caradoc clan."

A jagged bolt of fear zigged through Mary at the thought of Lynessa riding into her keep; delving into her safe shelter. The vixen could destroy all she held dear. Lynessa could flay her heart as thoroughly as she had destroyed Lady Cartwright.

She could take Erik away.

Mary's fingers gripped the stone until her knuckles blanched. "I believe we have no other choice."

Michael shook his head. "None that I can see," he agreed. "We do not have the resources for a full-on attack, and the Caradocs will be alert for any infiltration, given the success of your last endeavor. However, if we use Erik as bait, Lynessa will be hard pressed to ignore the lure of what she has wanted all this time."

Mary's voice was hoarse. "And what do I tell Erik?"

There was motion from the woods. A group of riders approached at an easy canter, and Mary's heart lifted as Erik's gaze met hers. She pushed all thoughts of Lynessa away. For tonight, Erik was hers alone.

Dinner seemed interminable, for all she could feel was the warmth of his thigh where it pressed up against hers, the gentle caress of his fingers as he handed her a fresh glass of wine. When they moved to sit by the fire, he leant against the base of the couch, drawing her in against him, and it was all she could do not to turn in his arms, to lay full across him and lose herself in his embrace. Then, as Lord Paul finished one of his stories, Erik turned his head to press a tender kiss against her throat. She could take no more. She turned to gaze up at him, her eyes full of longing and desire. The flare of passion in his own brought a smile to her lips. He made a mumbled apology to Lord Paul before sweeping her up in his arms, crossing the hall, and climbing the spiral steps in less time than she thought possible.

He shouldered the door to her room open, and for a minute she blinked in confusion. The room looked completely different. Gone was the massive canopy bed that had dominated the room all of her life. In its place was the low bed from Avoca's folly, piled with its dense blankets and soft pillows. The room was ringed with candles of all sizes, lining the mantle over the fireplace, the shelves, and the low table by the bed.

She turned her head to the fireplace. The mangled painting was gone. In its place was her tambourine, the stained leather replaced with new, fresh material. The oak shell was polished and gleaming.

Erik looked down at her, his eyes shining with respect. "You deserve a room that celebrates your strengths," he murmured. "One you can embrace as wholly yours."

He stepped to the bed, lay her down on it, and knelt at her side.

She put a hand up to his cheek, her body aglow, and then they were one.

* * *

Mary gazed down at Erik's sleeping form, soft tendrils of morning light just easing around the edges of the curtain. He blinked his eyes open, the corners of his mouth curving into a smile.

"You're up early," he murmured.

Her throat was tight. "I couldn't sleep."

His brow creased, and he raised a hand to lay it against her cheek. "What is it?"

She could barely get the words out. She knew once she started down this path there was no turning back, but she saw no other choice. "It is February thirteenth," she murmured.

His eyes immediately clouded. "I had lost track of – I'm so sorry. It is the anniversary of the burning of Cintersloe." He drew up to a sitting position. "Mary, if I could do anything to undo that night, I would do it."

Mary took his hands in hers. For a moment the still-new sensation of his strong fingers against her bare skin sent a delicious shiver through her body. It renewing the longing that could easily overwhelm her.

She pushed it away with effort. She could not give in to that now.

Still, it was a moment before she could speak. "There is one thing you could do for me."

"Anything."

. She could not hold his gaze and say it. She had to turn her eyes away, to stare into the low embers and draw strength from the flame.

Had Lynessa been involved in her town's destruction?

The thought gave her fortitude to continue - to speak the words she knew she had to.

"I want to invite Lynessa to stay at the keep."

Erik gave his head a small shake, as if he had not heard her properly. "You want to *what?*"

Her voice grew in strength. "I want you to tell her that the keep is now yours. That you have returned home and reclaimed your rightful place."

Erik pushed himself up to a sitting position, his jaw tight. "Whatever for?"

Mary shook her head. If she told him she was testing his loyalty to Lynessa, how could she trust any answer he gave? He would claim he was completely free of her charms - only to succumb when the blonde harlot next made her advances on him.

No. This was the only way to know for sure.

Erik's voice took on a steely tone. "So you want me to bring Lynessa here under false pretenses, and then continually lie to her? To act a role which is patently false?"

Mary's cheeks flushed with heat. She could feel the crispness of his motions - the distance spreading between them.

His voice was hollow. "Why, Mary?"

She turned at last, holding him with her gaze. "Because it is all I ask of you, in memory of my slain parents, my murdered friends, and the ashes of the village of Cintersloe."

He flinched as if she had hit him. Then he rolled to his feet, looking down at her with a shadowed gaze.

"As you wish."

He moved around the foot of the bed, pulled open the door, and then he was gone.

* * *

Mary ran a hand wearily through her hair, leaning against the wall's crenellation. Exhaustion seeped into every bone in her body.

Michael's voice was rich with worry. "You get on to sleep," he murmured. "I will keep watch for Erik's return."

"He should have been back hours ago," she insisted. "He was only accompanying the messenger to our borders."

Michael nodded quietly. "He was like this as a youth. When his mother gave him an order which upset him, he would roam the woods for hours. It gave him time to work the anger out of his system."

Mary pursed her lips into a line. In a way it *was* Lady Cartwright making demands from beyond the grave. The Lady's will was pushing Mary on a path she did not wish to follow.

Michael's voice was low. "You could always just tell him that –"

Mary cut him off. "No. Lady Cartwright made her wishes absolutely clear, and I am honor bound to follow them. I must turn over the keep to Erik's control. I cannot do that until I can prove beyond a shadow of a doubt that Lynessa no longer holds sway over him."

Michael nodded in understanding. "I just hate to see you torn asunder like this."

She smiled wryly at that, leaning her head against his shoulder. "I know, and I appreciate it. I will get through this."

There was motion from the distant forest. At last a lone rider cantered into view, the sure, steady motion speaking to a horseman comfortable with the terrain. Mary watched as Erik grew nearer, but he never looked up, never raised his eyes to hers even as he rode in beneath her position on the wall. She waited while he stabled his steed, but when he emerged he went straight toward the keep, not turning.

Michael gave a soft shrug. "Maybe at dinner we will learn more," he murmured.

But Erik did not join them at dinner, and his empty chair tugged hollowly at Mary's heart. The last course had barely been removed from the table before she was making her way upstairs. She slowed before his door, but could not bring herself to knock. Her own room seemed even more barren than usual, with only the low, empty bed to one side. The candles were all dark. The dim embers in the fireplace sent only the faintest glimmer against the cymbals of her tambourine.

Even the eyes of his painting were gone.

She climbed into bed and pulled the covers over her head, helpless to hold back the feeling of desolation that swept through her.

Chapter 10

Mary was being gently shaken awake, but she clung to her dream with all her might. In it, she and Erik were entwined in the solitude of Avoca's folly. The safety of the tower protected them, isolating them from all others. If only they could stay there forever, with no vows or promises to keep.

Tina's voice came insistently. "Lady Cartwright, the messenger has returned."

A jolt of fear shook away the cobwebs, and Mary sat up in bed. "Where is he?"

Tina blushed, looking down for a moment. "He came for M'Lord," she murmured, "not for you. M'Lord sent him back out with a message for Lord Paul."

Mary's cheeks heated, but she nodded. She had to accept this. It was her own plan, after all. She must live with the consequences.

"Of course," she agreed. "Has Erik said anything?"

Tina bobbed her head. "Apparently our guest will arrive this afternoon," she stated, her eyes showing confusion at the whirlwind of events going on around her. "She is to have the guest room - the one we moved the canopy bed into two days ago. Everything is being made ready for her arrival."

Mary's throat was tight, but she forced herself to continue. "And my sleeping area?"

Tina took a quick glance at the room around her. "My Lady, I am sure that we could –"

Mary shook her head. "I must not have anything at all reveal my station here." She smiled fondly at the girl she had practically grown up with. "And you must remember to call me Mary again, as you did when we were younger."

"Of course, My … Mary."

Mary chuckled, climbing out of bed. "If we only have a few hours, then I should start getting ready."

* * *

Mary sat on the top step of the chapel's entrance, pulling her wool cloak close around her shoulders. The whole of the keep had been turned out in the courtyard, and she swelled with pride in how orderly they looked. The soldiers had polished until they shone, and even Michael had traded in his leather armor for a dress tunic.

Her eyes went to Erik, and her breath caught. He was wearing his family colors, forest green, with the crossed sword emblem embroidered on his breast in silver. His blond hair shone in the sunlight, his muscles rippled as he walked over to talk with Michael, and he was all she could hope for in a man.

There was movement at the main gate, and Lynessa rode in on a beautiful bay, followed by two stocky men-at-arms and a small wagon. She wore a forest green cloak, her golden curls cascading down her back. She drew to a halt before Erik, and a page ran forward to hold the reins. When she dismounted, her cloak swirled open to reveal an elegantly embroidered dress of forest green and silver.

Mary closed her eyes for a moment. She felt she could see exactly how this scene should play out.

Lynessa would climb off her horse, her face glowing with satisfaction over how easily she had duped her naïve victim. She would stride arrogantly toward Erik. But wait! Erik would motion with his hand, and suddenly Michael would grab her from behind.

Lynessa's eyes would go wide with shock. "But Erik! I love you! I thought you loved me!"

Erik would look her over with a wry smile. "I did once, ten long years ago. But I was only a child then. Two weeks with this honorable, brave woman here, and I know now what my fate should be."

He would reach out a hand, and Mary would run into his waiting arms. They both would turn to watch as Michael hauled Lynessa away to await the sheriff's arrival.

Erik would gaze down at Mary in adoration. "I will never leave your side again," he'd vow. He would draw her again into an embrace –

Mary's eyes blinked back open, and she leant forward, her heart pounding.

Lynessa took a step toward Erik, her eyes gazing over him as if she could not believe he was real. Then she was tumbling into his arms, holding him tightly, and crying out in relief. There was a pause, and then Erik's arms came up around her, consoling her, reassuring her that he was all right.

Sharp twists of pain converged in Mary's stomach, and she took in a deep breath. Had she expected him to push the blonde away? To challenge her right there? To insist in front of the entire keep that Lynessa was a charlatan?

Yes.

Mary brushed away the tears welling in her eyes. She hadn't realized just how strongly she had hoped her nightmare would end in a manner straight from a troubadour's tale. It was silly, of course. Erik had been dedicated to Lynessa for over a decade. He had given up his family home, his heritage, and the love of his mother, all for her. He had endured who knew what hells in the Holy Land to prove himself worthy of her. Did Mary really think that undoing all of that would be the snuffing of a candle's flame?

She wondered if, in Erik's mind, Lynessa's delaying of the marriage was quite reasonable. The theft of the gold could be bad luck. Even the scene at the tavern and the church could easily be explained away.

As Erik himself had said, he held out hope that Lynessa was innocent in all of this. And, if Lynessa *was* innocent, for him to give up on her now would make all of his other sacrifices meaningless. He would be deserting the woman he loved just when she needed him most.

Mary squared her shoulders. It was up to her. She had to prove the existence of the twisted blackness which slithered beneath that gilded exterior. Lady Cartwright had known the challenge which awaited Mary and had prepared Mary over ten long years. Mary had known the mission would be harder than any other task she could undertake.

She could do this.

She had to do it.

It seemed an eternity before Lynessa released Erik and gazed up with adoration into his eyes. She hooked her hand firmly against his arm. He guided her up the stairs and into the main keep. Mary took her time, allowing the household staff to make their way indoors before entering the main hall.

At the other end of the room, Erik was leading Lynessa up the stairs toward her guest room. The two men-at-arms followed behind carrying a variety of leather bags and small wooden boxes. Mary's face paled at the thought of the woman sleeping in the keep, able to work her wiles on Erik whenever she wished.

Michael came to her side, following her eyes with his own.

His voice was even. "So much for the hope of Erik condemning her the moment she dismounted."

Mary blushed. Had her daydreams been that obvious? "It would have been nice," she muttered.

The corner of his mouth quirked into a wry smile. "And yet highly unlikely," he pointed out. "Ten long years? All his faith poured into her? He needs far better proof that she has been unworthy of his sacrifices."

Mary reluctantly nodded. "Erik is a man of honor. He will want to stand by her and trust that she is innocent. He would not abandon her just because she was unlucky enough to be robbed or happened across the brigands' hangout. I think he has suspicions, but he will want proof."

Michael's hand dropped to the hilt of his sword. His face was dead-pan. "So, we hang her from the wall and send ravenous boars at her until she confesses?"

Mary did smile at that, and the tension in her shoulders eased. "You do have a wild streak in you," she teased him. "No, Lady Cartwright had predicted it might come down to luring Lynessa to reveal herself. So my first step is to convince her to trust me, even a little."

Michael's gaze locked with hers. "Just let me know how I can help."

"For now, keep your eyes open. I'm sure Lynessa will be all sweetness and light until she gets that ring on her finger. So Erik should be safe until then."

Michael's eyes twinkled. "Safe is a relative term," he pointed out.

Mary's stomach twisted as she thought of the coming days. She knew it would take all her patience to play the part she had so carefully rehearsed.

* * *

The great hall had been swept, fresh rushes had been laid down, and the tables gleamed with polish. Most of the keep's inhabitants were already at their tables for dinner, murmuring with conversation. Mary tucked herself at the far end of a lower table, her crimson dress lost in the shadows of the flickering torchlight.

There was a stir at the far end of the room, and she looked up. Erik and Lynessa were just coming down the stairs. Mary's breath caught. Standing side by side, in elegant outfits of green and silver, with her golden curls and his blond hair, they appeared as if a matched set.

Dark hollowness pulled at Mary, dragging her down into its depths. For two long weeks Erik had been at her side, had gazed into her eyes, and had soared her to the heights of pleasure. Now it was Lynessa's hand he held as he walked along the back of the head table, approaching its central spot.

Mary flushed. Had those nights just been a casual distraction to Erik? A way to pass the time until he could return to his true love?

Lynessa's cultured voice carried easily across the hall. "That canopy bed is surely the most beautifully carved piece of furniture I have ever seen, Erik," she purred. "Thank you again for allowing me its use."

"It is my pleasure." His eyes swept the room, and for a moment they lit on Mary. He paused for a fraction of a second, a flit of emotion skittering behind his eyes. And then he continued his sweep, his expression still.

Lynessa's gaze moved to the carven throne before them, and her eyes lit up with delight. "Why, surely this was done by the same hand," she praised. "Such detail, such care! Is this where you sit?"

He gave a short shake of his head. "My seat is here, to the right."

Her mouth formed a perfect O. "Why then, this chair is for me! So I can be at your side! Why, you are indeed a chivalrous host." She moved around to stand before the chair and then serenely lowered herself into it.

A stillness settled over Erik, but he gave himself a shake and sat at her side. Then Zelda was in motion, her round curves moving more quickly than her size would suggest possible, pouring wine into pewter goblets.

Lynessa raised her goblet high, holding it toward Erik. "To my darling Erik, and the achievement of all he has ever dreamed."

Glasses and mugs were raised around the room, and choruses of "To Erik!" filled the air. Lynessa clinked her goblet against his, then took a long, satisfied sip.

The first course was brought around, a savory stew of eel and rosemary. Mary tried to take a few bites, but it felt like lead slugs falling into her stomach. It was all she could do to wash it down with some ale.

There was a throaty laugh from the head table, and Lynessa was leaning toward Erik, smiling widely in delight. Erik was nodding, an echoing smile drawing his lips into that curve she knew so well.

He still cared for Lynessa.

A chill flashed through Mary, and she pushed it aside with determination. Lady Cartwright had believed in Mary. The indomitable woman had made it her life's mission to train Mary in every way possible to break Lynessa's hold over her only son. Now it was time for the true test to begin.

She swept her eyes around the room, landing on the two men-at-arms, one light and one dark. They were side by side at the table on the opposite end of the hall, black curls and flaxen locks, conferring together over pints of ale. Her eyes narrowed for a moment, and then she sat back in surprise.

It was Bronson and Sander, two of the men who had ridden with Josiah in hunt of Erik. They were in Caradoc's employ – and they were here at Lynessa's beck and call.

Hope sprang up within her, but she pushed it down with steady resolve. Their presence here was hardly proof of anything. Lynessa could always claim she had no idea the men were involved with Caradoc. She had simply hired them for their skill at sword, nothing more. Mary would have to be patient and gather more information.

A smile grew on her lips. She knew just how to do it.

She drank down the last of her ale, then took her empty mug with her, crossing the back of the hall. She leaned down between the two men, offering a broad smile to each. "Is there room here for a third?"

The men rewarded her with large grins, each sliding aside to make room for her between them. She reached forward, pouring her mug full from the pitcher on the table, then raised her ale high. "To new friends."

"New friends," they echoed, drinking their ale down.

The next course was brought around, lamb with onions, a mouth-watering fragrance wafting from it. The trio dug in with delight, and Mary found her appetite returning. Another mouthful of ale helped her shoulders relax.

Bronson finally paused long enough to speak. "I'm Bronson," he announced, "and this here is Sander. We are looking after Lady Lynessa."

"I saw you come in with her," agreed Mary. "She seems quite a woman."

Sander gave a snort. "You can say that again," he murmured, drinking down his ale.

"How long have you been with her?" Mary took another bite of her lamb.

Bronson glanced up toward the head table. "Oh, we've known her for years and years," he grinned. He turned back to Mary. "So, what is your name?"

"I am Mary."

His eyes narrowed suddenly, and he leant forward, looking at her more closely. "Mary the singer?"

They had been at the tavern?

Mary could have sworn she had memorized every face which had come and gone in that slimy hell-hole, but somehow these two had escaped her notice. Had they been guards, secreted away in a back room?

There was a movement from across the hall. Michael half-rose from his seat, his eyes intent on her face. She gave a quick shake of her head. There was no way she was going to allow a minor inconvenience like a blown cover slow her down.

Clearly the first step was to gain their trust.

She leant forward against Bronson, pressing her bosom into his arm. "Yes, exactly," she murmured in a low voice. "You two were regulars at the Mangy Cur?"

Bronson flushed with desire at her contact, and he seemed to struggle to stay on topic. "Caradoc was in a rage. You vanished the same day Erik did."

She nodded in understanding. "Of course Caradoc was angry, but the fates were not kind to me."

His eyes seemed caught by hers, and his knuckles automatically rapped the wood table. "Fates can be cruel."

It came to her, suddenly. Bronson had been near terrified at the gates of Avoca's Folly. He had been certain of the curse and of the supernatural powers.

She fought to hold the smile from her face. She could put his fears to good use.

She pressed her body further against his and added a tremor to her voice. "It was my granny," she whispered. "When I went home that night, she told me that Caradoc's tower was cursed! She told me the spirits were angered by Erik's presence there, and that any who stayed with Caradoc would be stricken with horrible maladies. She warned me to run!"

Bronson drew in a sharp breath, and his fingers wrapped around hers. "Cursed?" he echoed.

She nodded with certainty. "I swear it on my mother's grave," she intoned somberly. "My granny always had a way of seeing danger coming. And sure enough, I heard that Caradoc's poor brothers were slain there!"

"They were, and an awful sight it was to see," he muttered. "Ripped open as if by wild boars."

Sander eagerly leaned over. "I was gored by a wild boar," he stated with pride. "Sliced my calf clean in half. Would you like to see?"

Bronson gave him a snarling frown. "She don't want to look at your festering wound," he snapped. He gazed back down at Mary. "Of course you ran, if your granny told you that," he soothed her. "Anyone would."

Mary looked up with plaintive eyes. "You won't tell anyone here that I once worked at Caradoc's tavern?" she pleaded. "If they knew I worked at that type of a place, they might toss me out in the cold."

He drew an arm around her, pulling her body closely against his. "Don't you worry, lass," he assured her. "I will take good care of you."

Sander leant forward with the pitcher. "We both will," he chimed in, topping off her mug. "You just trust in us."

Mary risked a glance toward Michael, and if anything his eyes held even more concern in them now. His fingers were on the table, drumming in a steady rhythm.

Despite her best intentions, her gaze slid left, along to the head table. Lynessa had her head back, talking to Tina, apparently asking for more wine to be brought, judging by the way she was waving her goblet around. And Erik –

Mary's mouth went dry. Erik was staring straight at her, his eyes holding cold disapproval. Then Lynessa was turning back to the table, his eyes returned to the blonde, and it was as if the moment had never happened.

Lynessa whispered something into Erik's ear, then drew to her feet. The men at the head table stood with her, then regained their seats as she headed toward a side door.

Mary's heart pounded in her chest. This was her chance. She had to make sure she talked with Lynessa before the woman recognized her. It would give her a chance to lay the same foundation she had with the two men.

Offering her apologies to Bronson and Sander, she stood and made her way along the back wall toward the garderobe. By the time she reached the quiet hallway, Lynessa was just stepping out of the small room. She pulled up in surprise as she came up to Mary, and then her eyes narrowed in recognition.

"You!"

Mary pitched her voice to be as full of pleading pity as possible. "Please, M'Lady, I meant no harm that night at the tavern. My only thought was to keep Caradoc safe. When I came across Erik here, I thought –"

Lynessa's mouth turned down in a scowl. "You thought to turn him in to Caradoc and gain all the credit for his discovery," she snapped.

Mary wrung her hands at her chest. "I know you are fond of him, M'Lady, but he's a ruthless killer! He killed Caradoc's own kin - Espan and Arbert." She widened her eyes in horror. "Killed them in an *awful* way." She drew her face into steady resolve. "You have to get clear of him, M'Lady, for your own sake. We have to let Caradoc know he's here. Caradoc lost two brothers. He deserves to take his revenge."

Lynessa looked down at Mary, her thin nose wrinkling in contemplation. "You love Caradoc?"

Mary bobbed her head enthusiastically. "With all my heart," she vowed.

Lynessa took a step toward her, causing Mary to press back into the wall. Lynessa's voice took on a sharpness. "And you would do *anything* for him?"

Mary was almost mesmerized by the focus in the blonde's gaze. She nodded mutely.

The edges of Lynessa's mouth curved up into a pleased grin. "Then you will follow my orders to the letter."

Mary's brow wrinkled with confusion. "I don't understand...?"

"I saw you with my two men-at-arms. You recognize them?"

Mary dipped her head. "Of course. They were Caradoc's men."

"Then you should trust that what I am doing has his blessing," she snapped. "Now stop confounding his plans." Her eyes narrowed with contemplation. "After all, it is *your* fault that Espan and Arbert are dead."

Mary brought her voice to a squeak. "My fault?"

Lynessa smiled with satisfaction. "Think about that. What do you think Caradoc will say when I explain to him how your foiling of my initial scheme led to his brothers' deaths?"

Mary dropped to her knees, holding her hands up to Lynessa. "I had no idea!" she pleaded. "Please, what can I do to make amends?"

Lynessa practically glowed with self-assurance. "Get back in there and stay with Bronson and Sander," she ordered. "Do whatever they tell you to do, and for God's sake, keep quiet this time."

Mary lowered her eyes. "Yes, M'Lady."

Lynessa turned and strode back toward the great hall, leaving Mary in silence.

Mary stayed down, her heart pounding.

Lynessa was guilty.

Mary had not admitted, even to herself, that there had been a tiny chance that Erik had been right – that Lynessa had been innocently caught up in machinations beyond her control. Mary had not been willing to admit that her plans could easily result in vindicating Lynessa.

She could have lost Erik forever.

Relief coursed through her, and she sagged back against the wall, brushing her hair from her face. She knew now that she was on the right path. What remained was to find incontrovertible proof that could be presented to Erik and to the sheriff. If the woman and Caradoc's band could be brought to justice, this whole nightmare would finally be over.

There were footsteps in the hall. Michael came around the corner, stopping in surprise when he found Mary sitting on the ground. He hurried forward, putting down a hand and gently drawing her to her feet. "Are you all right?"

"I am fine," she assured him, dusting off her dress. "Meet me on the wall when the moon is a quarter up."

He nodded, his brow creased in concern, and then he headed out again.

Mary waited a few minutes, then walked back into the hall herself, regaining her seat between the two men.

Bronson handed her mug to her. "There you are," he greeted. "We were worried about you."

She smiled reassuringly at him. "Just making myself ready for tonight's entertainment," she grinned.

His eyes drew down her curves, a hungry look firing in his gaze. "Oh?"

She smiled at him, then she stood, moving to the side of the room where she had stashed her tambourine. She turned, lifting it high, giving it a shimmering spin. A cheer went up in the room as she moved toward the head table, dropping into a curtsey before the pair.

Lynessa turned to Erik, her eyes bright with amusement. "How droll - a singer. You do think of everything, my darling."

Erik's gaze met Mary's. His eyes, normally so open and clear, were a mask.

Lynessa leant against him, turning to look down at Mary. "Do sing us a love song," she urged. "Something romantic and sweet."

Mary's jaw tightened, but she nodded, forcing a smile on her lips. "As My Lady commands, it is my pleasure to obey," she agreed, stepping back.

She raised her hands high, filling the hall with the rich, clear sound of her voice, swaying and shimmering the tambourine in time with the music.

"I have a young sister
Far beyond the sea;
Many be the gifts
That she sent me.

She sent me the cherry
Without any stone,
And so she did the dove
Without any bone.

She sent me the briar
Without any bark;
She bade me love my darling
Without any longing."

Mary spun and sang, holding her arms out to the audience, drawing them into her tune.

"How should any cherry
Be without stone?
And how should any dove
Be without bone?

How should any briar
Be without bark?"

Her voice caught, but all eyes were on her, and she pushed on, her voice filled with an emotion which was more than art.

"How should I love my darling

Without longing?"

She whirled in a circle to give herself time to regain her control, then drew in front of the head table.

"When the cherry was a flower,
Then had it no stone;
When the dove was an egg,
Then had it no bone.

When the briar was a sprout,
Then had it no bark;"

She could not help herself. She turned to Erik, holding his gaze with hers.

"When the maiden has who she loves,
She is without longing."

She gave one last shimmer of her tambourine, then dropped into a curtsy, lowering her eyes to the floor.

The room exploded into applause and cheers. Mary waited a moment before drawing back up into a standing position. She whirled in a circle before dropping into a fresh curtsy before the pair.

Lynessa was eyeing her with sharp attention. Her mouth curved into a smile. "You really do love him, this man of whom you sing," she murmured.

Mary flushed, but she nodded, willing herself to only look at Lynessa's eyes. "I do."

Lynessa's grin widened. "Well, then, remember our little talk," she advised.

Mary's eyes glowed with conviction. "I shall."

She turned before she lost her will and slid her gaze to Erik. Was he already so lost beneath Lynessa's spell that he had forgotten their time together? Her heart ached at the thought, but she focused on the path before her. In moments she was nestled between Bronson's dark curls and Sander's flaxen tousle, toasting the men and drowning herself in rich ale.

The conversation ebbed and flowed, the ale kept refilling, and it was only when the room began emptying out that Mary realized Michael's chair had been empty for a while. She pushed herself to standing, wincing as her leg wobbled beneath her.

Bronson was instantly at her side. "My dear, let me help you. Where will you be sleeping tonight?"

A tremor of nervousness slid through her. "I need to help Zelda in the kitchen, with some clean-up first," she demurred. "But when she gets through with me, if I am able to, I will come and find you."

He grinned, leaning back in his chair. "You be sure to do that," he growled, his eyes roaming her body.

She nodded, then turned, quickly hurrying out to the hallway. She drew a cloak from the small room to the left, then pushed open the main doors, walking through the dark, chill night as quickly as her injured leg would allow. She hobbled carefully up the long steps to the top of the wall. She made her way around its circumference, leaning against the outer edge for support.

Michael was standing alone at the eastern curve, a wool cloak wrapped tightly around him. He turned at her approach, his eyes holding a mixture of concern and frustration. She had barely pulled to a stop before his muttered words began.

"Where in God's teeth have you been? Do you know what time it is? To think what those two miscreants could have done –"

Mary put a hand on his arm, reassuring him. "I have my dagger on me," she soothed him. "And the hall was full of people. No harm would have befallen me."

He grumbled, but his gaze softened, and he shook his head. "So tell me what you know."

Mary leant against the wall. She started from the beginning, not leaving out any detail. Michael was a master of strategy, and she knew he might be able to spot something in her plan that she herself had missed. By the time she had finished he was nodding, running a hand through his greying hair.

"So we know they're up to something," he murmured. "I would assume it involves her marrying Erik, and then Erik somehow falling into Caradoc's hands so he could take his revenge."

To hear it said aloud ran Mary's blood cold, but she drew in a breath and nodded. "I would guess that's the gist of it," she agreed.

"So we know it but cannot prove it," sighed Michael. "How do we get the proof?" His mouth turned up in a wry grin. "Besides, of course, allowing her to become his bride and then seeing what happens next."

Hot anger shot through Mary at the prospect, and his eyes twinkled. He patted her on the arm. "You know I was only kidding," he added. "I love the lad as much as you do."

Mary's heart sank. "He's long past a lad," she pointed out, "and he feels he has waited over ten years for a virtuous woman. If we do not act quickly, it may be too late."

Michael shook his head. "I will do everything in my power to prevent that."

"As will I," stated Mary with determination. "There must be something that ties Lynessa to the criminals. Something more than her two bodyguards."

Michael brought a thoughtful finger to his lips. "Maybe something in that baggage of hers?"

Mary's heart lifted with hope. "There is a chance, at least," she agreed. "I will see what I can do."

Michael's gaze held hers. "Be careful," he warned. "That woman is a viper."

Mary patted the hilt of her dagger. "As careful as a cat in a den of wolves."

She turned, making her way back along the wall and across the quiet courtyard. How could she enter Lynessa's room without raising either alarm or suspicion? Mary was no longer sleeping on the upper floor, so she would have no excuse for being on that floor at all, never mind in a guest's room. If Lynessa were to find her –

She was grabbed hard by the arm, a hand was slammed over her mouth, and she was dragged around the corner of the keep. Her back was pressed hard against the cold stone, and her wide eyes lifted to see –

Erik.

Her shoulders sagged with relief, but his eyes were bright with fury as he released his hand from her mouth. His voice was a low hiss. "Expecting Bronson or Sander?"

It had been two nights since she last felt his body against hers, had breathed in his scent, and every part of her craved him. Her body arched against his of its own accord, and his eyes went smoky -

A creak came, of the main door being pressed open, and she realized her time was short. "Take Lynessa riding tomorrow," she insisted in a low voice.

Erik's voice was a growl. "Why?"

Lynessa's elegant voice floated out into the courtyard. "Erik, my darling, are you out here?"

Erik held Mary's gaze for a long moment, then he stepped back, moving around the corner. "Here I am," he called out to her. "I was just checking in with Michael on the state of the patrol before I turned in."

Mary dropped into a crouch, peering cautiously around the corner. Lynessa was putting an arm out to Erik, and he put his hand on it as easily as if they had been together for years.

Despair swamped Mary as if she were on a flimsy rowboat in the depths of a hurricane. Erik *had* been with Lynessa for years. He had loved her even before Cintersloe had been burnt to the ground. He had abandoned his mother to move in with Lynessa and her family. During the long years of his campaign in the Holy Land the two had written each other regularly. He had returned to live with her.

Mary shook her head. And how long had *she* known him? She had met him once, briefly, a decade ago. Since then she had dreamed of him, been jealous of him, fallen asleep with his eyes gazing down in steady focus. But in terms of actually talking with him, it had been a scant two weeks that they had been together.

Two weeks, and it felt like a lifetime.

She brushed her hair back from her face, standing to stare at the door in determination. She would prove to him just how corrupt that woman's heart was.

Mary nodded, her gaze steadying. She would prove beyond all shadow of a doubt that she was the one deserving of Erik's fierce and hard-won loyalty.

Chapter 11

Mary strode around the courtyard in the shimmering dawn light, pressing down on her injured leg with growing force. She smiled as the wound throbbed but did not impede her progress.

Michael chuckled, shaking his head. "Not yet, you don't," he warned her. "I know the bandage is off now, but you're not yet ready for sparring."

Mary's shoulders slumped. To see the men out in motion drew her strongly. She wanted to be in their midst, dodging a block, whipping the light wooden blade around against an unsuspecting hip. A longing throbbed in her so strongly that she could barely think, could barely –

There was a motion at the stairs, she turned, and her gaze met Erik's. Time staggered to a stop. It suddenly became crystal clear to her that the torment in her heart had little to do with the men-at-arms advancing and retreating across the smooth cobblestones. It took all of her will to stay in place, to hold back from running pell-mell into his arms and melting into him.

A flash of silver and green, and Lynessa stepped out beside him, tucking her hand around his arm. Mary turned, emotions twisting in turmoil within her. This was all her own doing. She had been the one to call for Lynessa to join them. Now every second was sheer torture.

The pair strolled across the yard to stand with Michael. Erik's voice was tight with an emotion Mary could not put a name to. "Good morning, Michael. Are you up for some sparring?"

Michael nodded. "At your leisure, My Lord."

Mary shivered. It was all sliding so effortlessly in place. Erik's station in the keep. Lynessa at his side, as if she had been born to be there. And in fact had she? Had this been her dream since she was a young girl?

The two men moved into the courtyard, saluted, and were in motion. Michael drove an attack at Erik's right shoulder. Mary waited for Erik to bring his own sword up in a block - to follow up with a sliding blow to the arm.

Instead Erik whipped his sword down hard on top of Michael's blade. The ringing noise echoed throughout the courtyard as the blades drove hard into the stone.

Michael's brow creased; he stepped back and reset. This time he dove at Erik's leg, the tip seeking to draw up and in.

SLAM. Again Erik drove his blade down on top of Michael's. Mary could see the reverberation of the strike travel up the older man's arm.

Lynessa's smile widened into a grin. "That's my warrior," she stated with pride. "Even when he was younger he could best any man for miles. Good skill to have when there are bandits about." She gave a shrug, then looked around. "The boys will be at it for hours. Come, let us go in and explore this marvelous keep."

Mary desperately wanted to stay. Something was wrong. Erik's attacks were brutal and sharp. Surely even Lynessa should be able to see that. But the woman was turning, heading back up the stairs, and Mary gave one last look at Erik's tense stance before following.

She could not give up the opportunity to spend time alone with Lynessa. Maybe this would be her chance to learn something valuable.

They stepped into the great hall, and Lynessa's eyes swept it in a calculating fashion. "First, of course, all these sword banners have to go," she insisted. "One can hardly have an elegant party with all those brutish symbols around."

Mary strove to keep her face calm. "Oh? What would you prefer?"

"Ivy, running in garlands throughout all of the rooms," the blonde promptly answered. "Ivy seems such an innocent vine, almost beneath notice. But did you know that over time ivy can bring down even the sturdiest of walls?"

Mary thought to the ivy which had worked its way through the curtain wall at Avoca's folly, and she nodded.

A smile came to Lynessa's lips. "And I think holly, for added color. That would seem quite appropriate."

Mary's brow creased in confusion. "Appropriate?"

Lynessa gave a small shrug. "Yes indeed. I shall keep the main chair and the canopied bed, of course. It will bring me great pleasure to sit in that chair each day and to stretch out in that bed each night." She glanced toward the stairs. "Shall we go examine the master suite?"

Mary flushed, but Lynessa was already in motion, striding across the hall and up the curved stairs. Mary's leg was aching by the time they got to the heavy oak door. Lynessa pushed the door in with a sweep.

She shook her head, going to each of the three windows and throwing open the curtains. "Just look at this," she muttered. "Barely fit for a servant." She glanced up at the fireplace and the bare hook above it. "And do they not believe in paintings in this place? The first thing I shall do is commission two paintings of me – one for the great hall, and one to hang in here."

Mary flushed, looking down. "Of you and Erik, do you mean?"

Lynessa gave a short laugh. "Having to see him in person is quite enough," she countered. Her grin grew. "Besides, your precious Caradoc is notoriously short on patience. I doubt we will have enough time to have a painting done of the current Lord of this keep."

A tremor ran through Mary, but she held it off with effort. "So it will be soon then, this plan of yours?"

Lynessa nodded sharply. "That should please you. I imagine you want to be back to that lover of yours as soon as possible."

The image of Erik's firm body, of the way his eyes smoked when he looked down at her, brought a flush to her face. "Yes, of course."

Lynessa laughed out loud. "God's teeth, woman, you wear your heart on your sleeve. You need to learn some self-control. Otherwise that man will leave you high and dry, when he realizes how easily he can wrap you around his finger."

"You are right, of course," murmured Mary.

Lynessa took a last look around the room, then shrugged. "Plenty of time to get things exactly right," she muttered to herself. She turned, walking from the room and striding down the hall to her own room.

She stopped by her door. "Time for me to prepare for my outing with Erik," she informed Mary. "You be a good girl and behave while I'm gone. It should only be another day or two before I have him properly hooked, and I have no doubt I can push for a quick marriage. Then we shall get you home to your Caradoc."

She turned, entered her room, and closed the door in Mary's face.

Mary was in a daze. Everything was happening so quickly, and Lynessa's ruthlessness staggered her. She stumbled down to the end of the hall, falling onto the padded bench that lay beneath the window overlooking the front courtyard. The men had finished their practice rounds. Mary could see Michael up on the front wall, conferring with two of the guards.

Erik was nowhere in sight.

She brought her knees up, hugging them in close. What if she found the evidence she sought in Lynessa's room, but Erik refused to acknowledge it? Surely Lynessa would have an explanation for any situation, and Erik seemed more than ready to believe in her. He had invested over ten years in this relationship, had gone to war for her, and had given up his family and heritage for her. What would one more minor inconvenience be to all of that?

A logical part of her reminded her that she simply had to tell Lynessa the truth about Erik's station – that he was not gaining control of the keep. That a marriage to him would not bring her the land and riches she desired.

Mary shivered. Lynessa was obsessed with gaining control of the keep. Now that the blonde had a foothold, she might not be deterred over a minor issue with legality. She might stay anyway, working her wiles, driving toward any solution that brought her closer to the prize. She would be like an invasive ivy, mining her tendrils into every spot of soft dirt. Burrowing until removal became nigh impossible.

Mary ran a hand through her hair. The only obstacle to Erik's claim on this keep was her word. She held the power, at any time, to turn the land back over to its true heir. She only had to determine that he was fit for the title. But with Lynessa present, handing over that key would also sign Erik's death warrant.

Her face hardened.

She would prevent that at all costs. Even if it meant taking on Lynessa with her own two hands.

There was a footstep at her side.

Her hand clenched, and she swung her gaze up–

Erik stood over her.

His gaze was shuttered; his jaw tight and angular. His breath came in long draws as if he were fighting to maintain control over some strong emotion.

For a long moment, Mary was caught. Only his eyes existed - those eyes that filled with a passion beyond anything her world had known.

There was a motion from behind them, the door swung open, and Lynessa stepped out, decked in a beautiful green and silver riding habit. Her curls were pinned up on top of her head, creating cascades down her back. Her mouth widened into a smile as she spotted the two at the end of the hall.

"Why, Erik, there you are. Come, let us head out on our ride. I look forward to spending some time alone with you."

Erik's face eased into neutrality with deliberate effort. Then he turned and nodded, moving forward to offer an arm. Mary found herself trailing behind them, lost in the shadows.

It seemed only a heartbeat before Erik was standing in the center of the courtyard in the late morning sunshine, holding

Lynessa's horse's reins as she mounted into her saddle. She looked elegantly beautiful in her embroidered green riding outfit, the silver tracery perfectly matching Erik's tunic. When he mounted and pulled over to her side, they looked like an image out of a bard's tale.

Mary knew she had wanted this outing to take place. Even so it was hard to watch the two of them heading through the gate, taking the road at a quiet walk, their heads bent together in conversation. Bronson and Sander followed at a discrete distance.

Mary's resolve steadied, and she looked back toward the keep. It was her duty to ensure that this place, and all within it, remained safe from harm. Her next step was to search Lynessa's room. With the party's departure, she now had the window of opportunity she craved.

She waited until the group was well out of sight. Then she turned and strode back into the keep, through the great hall, and up the stairs to the guest room door. Her heart hammered in her chest, and she drew in a deep breath. She should have a few hours to set about her task. She had to be slow and methodical in her search. Even the slightest clue could provide what she needed.

She pushed the door open to the guest room – and stopped in surprise. She hardly recognized the interior. Surely the large, ornate bed was part of the change, but Lynessa had managed to put her imprint on every corner of the room. The dresser was strewn with her brushes and mirrors. The open wardrobe in the corner was filled with her tunics. Several pairs of boots lined one wall. Even an embroidered pillow with an ornate letter "L" lay centered on the bed.

Mary shook her head. Ivy indeed. Lynessa was like a noxious weed, setting in her roots and preparing to overrun the entire keep. It was up to her to chop it back - to rip it out to its very core.

She moved over to the large, leather-bound trunk. She sat cross-legged before it, drawing her dagger from her hip. Lady Cartwright had been prepared for any eventuality, from Noah's flood to adventures of a more ignoble nature. Picking locks had been part of her training.

She carefully worked the tumblers, leaning her head close to the iron. After several long minutes she was rewarded by a soft click. Glancing around, she removed the lock from the chest and slowly raised the lid.

She shook her head. Lady Cartwright had certainly enjoyed her jewelry, but it seemed Lynessa could give the woman a run for her money. There was an elegant sapphire teardrop pendant, delicately balanced on a gold chain. A pair of ruby earrings twinkled to another side. Beneath those, a velvet pouch held an amethyst bracelet with gold and silver accents. Yet another small box held numerous rings.

Mary looked through the items with a growing sense of frustration. Lynessa had worn several of the pieces openly since she had arrived at the keep; she had not made any attempt to hide her ownership of them. They could not be objects that would connect her to any wrongdoing.

She sighed, looking at the chest again. Just what had she hoped to find? Perhaps a letter describing Erik's downfall in detail, with Caradoc's signature on it?

She closed the chest, re-sealing the lock. She moved on to the other two trunks, but with each search her heart fell further. The woman certainly owned finely embroidered clothing and leather goods of the highest quality. But nothing in any of the cases spoke of a direct connection with the bandits.

At last Mary stood, looking around the room in frustration. Clearly what she sought was not here – but somehow there had to be a way to prove her false.

She nodded in resolution. It was time for her to become even more intimate with Bronson and Sander.

Michael was waiting for her in the great hall when she descended. He was shaking his head at her expression before she drew to a stop before him.

"No luck, then?" he asked in a low voice.

"There will be something," she vowed. "I just need the time to find it."

He gave her a fond pat on the arm. "I have no doubt you will," he agreed. "But for now, you look as if you'll run yourself ragged with worry. Come and spar with me."

Her eyes lit up. "I thought you said I wasn't ready yet?"

He gave a wry grin. "Given the alternatives, I think this will be a fine way for you to expend some of that energy."

Mary did not give him a chance to change his mind. In a moment she was down at the barracks, sliding on her leather gear and gathering up the practice sword. Then they were walking out into the crisp sunshine, taking their place in the courtyard she loved so well.

A salute, a pause, and then they were in motion. Mary laughed out loud as she nearly landed a blow on his bicep, as he turned beneath her and deflected her away. Then she was sweeping her sword counter-clockwise, dancing out of the way of his counter. He nodded in approval, reset, and gave her a smile. She launched herself in, losing herself in the moment.

She drove herself to exhaustion, and she was drenched with sweat before finally agreeing to halt. She plunked herself down on the stone steps of the chapel, wearily raising her arms above her head so Michael could pull her leather jerkin off of her.

There was a call from above the gates. "Lord Cartwright has returned."

A chill flashed through Mary. So much was in motion. So much was taking on a life of its own, never to be reeled back in again. The main doors of the gate drew open, allowing the keep's master entrance, and at his side rode a glowing apparition in curls and green. By the triumphant glow in her eyes, Mary felt Lynessa must be nearing her objective. The two bodyguards came in a few lengths behind.

Lynessa turned with a beaming smile to gaze at Erik. "That was utterly delightful," she enthused. "Do promise me that we can go out again tomorrow. It would be my fondest wish."

Erik's eyes flickered to Mary for a moment.

Lynessa followed his gaze, her lips turning down in a frown. "My word, Mary, just what kind of a state are you in? I do hope you plan on cleaning up before entertaining us tonight."

Mary flushed, dropping her eyes. "Of course, M'Lady," she murmured.

Lynessa swept off her horse, and in a moment she and Erik were walking side by side into the keep. Mary forced herself to stay in place while they left. She had to focus on the task before her. She drew her eyes over to Bronson and Sander. The men dismounted as she approached, looking over her form with hungry eyes. She realized that her exertions had made her dress moist, and it clung to her body more tightly than she had imagined.

Bronson's voice was a warm growl. "Miss me?"

She forced her lips to curl up in a smile. "Absolutely," she agreed. "Do you really have to go out with her tomorrow?"

He gave a shake of his head, his eyes steady on hers. "Not if M'Lady has her way," he countered. "She intends to get Lord Cartwright out there alone, and she usually gets what she wants."

Mary flushed at the idea of Erik alone in that woman's clutches, but she pushed the thought aside. The more time she could spend with these two men, the more likely she was to discover what she needed to know.

She lowered her voice to a purr. "That sounds perfect, then."

Sander edged forward. "I will be free as well," he pointed out.

She gave a low laugh. "Maybe you two will have to throw dice for me," she teased.

Sander's eyes lit up with delight. "Do they play dice here?"

Mary's eyes flashed to Michael, and her smile grew to a grin. "Absolutely," she agreed. "I am sure we can put together whatever type of dice game you crave."

Now both men's eyes were gleaming with avarice. Bronson looked as if he were counting the coins already. "The more the merrier," he insisted. "We even have our own lucky dice."

Mary bet that it was more than luck that caused their dice to fall a certain way, but she nodded warmly to the pair. "As soon as the two lovebirds leave on their ride tomorrow, we will have the best dice game you have ever seen, with the finest ale as well."

The smiles on their faces were all she could have hoped for.

* * *

The roast venison was being passed down the table, and Mary did not know if it was Sander or Bronson who was the more flirtatious. If one was pouring her ale, the other was complimenting her on the curls of her dark hair or the bright gleam in her gemstone eyes. Michael's watch over her had settled into a steady simmer. She had no doubt she'd get an earful from him once the dinner was over and she was able to talk with him in privacy. But for now the room throbbed with conversation, the simmered turnips were sheer perfection, and she took down another swallow of ale.

Bronson pulled her back against him, his dark curls shining in the torchlight, and she gave a laugh as he tickled her ribs.

There was a call from the head table, and all eyes turned.

Erik was standing, his gaze steady on her, his face edged in shadows. "Singer! It's time for a song."

Bronson's face darkened, and he muttered to Sander under his breath. "Can't be too soon for my liking."

Mary flushed. She dropped her eyes and strode to grab her tambourine before walking the length of the hall. Her leg was feeling much better, thank the Lord. Her thoughts went to the wound Erik had endured. How was it healing?

She was filled by the image of him riding toward the Folly, wounded, focused solely on her safety. With the memory came a longing which nearly overwhelmed her. She pushed the feeling away as she drew before the head table.

She kept her eyes lowered. "What is your pleasure, M'Lord?"

There was a pause, and then his voice came, tight. "Favor us with a song about a woman who misses her true love."

Lynessa's voice was rich with pleasure. "Oh, as I missed you when you were away fighting in the Holy Land! An ideal request, my love."

Mary nodded, refusing to look up. She felt his absence keenly. She was drowning in the blackness … slipping into the hole swelling within her until it threatened to consume her every thought.

She searched through her mind for a song that was as short as possible. She worried that, if she sang on the topic for too long, she might break down in sobs. That would not serve her purpose well at all.

Ah, there it was.

She drew the tambourine in a shimmering arc, swaying in rhythm. She drew out each line, filling it with the emotion that roiled within her.

"My love has gone away
Alas, why has he left?"

She dropped her eyes, sorrow filling them.

"But I have pledged a vow
I cannot follow him."

She spun in a circle, feeling the truth of it echo in every word.

"He has my heart in his keeping
Wherever he rides or goes."

A final spin.

"My love is true,
A thousand fold."

Mary dropped to a curtsy, giving a trilling ripple to the tambourine.

The room burst into applause, and it was a long minute before it quieted for Lynessa's voice to be heard.

"That was wonderful, dear Mary. And just perfect, too! For I could not follow Erik into the Holy Land, and I waited eagerly for his return to me."

She gave a low laugh, and Mary looked up. Lynessa was turning to Erik and smiling up at him. "Although I did of course know *why* you left me," she added. "It was all your mother's fault and that insane declaration of hers. To think that it took you this long to regain what was rightfully yours! We could have been here ten years ago, side by side, if not for her."

There was a flicker of emotion lighting his eyes, and then it was gone. He quietly nodded at her. "Of course."

Lynessa reached into the pouch at her side and withdrew a small coin. She flicked it toward Mary. "For your delightful song," she offered with a chuckle.

Mary deftly caught it, then bowed again. She returned to her seat between the two men.

Bronson gave a scoffing laugh. "What'd she give you? A piece of tin?"

Mary turned the coin around in her fingers. The markings on it seemed odd. "I don't know," she admitted. "I've not seen one like this before."

Sander took a glance, and then gave a low laugh. "That's 'cause it's from the Holy Land," he explained. "Worth less than nothing until you get Caradoc to change it into proper money for you. She's reminding you that you're hers until we return to Caradoc." He glanced at Bronson. "It's all she's paying us in, for the same reason. Even though she has plenty of good English money up in that chest of hers as well."

Mary's heart pounded against her ribs. Lynessa was traveling with large amounts of money? Including money from the Holy Land? That could be much harder to explain away. This could offer proof that the theft of Erik's money had all been a ploy.

Surely that would be enough for him?

Her brow creased. "You say the money is in her chest?"

Bronson nodded his head. "It sure is. Why?"

She could hardly admit that she'd already picked the lock and found nothing within.

Her mind sought for another approach. "Isn't that risky? What if a maid came in while Lady Lynessa was selecting out some clothing from the chest and the maid saw all the foreign money?"

Bronson looked uncertain. "I'm not sure I should –"

She leant against him. "I am one of you," she purred. "We are all in this together. The more I know, the more I can help!"

His face flushed. "Right, of course, together," he murmured, looking down at her. His voice dropped to a whisper. "There is a secret compartment in its base. That way Erik has no chance of finding it."

Her eyes lit up. "How does it open?"

He patted her on the arm. "Don't you worry about that. Just know that we'll be well paid when this is all through. I will be able to support you in a manner of which you've only dreamed!"

Sander leant over with a gleam in his eye. "Mutton every night!" he promised. "Ale that flows eternally!"

He dropped an arm around her shoulder.

There was a movement from across the hall. Michael had drawn to his feet. His face made it clear that either she either extricate herself immediately or he would come over and do it for her.

She looked up between the two men, tingeing her gaze with reluctance. "I'm afraid it's time for me to head into the kitchens again. With all the excitement over Lady Lynessa's presence, we are worked until we drop right now."

Bronson's smile faded. "There's no chance of you getting away?"

She shook her head. "Not tonight - but I will be all yours tomorrow afternoon," she pointed out.

His smile returned at that, and she was able to draw away from them. It took all her strength of will not to look up to the head table, not to soak in one last glimpse of Erik before heading to her lonely mat in the corner of the pantry.

Chapter 12

Rain thrummed on the roof of the chapel, nearly drowning out the priest's rumbling voice. Mary looked at her hands, willing away the frustration that roiled like a spring river. Clearly there would be no riding today. Her hopes of dragging more information out of the degenerate duo would have to be postponed. And that gave Lynessa even more time to seduce Erik with her clever wiles.

Mary's thoughts spun in circles around that chest in Lynessa's room, despair seeming to envelop her at every turn. Lynessa seemed to have a plan for everything. Even if Mary did find her way in to those coins, and presented them to Erik, what would Lynessa say? Perhaps that she had found the thief and had been planning to give the money back to Erik as a wedding present - as a delightful way to start their new life together.

Shadows wrapped themselves around Mary until she could barely see the candles flickering along the side wall or the wooden cross hanging at the far end of the altar. She barely heard as the priest finished his sermon. Out of habit she slid from the pew, pulled her cloak hood up over her head, and plodded her wet, weary way across the courtyard and through the open gate. She turned left, walked the length of the main wall, and then made her way up the small hill to where a low stone wall marked the perimeter of the cemetery.

Lady Cartwright, of course, had the most elaborate grave marking Mary had ever seen or heard of. A slab of stone covered the entire top of the grave, carved with praise in Latin and crossed swords engraved at the front. A statue of a guardian angel stood at the head, his hands holding a sword point-down, his face stern and defiant.

Mary moved to the row of flowers planted in the space between the angel's feet and the start of the stone slab. The snowdrops were just beginning to bloom, with the steady shower of rain adding a glistening light to them. Mary tended to them with focus, cleaning dirt off of one, lifting stray grasses off another.

At last she sat back on her heels and looked up at the stern angel. Somewhere up there Lady Cartwright was staring down at her, scowling at her. Wondering why Erik's assigned guardian angel was failing him.

Mary's tears mingled with the falling rain as desolation poured through her. She put a hand out to the slick stone, laying her fingers on the sword, desperately praying for the strength to see this through.

A woman's voice came from behind her. "And what are you doing here?"

Mary turned in surprise; this had always been her quiet time of contemplation. Who would be interrupting her?

Lynessa and Erik stood side by side in the rain, staring at her from beneath their hoods. Their faces were lost in the shadows.

Mary flushed and stood. Her mind raced to think of an excuse for why she was here. "The cook said she normally came out to pay her respects for the grave," she stammered, "but with the rain she is feeling poorly. So she asked me to come out for her."

Lynessa's mouth turned down. "Well, you've done as she asked," she snapped. "Erik here would like some time alone with his mother now." She slid her arm through Erik's, and her eyes brightened. "And I shall remain, of course."

Mary dropped her eyes, unwilling to look into his, and gave a short nod before scurrying past them.

The hall was packed full of people when she wearily pushed her way through the main doors. The ale was already flowing. Normally Mary would have relished a rainy day of fun and carousing, but the thought of Bronson and Sander man-handling her all afternoon turned her stomach. She slipped her way down into the kitchens, tucking into a corner and making herself useful cutting carrots and turnips.

The hours dragged on, the shadows lengthened, and at last the main meal began. She poked her head into the main hall – and sighed. The two men were laughing uproariously at some jest, their red cheeks and noses clear signs of just how much they had consumed over the afternoon. She squared her shoulders. She could get through this.

The men's eyes lit up in delight as she approached them, and a place for her was immediately cleared. Bronson wrapped a beefy arm around her waist. "There you are! We were about to go searching for you! That cook can't keep you busy forever."

Sander leant over to fill her mug to the very brim. "Drink up!" he insisted. "You are at least twelve mugs behind us already!

She reached forward to grab a warm loaf of bread and ate a bite before downing some of her ale. "So, no gambling today, I take it?"

Bronson shook his head, his eyes warm on her. "That's fine, the rain should let up tomorrow." He raised his mug in a toast. "Then Lynessa goes out on her quest, and we head downstairs for ours. We'll get every coin possible out of these sheep before we leave." He drank down his mug in one long draw.

Mary shot a glance at Michael, who was glaring at her with steady focus. "Are you sure Lynessa will appreciate you fleecing her flock?"

Bronson gave a low laugh. "With all she is getting for her end of the bargain, she can hardly complain," he growled. "And besides, she wants her soldiers poor and needy. That way they are more dependent on her and her generosity. The more they need her, the less she can pay them and still know they'll stick around."

Sander poured Mary's glass full again. "That's right," he chimed in. "She'll want them as destitute as possible. Willing to do anything she asks. That's the way she is."

Bronson draped an arm across Mary's shoulder, pulling her in. "So we want to get as much as we can out of them tomorrow, because it won't be long now, my darling." His face closed in on hers. "And then you'll be all mine."

A deep voice rang out from the head table. "Singer!"

Mary's heart quickened at Erik's call, and she pulled herself free of Bronson. Gathering up her tambourine, she made her way across the open floor to stand before the head table. She kept her eyes lowered. "What do you wish of me, M'Lord?"

There was a long pause, and finally she looked up. He was standing at the table, looking down at her, his eyes shadowed, his face almost a mask.

The words slipped from him, as if beyond his control. "Tell me your plan."

She paled. "My plan, M'Lord?"

He gave a small shake of his head, and after a moment his voice rumbled out in a steadier tone. "For tonight's entertainment."

She let out her breath. "Oh. I suppose it is Sunday, so I should sing something appropriate."

He held her gaze for a moment longer, then nodded, lowering himself to retake his seat.

She spun in a slow circle, drawing her eyes across the audience as she went.

"Lully, lullay, lully, lullay,
The falcon has borne my mate away.
He bore him up, he bore him down,
He bore him into an orchard brown."

As she sang the melancholy tune, she felt the longing of the song, felt the ache in her heart. She gave a shimmer with her tambourine to cover her emotions.

"In that orchard there was an hall
That was hanged with purple and pall.
And in that hall there was a bed:
It was hanged with gold so red."

Her throat closed up, but she forced herself to sing, to swirl. Her performance had to be perfect. Erik's life depended on it.

"And in that bed there laid a knight,
His wounds were bleeding day and night."

She could remember vividly receiving the letters that told of Erik's being in battle, of his serious injuries. She recalled how her heart had been pierced with worry. To think of all he had endured …

"By that bedside knelt a maid,
 Weeping for him night and day."

Mary knew the song was religious, was about places and people greater than herself, but the ache in her heart was for one man alone.

"By that bedside stands a stone:
Corpus Christi written thereon."

Mary dropped to a deep curtsy before the table.

There was a long silence, then the room burst into applause and cheers. Mary held her pose, blinking away the tears that threatened to fall. At last she felt it safe to rise, to look up at the pair before her.

Lynessa was leaning forward with a wide grin. "Why, Mary, I think you have touched Erik deeply! I never knew him to be such a religious man." She turned to Erik with a smile. "Why, maybe you will have visit Jerusalem at some point!"

Erik's gaze was steady. "I was stationed there for four years."

Lynessa's eyes widened with surprise. "You were?" Then she blinked, coughed, and her confusion slid into smug assurance as easily as a swallow turned in flight. "Oh, of course, I was only teasing," she insisted. "Your letters were quite touching. Maybe sometime we can go together and enjoy a restful vacation there."

Mary stared at her as if she had lost her mind. Surely Lynessa had a different definition for "restful" and "vacation" that Mary was previously unfamiliar with.

Erik calmly held Lynessa's gaze. "If you feel my time in Jerusalem was restful, then we could also visit that city I helped lay siege to."

Lynessa nodded eagerly. "Of course! What was it again, Antioch? Arabia? Andorra?"

The name was ringing in Mary's head. *Acre! Acre! Acre!* How could Lynessa possibly forget it? How could she not remember the brutality of the fighting and the horrific treatment of the prisoners? Mary knew how much Erik had been troubled by it all; his Commander had seen Erik writing long into the night, pouring out his concerns in his messages to Lynessa.

Apparently, if the woman had even seen the messages, she had not cared much about their contents.

Lynessa's voice sparkled with playful teasing. "Alabaster?"

Erik's response was soft, and Mary could not quite name the emotion hidden behind his eyes. "It was Acre."

Lynessa clapped her hands together in delight. "Ah, of course. Acre! Certainly, we can visit there, and you can show off all the locations of your triumphs."

Mary could not take any more. She turned on her heel and strode back to her place between Bronson and Sander. They had a full mug of mead waiting for her, and she drew it down in one long pull.

Bronson wrapped his arm around her shoulder, giving her a fond squeeze. "That's my songbird!" he proclaimed with pride. "I bet you could drink any man under the table." He reached forward with his free hand to refill her mug. "Another?"

Mary had the mug to her lips before Michael's sharp eyes caught her gaze from across the room. He made a sharp motion with his head toward the main gate. Then he headed out into the dark night.

Mary sighed. "I will be back soon," she assured Bronson. It was like pulling free of a briar, but at last she was standing again. She made her way to the front steps.

The rain had eased up, and only a light mist drifted through the courtyard as she crossed. She held up her dress as she ascended the long, stone stairs. By the time she reached the back corner Michael was standing there waiting for her, a cloak draped over one arm. He tucked her within it.

She eased down onto the small wooden stool in the corner of the wall, leaning back against the stone with a sigh.

His voice was low and tense. "God's teeth, Mary, what do you think you are doing with those two? They are wolves. The moment they have their chance they will pounce. What you are playing at is beyond dangerous."

She shakily ran a hand through her hair. "If there were any other way, I would take it," she insisted. "We know Lynessa has the money. However, I am sure she will have an excuse for why it's in her possession. We must separate her from those two. If I can get the two men gambling, their greed will be their undoing."

She looked up at Michael. "The men will want to use her money in order to bet as much as possible, to fleece our troops before they leave. When Lynessa finds out about this, she could turn on them. They could turn on her. We could finally have them arguing, and prove to Erik beyond a shadow of a doubt how involved she is in all of this."

Michael's brow creased in uncertainty. "Surely she'd just claim she didn't know what the two miscreants were up to."

Mary shook her head. "There's only so much she can cover for," she pursued. "If Erik overhears her fighting with the men, and describing her plan, how can she then deny her role? At some point it will be too much to explain away. We just have to leverage them apart."

Michael's lips pressed into a thin line. "If this is going to be an afternoon of heavy gambling, then I will absolutely be there by your side."

Mary patted him reassuringly on the knee. "I am sure the wolves' heads will want to take all your money as well as the other soldiers'," she soothed him. "You will have a quite proper reason for being there. The more potential gain we can lay out for them, the more likely they are to go visit their *bank*. And then we simply make sure Lynessa finds out about it, and that we have Erik nearby to hear the fallout."

Michael sighed. "It does seem we need to bring things to a head, and soon," he agreed. "I only hope this works out well."

Mary looked down at her boots. A cold mist seemed to swirl around her feet, and she felt more alone than ever. "As do I."

There were quick footsteps along the wall, and Erik strode toward Michael, his face tense with worry. He began without preamble. "Have you seen Mary? I've looked everywhere for her. Those wolves' heads are beyond drunk tonight, and I'm afraid that –"

Michael nudged his head right. Erik followed his gaze, and his shoulders slumped with relief as he spotted Mary in the shadows. "There you are."

For a moment the world fell away, and Mary felt as if she were staring through the barred window of the prison door at Erik. He was gazing at her with concern and steady determination. It seemed to her that his message was clear.

He wanted her to stop the dangerous course she was on.

She gave her head a shake. She was going to see this through, no matter what the cost to herself. It was her sacred vow.

She dropped her eyes. "M'Lord." She stood and quickly moved past him, before she said something she would regret.

Somehow she was able to thread her way through the shadows and into the kitchen without being seen by either of Lynessa's guards. In short order the doors were closed and the women were stretched out on mats, blankets mounded over forms large and small. A steady snoring echoed amongst the pots and knives.

Mary pulled her blankets over her head, but it was no use. She had become accustomed to the years of sleeping at the foot of Lady Cartwright's bed, and the woman had slept as still as marble. The Lady was sensitive to even the smallest noise, so Mary had quickly learned to lie as motionless as possible, not even turning in place.

This cacophony was stretching her to her very limits.

At last she could take no more. She had not had one good night's sleep since … she blushed, thinking back to the feeling of Erik's arms around her, of his sturdy, broad chest pressed against her body.

If she were going to be any good to anybody tomorrow, she needed to rest.

She carefully eased up from her mat, but she needn't have worried – the women around her snored in contented abandon. She crept to the door and slid it open just enough for her to slip through. Then she walked surely through the dark hallways, knowing every turn and step even in the deepest shadows. She nodded to the guard at the keep doors, then moved across the moonlit courtyard to the stables.

She smiled as she stepped into the dark building. The low rumble of the horses' breathing was exactly what she needed. She pulled one of the blankets from the shelf, headed to the empty stall in the far back, and pushed the gate open.

Perfection.

She laid out the blanket, made a small mound of hay beneath one end for a pillow, and gave a sigh of contentment. She would finally get some sleep. She took a step forward toward her makeshift bed.

The main stable door creaked as someone pushed it in.

Her hand flashed to her hip. God's teeth, would those men never let up? How had they seen her come in here? Well, they would learn something about pushing their limits too far. She moved to the side of the stall entrance and crouched down, drawn dagger in hand.

The footsteps came closer, cautiously, and she waited … waited …

He stepped into the stall.

She was on him in an instant, her arm high around his neck, her blade against his throat. Her voice came out in a hiss.

"I tell you once and for all, I will not be yours - not if you plan to force me!"

Erik's voice was a guttural growl. "Who assaulted you? I'll kill him!"

Mary blinked in surprise, releasing him in an instant. Erik turned on her, his face half fury, half wild concern. "Did they hurt you?"

She was shaking her head before he finished. "No, no," she soothed him. "They have not laid a hand on me."

His face darkened. "That is hardly true," he snapped.

She slid her knife back into her scabbard. "Not in any meaningful sense," she promised. "And soon it will all be –"

She flushed, realizing suddenly who she was talking with.

His eyes were sharp on hers. "Soon it will all be *what*?"

She took a step away from him, trying to shake off the mesmerizing heat of his body; the nearness of the strong arms she so longed to curl within.

Her eyes dropped to the mat. "Soon I will finally get a decent night's sleep," she murmured.

His eyes followed hers, and understanding lit his gaze. "So that is why you came out here?"

She nodded. "I love the staff here dearly, but laying in that kitchen is like trying to sleep beneath a waterfall."

He glanced up in the direction of the keep. "Surely we can set you back up in the master bedroom."

She gave a sharp shake of her head. "No. You know I cannot. You are Lord of the keep – that is your room."

He drummed his fingers against his leg. "Then perhaps we could –"

Mary gave a gentle smile. "Truly, Erik. I prefer to sleep here for now."

He looked around the stall, gazing at the hay for a long moment. Then at last he sighed and nodded in acceptance. "Then I shall stay here with you."

She blanched, her eyes meeting his in shock. "But you cannot! If Lynessa were to catch you –"

"She won't," he promised, "and I won't allow you to sleep here unguarded." His eyes darkened. "There are too many wolves prowling."

A large yawn erupted from Mary's mouth, and she realized she was beyond exhausted. She ran a hand through her hair. "Fine," she sighed. "I am getting to bed. I haven't had a good sleep in ages, not since –"

The image of his arms around her flooded her memory, and she flushed crimson.

He stood in the doorway for a long moment, his eyes on her, and then he turned, closing the gate behind him. There was a rustling noise, and Mary realized that he had hunkered down immediately outside her stall.

The thought warmed her, and she climbed in under her blankets. Her head had barely touched her hay pillow before she fell into a deep sleep.

Chapter 13

Mary blinked her eyes awake, feeling more rested than she had in a long time. The sweet smell of hay rose around her, and the late morning sun danced through the shuttered window with a golden glow. She pushed herself up onto her elbows. To her right the hay was dented, as if someone had knelt on one knee for a while, watching over her as she slept.

She put a hand to the spot, warmth coming to her heart.

She sprung to her feet, moving to the gate, pushing it open –

He was not there.

The stables were quiet. Only the soft *whisk* of horses' breath sounding from the stalls.

She ran a hand through her hair. Of course he had gone back to the keep. It would not have done for them to be found in the stables together. She knew it as well as he did – and yet she felt an empty hollow within her. For a few hours, at least, they had been close again. She found she missed that more than she had thought possible.

There was the sound of footsteps, and the main stable door pressed in. Michael stepped through, his head sweeping, and he gave a shake of his head when he took in Mary.

"Aiming for the role of scarecrow, are we?"

Mary looked down her dress. She was, indeed, covered with bits of straw, and she was sure her hair was no better.

Michael chuckled, then moved to one of the stalls. "Erik and Lynessa are nearly ready for their morning's ride. He stalled her as long as possible, to give you time to wake, but we need to get the horses saddled." He took a blanket from the bench and brought it over to Lynessa's elegant steed.

Mary turned to pull open Erik's horse's stall door. "Where are the stable boys?"

Michael gave a low chuckle. "They were kept away as well, as you might imagine."

Mary looked up in surprise. "But the poor horses!"

"I'm sure they will survive having their grooming a few hours later than normal," he assured her. "Erik saw to their food and water."

Mary ran a fond hand along the neck of Erik's steed. He was a fine animal – sturdy and steady. For a moment she envied the horse, that he would be able to spend the afternoon at Erik's side.

Michael gathered up both sets of reins, then gave a nod of his head toward the keep. "All right, you. Go out the back way and over through the kitchen entrance. You need to get cleaned up, if you are going to be joining me for our gambling this afternoon."

Mary's brow furrowed. "Is everything ready?"

He nodded shortly, his gaze serious. "If this is going to be our chance to break the group apart, we need to do everything we can to draw them in. I have instructed all of the soldiers who are free to be available, and to bet whatever they have. We want to drive the stakes so high that the two men are willing to do anything to take advantage of the situation. If we can get them to risk stealing the coin, and maybe even her jewelry, then we should be able to breach their alliance."

Mary nodded. "And if we can ensure that Erik is nearby when they go for each other's throats, that should prove to him for once and for all that Lynessa is deeply involved in this treachery."

Michael held her eyes for a moment. "I will do everything I can to bring that about."

She smiled. "I know you will."

Lynessa's voice called from outside, imperious and demanding. "Where are our horses?"

Michael's eyebrow rose, but his voice was placid as he called out, "Coming, M'Lady." He pushed open the door and moved into the bright sunshine, leading the two steeds.

Mary stayed in the shadows, but she could not help gazing out through the glowing rectangle of space to look for Erik. There he was, his blond hair glistening in the sun, his sturdy build seemingly prepared to take on any enemy. He stood alongside Lynessa, who was elegantly garbed in a close-fitting dress of rich purple.

His eyes swept to Michael, and then past, and for a moment Mary felt that he was staring directly at her. The connection was palpable. She put a hand to her chest and drew in a deep breath, her body tingling with life.

Then Lynessa was taking his arm, leading him toward the horses, and he was gone.

The absence was like the darkest shadow crossing over her soul. It was all she could do to turn to the back door, slip through it, and make her way to the keep.

As Michael had said, the kitchen crew was ready for her with a half-barrel of rose-scented bath water and a small jar of wood ash soap. They had rigged up a ring of curtains to shield her, and she dutifully moved within, scrubbing away the dirt and grime of the past week. She lingered for a while, soaking in the bliss of the warm water and the delicate scents. Then at last she dried herself off and donned a long chemise.

Her team had been busy. A newly sewn dress of deep crimson awaited her, even more revealing than the one she had worn until now. She shook her head as she pulled it on. Hopefully it would be just for this one afternoon - just enough to draw the men into taking any risk and indulging in any whim. This one afternoon and it would all be over.

She took the small, spiral stairs in the corner down into the basement. She was in the storage area. Boxes of cheese, crates of wine, and a plethora of other supplies surrounded her on all sides. She wended her way through them to the front half of the level. She knew this open area would be where they would be gambling.

She pushed open the door.

There was a hush, and the entire room of men turned to stare at her. There was a large round table at the center of the torch-ringed room, with eight stools pulled up around it. Bronson and Sander were side by side, facing six of her men, including Michael. Another twenty or so soldiers were standing and sitting around the group, drinking mugs of ale or eating loaves of bread.

They all stared at her, eyes round, mouths agape.

Mary flushed. It was one thing to dress this way, to act this way, in a seedy bar where none knew her. It was quite another to be a harlot within her own home.

In order to keep Erik from determining her true mission, the keep's staff had been told nothing. They had simply been asked to call her Mary again and to treat her as a visiting singer. They had trusted in her. They had done as she had requested without question.

She wondered what they were thinking now.

Bronson and Sander recovered first, launching to their feet and dragging over a chair to seat her between them. Mary headed over to them, and Bronson shook his head while he looked her up and down.

"I thought you were gorgeous before, Mary, but now you are a goddess," he stated with certainty. "You stay here right by me."

Sander spoke up. "And by me," he chimed in. "We will make sure you have everything you could possibly need." He pushed a mug of mead before her as she sat.

Michael's eyes were shadowed, but he nodded to her as he brought his attention back to the table.

Mary looked at the cards and the piles of coin before each man. It looked like they were already well underway – the stacks before Bronson and Sander showed their success thus far.

Good. It would lure them into the trap.

Michael spoke up. "I believe it was your hand, Bronson."

Mary leant back in her chair, taking a long drink of her mead. She knew her job well enough. She was to flirt with the men, encourage them to bet, and make it clear just how impressed she was with their skill.

Anything to drive them to raiding Lynessa's storehouse of wealth.

Mary lost all sense of time as the cards were shuffled, the coins were moved, and her men changed places at the table as their luck ran out. There were no windows in the basement - only the flickering of the torches and the coming and going of maids with more ale or food. She cheered with delight when Bronson won a hand and encouraged him to try again when luck went against him. The piles before Bronson grew, and the avarice glowing in his eyes became a steady beacon.

It seemed no time at all before it had come down to just Bronson and Michael. Michael had an impressive collection of coins before him, and Bronson was practically drooling at the sight. He made a quick tally of his own stash, then turned to murmur to Sander.

"We don't have enough here. Do you have any more?"

Sander shook his head. "Everything I own is on the table."

Bronson pressed his lips into a thin line. "We are so close ..."

Mary leant against him, tenderly wrapping her fingers around his arm. "But surely, you said that there were other funds available to you? In times of emergency?"

Bronson's eyes flicked furtively to the side. "We aren't supposed to touch that," he growled.

Mary patted his arm soothingly. "You won't be touching it, not really," she assured him. "You will just borrow it for five minutes, maybe ten minutes at the most. Then it goes right back where it belongs. And you own every item of value in this room."

Bronson drew in a deep breath, his face nearly glowing with desire. "Does that include you?"

Mary's breath caught, but she forced herself to nod. "Of course it does," she promised him. "You will be the wealthiest man for miles. Who else would I want to be with?"

His eyes moved down her form, and his smile widened. He glanced for a moment at Sander. "You stay here and guard our winnings. Mary and I will go and fetch more funds."

Sander's face darkened in jealousy. "Why do you get to go with her?"

Bronson drew to his feet. "We can hardly leave her alone here, with these drunk, lecherous men," he contested. "Besides, I know the technique better than you do. It could take long enough as it is, and time is of the essence. If Lynessa were to return –"

Sander's frown deepened. "All right, all right," he conceded. "Go get it, and be as quick as you can about it."

Mary darted a glance at Michael. He gave her a nod, his eyes moving to the table. Mary held in a smile. It was all going as planned. As long as Michael could win the next few hands, disaster would crash down on Bronson and Sander. Once Lynessa came home, no matter where they had their *discussion*, Mary would be sure to be there, with Michael and Erik in tow. She knew every in and out of this keep.

Bronson turned, and she dutifully went at his side, first up the main stairs into the central hall, then up the back stairs toward the bedrooms. He glanced around cautiously, but there was no one in sight. Mary smiled. She knew Michael had been explicit with the staff in leaving this floor completely empty for the afternoon. There would be no interruptions in what Bronson was about to do.

Bronson nodded, satisfied that they were alone, then he pressed open the door. They stepped through, and then Bronson closed it firmly behind them. He strode with determination to the largest chest, unlocked it with a key from his belt, and quickly but carefully removed each item from it, placing them in a row to the left. Once the chest was empty, he knelt before it, staring at the front face.

Mary sat at his side, her face aglow with curiosity. "Now what do you do?"

He motioned to a pair of knots located to the right of the lock. "It has to do with these."

He put a hand on each knot. He leant his ear against the face of the chest and began slowly turning the knots. The right one moved clockwise, while the left one rotated counter-clockwise.

Mary's heart pounded in her chest. She wanted with every fiber of her being to take over for him, to break into the chest herself. He was taking an eternity, muttering and grumbling as he went. She had trained at this very task for months on end. If only she had known -

She reigned in her impatience. She did not want to interfere with him - not now when they were so close. If anything, it would be perfect if Lynessa returned while he was breaking into her stash. The fallout might be exactly what Mary craved.

There was the softest of clicks.

The inner floor of the chest rose, and Bronson smiled in satisfaction. "Here we go."

He reached forward with both hands and lifted off the false bottom.

Mary gasped in surprise at what was revealed. She had known the coin was in there, of course, but she was still not prepared for the sight of so much wealth in neatly laid out rows of glistening metal. No wonder it had taken the two men to lift the chest. It held the weight of not only the piles of Lynessa's jewelry but also this hidden wealth lining its base.

Bronson's eyes ran down the coins, calculating. "We'll probably need these three rows," he muttered. His gaze moved to a large ruby necklace, and his eyes gleamed. "In a few days, you'll be back home with me, and I'll dress you up proper," he promised. "My mum will be right shocked to see how well her only son's done."

Mary's brow furrowed. "I thought you had a brother, Arthur?"

He glanced over with sharp eyes. "Who told you that?"

Mary paled. Where had she heard the story? She hadn't even seen Bronson until he arrived here at the keep. Except, of course, for the two brief times he had been at Avoca's Folly …

Her breath caught. That is where she had heard about Arthur. Sander had made a comment implying that Bronson's brother had committed suicide.

She swallowed. "I … I imagine Caradoc must have said something," she stuttered. "I'm sorry, is it a sore topic?"

His gaze was piercing. "It is never spoken of," he growled. "Never."

Mary dropped her eyes. "Of course. I apologize."

She could feel Bronson's eyes still on her, and when his voice came, it had a sharp edge to it. "Well, once we have all this money, we can afford to light a candle for his soul. As you might for your dear departed Grandma?"

Mary nodded. Thank goodness, he was going to accept her slip as an understandable mistake. There was still a chance that the afternoon could play out the way she had planned.

She gave a sigh of relief. "Of course, we can light candles for our loved ones," she agreed. "I would like that."

There was a long moment of silence. At last he said, "Well, then, we need to get this money tucked away. Why don't you grab a few of those leather sacks and we'll get started."

Mary gave him a warm smile. She turned to the right, reaching for the items.

A solid blow landed on the back of her head. The world shimmered, disintegrated, and ebony stillness swallowed her whole.

Chapter 14

Mary's head ached with liquid pain, and her stomach roiled as if it had discovered a way to digest itself from the inside out. The world swayed and swirled around her. She blinked her eyes open, but her vision remained pitch dark. Baffled, she went to raise a hand to her head – but it came up short, tied in place with a sturdy rope. She began to roll to a sitting position, but her shoulders and legs met solidly with a wooden frame.

Her world gave a jolt, there was a whinny, and suddenly the pieces connected together.

She was wedged into the chest. She was being transported somewhere on a wagon whose every moment jostled her sorely.

Her heart pounded against her ribs. How long had she been unconscious? Who was kidnapping her? Did Michael and Erik know what had happened?

She kicked solidly at the chest's wall, hoping beyond hope that they were still within the courtyard. Her mouth was gagged with a thick cloth, but she screamed through it with all her might.

The wagon came to a stop.

The lid was lifted, and a brilliant orange sunset blinded her with its focused glow. She blinked furiously against it. A shadow fell across her, and Bronson's face came into focus. He seemed amused, and he reached a hand out to stroke her cheek. She flinched back, but there was nowhere to go. He grinned at that, letting his hand linger on her skin for a moment before giving a shrug.

"Guess we're nearly there anyway," he mused. "And Lynessa wants you good and healthy before we start the fun."

A shaft of fear shot through Mary. She struggled to a seated position, looking around her. She did not recognize the stretch of woods around her. Clearly they had gotten quite a distance from the keep since she had been rendered senseless.

Why had Michael not sent out troops to find her? Surely the keep's men could have overtaken this slow wagon without much effort.

Bronson grinned at her confusion, then turned and gave a shake to the reins. The wheels creaked into motion again, and when the slender path turned a corner Mary could see a small stream up ahead. A horse was standing in the gentle cascade of water, with two lanky teen boys mounted on it. They gave a wave as the wagon pulled to a stop next to them.

One of the pair shook his head, his grin lopsided. "You're late."

Bronson shrugged. "Had to head north first, to throw them off the track," he pointed out. He moved around to the back of the wagon and removed several large leather sacks. The boys dismounted and hooked them to various parts of the saddle. Then Bronson swept Mary up in his arms and moved her over to sit on the horse. Every instinct within her told her to struggle, to run, but after hours of being cooped up within the chest it was all she could do to stay balanced on the steed.

Bronson turned to the boys. "All set with the plan?"

One of them gave the other a playful shove. "Ding, dong, done," he agreed.

The boys clambered up into the wagon's front and took the reins. Without another word they headed on, and within minutes they were lost in the dense wood.

Bronson nodded in satisfaction, then climbed up behind Mary and began guiding the horse down the stream, staying within its running water.

It seemed at least another hour before he finally drew them up the bank and to a rough lean-to, nestled against a rock face. Bronson helped Mary down and left her propped against a decaying stump. He settled the steed within the shelter, removed its gear, and supplied it with food and water. Then he turned his attention back to Mary. He unceremoniously slung her over one shoulder and brought her to a small clearing behind the structure.

He gave her a long, amused look. "I'll remove your gag," he informed her, "but you make one loud noise and you'll be knocked out for the night. Understand?"

Mary nodded. She needed to conserve her strength until the time was right. It would do no good to scream where none would hear her, and risk a concussion – or worse.

Bronson reached over to pull the gag loose, and her mouth ached where the cloth came away from her skin. He handed a leather skin into her bound hands and she brought it to her lips, drinking down the warm ale with gratitude. He turned to the ring of stones before him, and within minutes he had a warm fire blazing before them.

He reached into the lean-to and brought out a large leather sack. He drew out two loaves of bread, throwing one to Mary. She caught it and began gnawing at it, hunger growling within her.

She looked over between bites. "So, where are we going?"

His mouth quirked up into a smile. "You will find out soon enough," he assured her.

They settled into silence. Mary strained every sense for signs of approaching rescue. Surely by now Erik, Michael, and Lord Paul would be out scouring every inch of the forest for her. At this very moment Erik would stealthily be approaching their position. He would be –

There was the tiniest sound of a foot on a branch, and her heart leapt. He was here! He had come for her. Her gaze flickered to Bronson, but he appeared oblivious to the danger he was in. He stared into the fire, resting an arm on one knee.

Mary's heart thundered. Just a few more moments. Erik would charge in and she would be saved.

There was a movement opposite her, and Bronson looked up with a smile.

"There you are. About time you arrived."

Lynessa's eyes shone as she stared down in satisfaction at Mary's trussed form. Her mouth spread into a wide grin.

"I wouldn't have missed this for the world."

Chapter 15

Lynessa shook her head at Mary as she stepped into the ring of firelight. "Somehow you are always bungling into my plans," she sighed, brushing dust off of her elegant riding outfit. Her gaze swept the rough lean-to and the surrounding forest before coming back to pin Mary. "And now I hear that you are the reason Erik first escaped from Caradoc? You were involved in that fiasco which resulted in Caradoc's brothers being slain?" Her mouth grew into a toothy smile. "I am sure Caradoc will be quite interested in hearing all about that."

Bronson let out a heavy sigh, stirring at the flames with a long stick. "Such a shame."

Lynessa raised her eyebrows, looking down at the man.

Bronson pointed at Mary with the glowing tip of his branch. "Just look at the perfection of those curves. I thought I was close to having that all for myself." He shrugged. "And it was all an act."

Lynessa gave a barking laugh. "Just make sure you get her to Caradoc in pristine shape," she reminded him. "I'm sure he is even more certain this time that he wants to draw out her punishment as long as possible. He will want her as healthy as a fatted ox when he starts, so that she lasts as long as possible."

Bronson's eyes lit up as he examined Mary's bound form. "You know, with all I have been through, perhaps Caradoc will allow me to take part in the *humbling process*."

Lynessa gave a dismissive glance to the woman trussed by the fire. "More likely Caradoc will want to savor every moment of that himself," she countered. "Even so, I'm sure Caradoc will shower you with ample reward for bringing her back to him. You can buy yourself four more just like her."

Mary had been carefully observing the interplay, looking for a weakness she might exploit. Bronson's avarice was exactly what she needed. She turned to him, holding his gaze with steady eyes. "I am still the rightful Lady of Cartwright," she reminded him, proud of the calm tenor of her voice. "I have access to a substantial amount of funds – both from my own keep and those of my neighbors. Just tell me what you wish. I can give you anything you desire."

Lynessa laughed out loud in delight. "My naïve girl, do you really think you have any hold in Cartwright after today?"

Mary's blood ran cold, and she swung her gaze to the blonde. "What do you mean?"

Lynessa took a step forward, towering over her. "I have to say, I owe you a hearty thanks for all of your bungling. Back when I first entered the Mangy Cur Tavern with Erik on my leash, I had given up hope of ever laying claim to the Cartwright Keep. I was ready to count myself lucky to have achieved his money. I would put him out of his misery and move on to a new conquest." Her smile turned brittle. "It was a hard decision to make, after over a decade of planning to be Lady Cartwright. But it seemed it was not fated to be."

Her eyes sparkled. "And then you leapt into the fray, and suddenly my fortunes reversed. Erik was granted a warm welcome at his keep. His mother lay moldering in her grave, no longer able to interfere. Best of all, Erik had blindly missed the true import of the previous events. He invited me into his home; he gave me an honored place by his side."

Her grin sharpened. "Do you truly think Erik's loyal staff would turn him out now, no matter *what* you said? And do you think Erik, after all the sacrifices he has made to win me, would give up on me now, when his dream was just within reach?"

Mary's heart thundered in her chest. She knew Lynessa was a master at manipulation. And yet, there was a thread of truth to what Lynessa was saying. Her throat closed up, but she forced herself to speak.

"I am sure Erik –"

Lynessa burst into laughter, cutting Mary off, and it was a moment before the blonde could speak. "If you know anything about Erik, you know how he values loyalty. I get the sense that you dallied with him during your two weeks together. And yet, the moment my men-at-arms walked in the door, you were practically climbing into their arms. Erik all but burst into flame with his disappointment in you. How could you have missed his reaction?"

Iron bands constricted around Mary's heart. She had known she would upset Erik with her plan, but she had figured the end result would be worth it. Had she lost sight along the way of what truly mattered?

Lynessa shook her head in amusement. "The whole keep knows how you and Bronson have been at it. Half the guards saw you in that indecent crimson dress that not even the lowest wench would wear. Even if Erik had been inclined to believe in you, how could he hold out against the voices of those he trusted - those he had known far longer than you?"

Mary could barely breathe. She knew Lynessa was far from trustworthy, but the blonde's smile was just too bright. She was telling the truth.

Lynessa dropped her voice to a seductive purr. "When my darling Erik was told that you and your lover had run off for the Scottish border, with half of my jewelry stolen as well, he was beyond furious. Within minutes every spare man was streaming north to bring you and your paramour to justice."

Mary fought desperately to find a hole in Lynessa's story. Lady Cartwright had trained Mary for years for this very purpose. Mary knew just how devious Lynessa could be.

Michael.

She sighed in relief, unclenching her fingers. Michael knew the truth of it all. Surely, the moment Michael had realized she had been taken hostage, Michael would have revealed the whole situation to Erik. Lynessa was twisting the truth simply to keep Mary quiet until Bronson could safely get her to Caradoc's dungeon.

Lynessa raised a brow at the change in Mary's mood. "Thinking of Michael, are we?"

Mary paled, her heart stopping.

Lynessa patted her gently on the cheek. "Oh, child. You do concoct such rosy fantasies. I'm afraid Michael was tracking you and Bronson long before Erik and I returned to the keep. By all reports Michael drove hard north, aiming to cut Bronson off before Bronson got you across the northern border. Poor Michael was in such a state that he didn't stop to leave a message at all."

She gave a delicate shrug. "So whatever you think Michael might have told Erik, that won't happen for weeks. Not until Michael gives up the chase."

A chill settled through Mary's body, settling into her very bones. It had not seemed that one word Lynessa had spoken was false. It was as if the woman felt there was no need to lie – that the truth was damning enough.

Lynessa ran a hand through her golden tresses, smoothing them into place. "So, for now, it will be just me and Erik in the keep. It won't take me more than a day or two to convince him that you and your bandit lover are gone for good. After that, I will cling to him with misty eyes and whisper how all the chaos has shown me just how brief life truly is. That we should wed immediately."

She brought her hands together in an attitude of prayer, placing them just over her heart. "After all these long years, I know how thrilled he will be. He will want to wed as quickly as possible before something else separates us."

Mary lowered her gaze to the ground, desolation pouring into every corner of her being. Lynessa had Erik wrapped around her finger. Mary could imagine the days playing out exactly as Lynessa had described. Lynessa would know exactly what to say to Erik and the perfect tone to draw him in. The accomplished liar had benefitted from decades of practice.

Only the iron core forged by Lady Cartwright's years of training insisted that there must be some way – any way – to ruin Lynessa's well-laid plans. Mary sorted carefully through all she had learned over the past few weeks, searching for a path out of her predicament.

Ah – Lynessa had seemed far from bosom buddies with Caradoc. Maybe this could serve as the lynchpin. Any delay Mary could cause would give Michael a chance to turn back - to meet up with Erik and put things right.

She set her face to hold rational calm when she looked up to the blonde. "You are hardly in need of money now, between your stolen funds and your access to the full keep's resources. Why not keep me yourself as a hostage? Play me off of Caradoc and Erik. See who would grant you more concessions in return for handing me over. Within a short time you might have doubled your land holdings, or gained who knows what other accomplishments."

Lynessa laughed out loud. "Oh, you would enjoy a delay, wouldn't you," she grinned. "But I am afraid that, after so many years of waiting, I want my wedding day over as quickly as possible. No negotiations or other distractions will interfere with that." She glanced at Bronson. "You see how quickly she turns on you? Now she wants to cheat you out of your reward."

She tapped a finger to her lips. "Speaking of which, I would appreciate having my jewelry back now."

Bronson shot a sharp look at Mary, then his shoulders fell and he nodded. In a moment he had retrieved the bags from the shed and brought them over to Lynessa. She knelt by the fire and went carefully through each bag, checking over the items within. At last she nodded in wry satisfaction.

"Nothing missing. Good."

She stood, hefting the bags over her shoulder. "Bronson, you get her safely back to the old keep and into Caradoc's hands. I will be by as soon as I can." Her grin sharpened. "I wouldn't miss this event for all the fish in the ocean. It will make the perfect wedding present."

She turned on her heel. In a moment she was lost in the depths of the forest.

Bronson gave a low chuckle, then sat back against the aging lean-to. "Sleep well, Mary," he advised her. "It might be the last good night of rest you have left in life."

Chapter 16

Mary slowly blinked her eyes open. She took in the familiar damp stone walls, breathed in the dense, musty stench, and winced at the guttural laughter of her guards. The men sprawled around the same worn table she herself had sat at only a few weeks earlier.

Her arms were throbbing in pain, and she tugged uselessly at the ropes to try to bring even slight relief to her state. Her wrists were tied high and out in a Y position. Torches guttered in iron brackets on the walls. She had no idea if it were dawn, dusk, or the darkest depths of night.

It had been but a few hours' ride the morning after her capture to reach Caradoc's base, but after that her memory became hazy. They had fed her mead with an herbal flavor to it, and she sensed it was drugged, based on her foggy perception. Guards had come and gone, the torches had flickered, and it could have been one day that passed or five.

She turned her head toward the table. Bronson was waving his mug before him, holding court with the four guards who hung on his every word. He was re-telling the grand adventure he'd had at the keep, presenting an embellished and self-aggrandizing version that Mary barely recognized.

Mary swept her gaze across the dust-caked floor to the heavy, barred door and the small, grated window in its center. The landing beyond was dark. No sound came from the stairs.

Thank all that was Holy that Caradoc had not arrived yet, but Mary knew her luck could not hold out forever. He would be here, soon enough, and then she might desperately wish for the luxury of her time bound in the wooden chest. She knew the only reason the guards had not abused her in any way was that Caradoc had far worse planned for her.

She swallowed. She had been around Caradoc and his men long enough to know just how ruthless they were. She would be made an example of. She would be used to show others just how important it was that they stay in line.

And then, eventually, of course, she would be dead.

A sense of clarity kindled within her, small at first, then growing with every passing moment. She had done her best. She had dedicated her life to following Lady Cartwright's orders. She had taken on every challenge presented to her. She had unraveled the threads to show Lynessa for what she was. Surely Michael would quickly realize that he was chasing a ghost and would return to Erik. Michael would reveal the entire situation to Erik, and Erik would drive Lynessa from the keep. The blonde was, after all, just one woman. She could not hold out against the combined forces of Erik, Michael, and Lord Paul.

Mary's job was done. Her time of living her life for Lady Cartwright must be over. For the first time in over ten years, Mary would forge a path of her own. She would act as she believed with all her heart.

All else had been stripped away. All other doors had been closed. The one thing left available to her was to die with honor.

She smiled.

It would be enough.

She would have to watch carefully for her opportunity. Maybe a guard would have a knife which came within reach of her bound fingers. Maybe Caradoc would be less than alert when he first handled her.

However she managed it, she had to draw them into a fight, and either escape or be slain. It was a far better option than to let herself linger.

She closed her eyes, soaking in the calm. Somehow she would find that option.

And with it, peace.

The quiet thud of footsteps came to her ears, and she nodded. It had begun. Caradoc was finally here to extract revenge for the death of his brothers. Somehow she would convince him to release her right hand. Just one hand would be enough. And then she would either kill him – or make sure she herself was slain.

The steps drew down to stop on the landing.

There was the softest shimmer of sound.

Mary's heart stopped. She intimately knew that sound. As a young child she had fallen asleep to it when her mother sang her lullabies. She knew exactly the number of small metal cymbals; knew exactly the feel of the worn wood within her hand.

Her eyes flew to the barred window. It could not be –

Erik's blue-grey eyes held hers, calm, steady, and determined.

Mary's face paled in shock. No. He could not do this. He could not walk into this room - not after all she had done to set him free. She had already accepted her fate.

She gave the slightest of shakes to her head.

He smiled at that, a wry smile that nearly broke her heart. And then he knocked on the door.

Bronson glanced up in surprise, and his eyes hardened to marbles when he realized who was standing there. His hand fell to the hilt of his sword, and he strode over to the door. Before he could say anything, Lynessa's voice floated through the bars. "Bronson, it is me. Open up for us, please. We have some important business with your captive here."

Bronson's brow creased in confusion, and he glanced back at the other men who were now standing as well. His voice was gruff. "Caradoc's orders were clear," he growled. "No arms within this room, except for our own guards."

Lynessa's voice was lightness itself. "Of course," she agreed. "We spoke with Caradoc personally, in the courtyard just now. Erik left his sword in Caradoc's care."

Mary's heart thundered against her chest. It could not be true. Erik had come down completely unarmed, a sheep to the slaughter?

Bronson's grin grew at that, and his shoulders relaxed. He looked again to his men, and they ranged along either side of him. Then he pulled open the door and stared at the two people standing on the other side.

Lynessa stepped forward and gave Bronson a grateful hug. "My dear Bronson, Sander realized that what he first told us was incorrect. He had thought Michael was chasing after a pair of fleeing lovers. But then, after talking with me, he realized that Mary here was the real thief – and that you were simply bringing her here for proper justice. It is all due to your quick thinking that you were able to discover who had stolen my jewelry. Words cannot express how grateful I am that you captured her."

She made a fluttering hand motion to Erik. "I have explained everything to Erik here. How Mary had been routinely stealing from Caradoc, and how you and I had been watching her carefully since our arrival. How it was only right to bring her back to Caradoc, given the enormous harm she has done to him during these past weeks."

She flushed in embarrassment and looked to Erik. "And of course, Erik now understands that his previous challenge with Caradoc was just a misunderstanding. We have that misfortunate affair all resolved now. He reassures me that far worse confusion happened in the Holy Land, and that the important thing is to put it behind us." A look of angelic sweetness came into her gaze, and she folded her hand into his arm. "Especially now that we are to be married."

Mary's heart nearly hammered out of her chest in panic.

It could not be true. It simply could not be.

Bronson looked between them with a carefully neutral gaze. "Congratulations are in order, then. How can I be of service?"

Lynessa gave a wide smile. "It turns out there was a minor legal hurdle to our marriage," she explained. "Despite all of Mary's heinous crimes, somehow the woman is, technically, still Lady Cartwright. Erik's poor mother was probably taken in by the girl's swindling as well. It is time to wrench this chit's grasp from the Cartwright family for once and for all."

She gave a delicate shrug. "So we just have to get her to sign a release, to turn the keep over to Erik, the man who rightfully owns it. Once that is done, we can at long last marry and have full ownership of our keep."

Mary's body was trembling with emotion. There was no way on God's green earth she would turn over the keep to that vixen. No matter what it took, no matter how she was tortured, she would refuse to sign. Her eyes moved to Erik's, hoping for even the slightest sign that he was not fully under Lynessa's manipulative spell.

There was a soothing in his gaze, a reassurance, and a kindle of hope swelled within her chest. Could it be that Michael had talked with him? Did he realize the fullness of what had gone on these past few weeks? The thought brought a tangled mixture of hope and agony. If it were true, then he was here to try to rescue her.

Her eyes dropped automatically to his hip, to where his sword should have hung.

The space was empty.

Bronson's eyes were also directed at the bare spot at Erik's side, and a relaxed chuckle came from him. "So that's all you need? Just a signature, eh? Sounds easy enough."

Erik's gaze was neutral when he turned to Bronson. "Just a few minutes and we'll be out of your way for good," he agreed. "But in order for her to sign this legally, you'll need to untie her right hand."

Bronson shrugged. "Sure thing."

He stepped forward to stand before Mary, carefully unknotting the heavy rope. It took him a few minutes, but at last it came undone.

Mary only half-feigned the exhaustion which cascaded along her muscles when the support was freed. She slumped wearily down against Bronson.

He smiled at that, pressing his body in against hers. He murmured low in her ear. "One last time, my dear, before the true fun begins."

That was all Mary needed to hear.

She lunged for the hilt of his sword, drew it in one long pull, and tossed it into Erik's waiting hand. He spun, slashed, and two of the guards went down in geysers of blood. Erik leapt to put himself before Mary, and Lynessa vanished up the stairs without a sound.

Less than ten seconds had passed.

Bronson grabbed the sword of one of the fallen men, then turned to his two remaining companions. "What are you waiting for? Get him!"

A pair of yells, a flurry of action, and both lay bleeding in twisting agony on the floor.

Bronson's grin grew wolfish. "This is perfect," he taunted Erik. "Now I kill you, and there are no witnesses left to see what I do to your beloved Mary. Lynessa is undoubtedly a county away by now; it could be hours before the next guards come down to check on us. By then, I would have had my fill of this whore and killed her." His eyes sparkled in delight. "And then I will simply knock myself out and claim you were responsible for everything."

Erik's gaze darkened with emotion, but he did not say a word. He held still before Mary, guarding her. He waited, steadily, for Bronson to approach.

Bronson raised his sword high, gave a screech, and then dove in. The men were a flurry of motion, twisting, slicing, jumping back, moving over the tangle of bodies at their feet.

Mary tugged desperately at her left hand, but she could not release the rope which still bound her to the iron ring on the wall. She looked desperately for anything within reach – a knife, a sharp piece of metal – but there was nothing she could get to. All she could do was watch, heart pounding, as the two men battled for their lives.

Bronson was edging his way left, trying to get closer to Mary, but Erik resolutely held himself between the two. Bronson's foot slipped in a pool of blood, and he caught himself, his breath coming in long draws. He looked up at Mary, and his eyes grew crafty.

He slid his eyes down the low-cut front of the crimson gown she still wore, directing his question to Erik. "Did she tell you?" He gave a guttural laugh. "Did she tell you how eagerly she came into my arms at night? How sweet those curves felt under me?"

Erik gave a low growl, but he did not move forward from his guard position.

Bronson's gaze darkened. "She is mine," he challenged. "And after I'm done with you, I will prove it!"

He dove at Erik, bringing his sword high and right, aiming to take off Erik's head with one massive strike.

Erik dove forward into the attack, driving his sword straight into Bronson's chest, forcing their momentum to send them backwards. Bronson's outswept sword shaved a thin line in Mary's dress as they tumbled to the ground.

Erik yanked his sword free of Bronson, standing above him, his chest heaving with the exertion. There was a long moment of silence as he stared at the body, watching the last spark of life leave Bronson's eyes.

Then he turned.

Mary's heart pounded against her chest as she looked at him. His leather jerkin was streaked with blood, his eyes blazed with determination, and she knew with all her heart that she belonged to him.

Her body rang with the truth of it, and she gave him a wry smile.

"I love you."

His breath eased out of him, and then he had crossed the space between them and drawn her into his arms, holding her as if he would never let her go. She was laughing and crying, and he pressed his lips against her neck, his breath warm against her skin. It was a long moment before he drew back and cut away the remaining rope; before he lowered her down to a stool.

He reached for the mead, but she shook her head. "I think they did something to it," she warned him. "I feel sluggish."

He gave it an experimental sniff, then poured it out onto the ground. He went to the ale instead and took down a swallow himself before nodding and handing it to her. She drank it down gratefully, drawing strength from the rich flavor.

He moved to one of the smaller men and removed the belt and scabbard from him, returning to settle it on Mary's hip. "Just in case," he murmured.

Mary glanced at the stairs. "Is Caradoc really up there?"

He nodded, his lips in a thin line. "Caradoc and all fifty of his men."

Mary blanched. "Why didn't they come thundering down when Lynessa told them what was happening?"

Erik gave a wry smile. "If I know Lynessa, the last thing she would ever admit to is that she helped in any way to bring me in to save you," he pointed out. "My guess is that she made her way outside the gates as quickly as possible, and she is likely still running."

He put a hand out to her. "Ready?"

She nodded and settled her own hand into his. "With you at my side, absolutely."

Erik led them through the door and slowly, carefully, up the stairs, stopping every few steps to listen. When they reached the top he quietly approached the door and peered around it. He smiled back to Mary. "All clear," he reported. "They must all be out in the courtyard making their preparations."

They stepped into the small chamber. Mary took a look around the low fireplace, at the small table and chair.

Erik raised an eyebrow. "I don't suppose I could convince you to wait here," he murmured.

A fierce anger swept through her. "After all I went through, do you think you could –"

He gently shushed her, drawing her in against his chest, soothing her. "No, I didn't think so," he agreed. "Just stay on the steps, like last time. Let me see this through." His gaze grew serious. "If they take you hostage, and threaten your life –"

She nodded in understanding. "I will stay clear of the fighting," she agreed. "I know, in my current state, that I could too easily fall."

He took her hand in his, gave it a squeeze, and together they pushed open the door.

Chapter 17

Mary blinked in surprise at the scene before her. The courtyard was ringed with torches which blazed brightly against the night sky. The moon was high overhead, and stars twinkled in festive abandon. Men were standing on all sides drinking mugs of ale and gnawing on skewered meat. A pair of men were strumming lutes and singing a bawdy song. By all looks it was a night of a winter faire, with a full fifty men carousing and enjoying the celebration.

Then Caradoc spotted them, taking in Erik's sword and the spray of blood covering his body. His yell brought instant silence across the courtyard.

Caradoc stalked across the uneven stones, and the men fell back into a ring. The gleam of stares was bright in the ebony night, a circle of eyes, all focused with delighted anticipation.

Caradoc came to a stop before them, his face glowing with fury. "I should have known better than to trust that blonde trollop," he ground out, his eyes fixed on Erik's. "She will get her just reward soon enough. But right now, this is between you and me." He looked around to the ring of watchers. "Men, you were cheated of your arena before, when Erik escaped from our clutches. It looks like you'll get a special treat tonight! Blood will flow!"

A rousing cheer went up around the courtyard, and mugs were raised in celebration.

Caradoc waited for the noise to subside before turning to Erik again. He eyed him for a long moment, the corner of his mouth turning up. "Speaking of blood, I bet your mother never told you."

Erik kept his sword in a guard position, his eyes not leaving Caradoc's. "Told me what?"

Caradoc chuckled. "Of course she didn't. It would have marred her perfect image. Did you know that you were nearly my nephew?" He gave a snort. "Wouldn't that have been something? That aunt of yours was inches away from becoming my wife before she took that tumble."

Erik stilled. "You were harassing my Aunt Avoca?"

Caradoc's barrel chest rumbled with laughter. "Oh, I don't think the woman considered it harassment," he grinned. "She rather enjoyed the attention. Always in the shadow of her older sister, she was. Your mother was domineering; poor Avoca never had a chance. She was a ghost of a woman." His grin widened. "At least until I got involved."

Erik took a step forward, his gaze hard. "What did you do to her?"

Caradoc's eyes twinkled in delight. "Oh, nothing that any man in the world hasn't done once or twice. I convinced her that she should seek some pleasure in the world. That she should think of herself for once, and not put that damned Lady Cartwright first all the time."

Erik's voice was a low growl. "You drove her to jump!"

Caradoc's brows raised in surprise. "Me? I wanted the woman alive and wearing my ring! That way when your mother suffered an untimely death, sweet Avoca and I could act as your regents and take control of the keep in your name." He rolled his shoulders to loosen them. "Then, of course, something tragic would have happened to you as well."

He held Erik's gaze for a moment, his eyes narrowing. "No, if anyone was responsible for Avoca's death, it was that mother of yours. Somehow she found out that Avoca was planning on eloping with me. She tore into her sister something fierce. Berated her. Ridiculed her." The corner of his mouth tweaked. "Well, you know how your mother was."

Mary looked between the two men in shock. As much as she wanted to accuse Caradoc of making the whole wild tale up, the truth of it echoed in her core. Lady Cartwright had always seemed wracked with guilt on the anniversary of Avoca's death. Mary had wondered if it was simply the sadness of an elder sister who had not done enough to watch over her younger sibling – but it had seemed much more than that.

Erik took another step forward, keeping himself between Caradoc and Mary. "You would have cut a swath of death through my family," he growled. "It is only fate that you were held to one victim." He gave his sword a spin. "This ends here."

Caradoc reached his hand down to draw his own sword – and instead he snatched the dagger from his belt, whipping it straight at Mary's chest. Erik leapt left to block it with his own body, and the blade drove deep into his left arm. Caradoc was arcing his sword high, driving to cleave Erik's head in two, but Erik swung his blade to intercept, continuing to dive left, causing Caradoc's blade to slide down and off.

Caradoc gave a snorting laugh. "That woman is your weakness," he taunted.

Erik shook his head, resettling himself into a low stance. "She is my greatest strength," he countered. "I would die for her."

Caradoc chortled. "I will be happy to help with that." And then he dove in.

Mary could not move, could not leave the steps from which she watched the battle. The drugs still held her in their grasp, still caused the world to fade in and out, and she knew she would cause more harm than good if she tried to interfere. But her soul wrenched in twisting agony as Caradoc drove hard at Erik, his barrel chest and beefy arms hammering as surely as if he were flattening an axe blade on a smithy's anvil. Erik was quick, precise, but blood trailed steadily from his left arm, and his movements were infinitesimally slowing with each stroke.

Mary took in Erik's dragging reactions, the slight stumble in his footwork, and it suddenly struck her that she might have been hanging in that dungeon, drugged, for days. Had Erik gotten any sleep at all in that time? How many miles had he ridden? What had he driven himself to before beginning tonight's battles?

There was a hoarse cry, and Mary's heart stopped. The men had separated and were staring intently at each other. It took all of Mary's self-control to stay where she was, to resist the urge to run forward to be at Erik's side.

Then Caradoc sagged to the ground as if all the strings holding him upright had been cut through with a razor. His eyes stared into the cobblestone ground and lost their focus.

The men in the ring went silent in shock. The only sound Mary heard was the wild beating of her heart. Then a throaty roar of anger rose, threatening, echoing, circling the courtyard.

Mary's blood ran cold. There was no way they could hold out against this many men. *No way.*

Erik put two fingers into his mouth and let out a high, piercing whistle. And then it was as if the very earth answered him. There was a trembling, the torches in the ring shivered, and a thundering noise filled the air. Caradoc's men looked around in fear, and then through the gates of the outer wall burst a wall of horses. Mary spotted Michael, Lord Paul, the sheriff, and a wealth of familiar faces.

Relief coursed through her as the incoming forces swept through the bandits, mowing them down. Erik took up a station before her, preventing any from reaching her to use her as a bargaining tool. It seemed only minutes before the sounds of battle had subsided. Soon there were only the whinnies of horses and muted conversations.

Michael strode to her side, drawing her into his arms. "God's teeth, are you all right, lass?" He ran a hand down her hair, shaking his head. "When I realized you had gone, I was beside myself with fury. I could not believe they had stolen you under my very nose. I thundered through that gate without a second thought, desperate to get to you before he could harm you."

"I am fine, truly I am," she reassured him. "They did not hurt me."

Lord Paul joined the group, giving her a fond pat on the shoulder. "I knew you'd hold up," he smiled. "Toughest woman I've ever met."

An arm slid along her waist, and Erik was by her side. "It is time to get our tough woman back home, where she belongs," he added with a weary smile. "I think we have had quite enough of this place to last a lifetime."

The sheriff spoke up. "The local church has asked to use the stone to build their new church. I think it's a fine idea."

Erik nodded. "Take it down. Take the whole thing down."

Mary looked to Erik. "And Sander?"

Michael was tying a bandage around Erik's arm, and glanced up at that. "Last we heard, he was half-way to Scotland. Apparently he has cousins up there. So that much, at least, was true."

And what of Lynessa?

Mary's throat closed up. She knew she should ask, but she could not bring herself to mention the woman's name aloud. She seemed a force of nature, malignant, unstoppable.

Erik's eyes creased in concern, and then he sighed and drew Mary in hard against him. "Lynessa is long gone," he promised her. "She was one for subtle manipulations, not open conflict. She will undoubtedly flee to Gaul, or Rome, or to some other far-off place to hatch new schemes. She knows her plots here have failed for good."

Mary could barely speak. Lynessa had been such a potent force in her life for so long; she could hardly believe that it was finally over. "But what if she returns?"

He gently kissed her forehead. "Then we shall bring her to justice."

An ache pulled at her heart. "But you – you cared for her."

He shook his head. "When I was hanging on that dungeon wall, it was as if everything else was stripped away. Clarity swept through me. I could suddenly see everything she had been doing - see it as if it were etched in glass. I realized exactly the steps she was taking."

It was almost too much for Mary to take in. "But you said – you said that you half-believed she was innocent."

He ran a hand tenderly through her hair. "I said that when I was taken at the church that I still had a kernel of doubt," he gently corrected. "But locked in the dungeon, with all else lost, and only my death before me, I saw things for what they truly were. I realized that I had never loved Lynessa. I had only built a childhood fantasy around her, and then clung to it. I realized how, even when we first met, she had manipulated me and guided me."

He tucked a hand beneath Mary's chin, raising her eyes to hold his. "I am only sorry I did not realize that years before, and come home to apologize to my mother. To meet you."

Tears were streaming from her eyes, she raised her lips, and then they were lost in each other.

Chapter 18

Dawn was easing golden shafts of light over the tower's crumbling curtain wall when they set in motion toward home. With the adrenaline of the fight several hours behind her, Mary found she was beyond exhausted. It was all she could do to keep herself in the saddle. Erik rode by her side, and she knew he had to be even more wrung dry than she was. Still, she could not have known it from looking at him. His stance was alert, and his eyes ranged from Michael's men before them to Lord Paul's behind.

Mary reached out to hold his hand. "The sheriff did say all of Caradoc's men were accounted for," she reminded him. "He had planned for this festivity to be sung about for centuries to come. Even more extravagant than his last one."

Erik turned to her with a wry smile. "You mean greater than *my* death celebration?"

She chuckled. "Yes, that would have been the one," she agreed. "I'm grateful neither festival went the way he planned it." Her arm gave a twinge, and she winced. "This time, I was en route to being the main course."

His gaze shadowed. "We were barely in time," he murmured. "Another few hours and it could have been too late."

She looked at him in curiosity. "So, how *did* you know that I had not run off to Scotland with Bronson? Lynessa was fairly sure that her cover story was foolproof."

Erik glanced forward to Michael for a moment. "I wasn't sure what exactly you had been up to, this past week, but I at least felt assured that Michael was involved with it. The only reason I went along with your requests was I knew Michael was watching over you."

He let out a long breath. "So when Lynessa and I came back from our ride, and the keep was in an uproar, my only thought was to find Michael. I knew once I found him that I would get the truth of the matter. To do anything else would be to waste critical time."

"And Michael was riding north?"

Erik nodded. "Riding hard. So I pushed my steed to his very limits. I knew if I did not catch Michael quickly, your life would be forfeit." He looked down and was quiet for a moment. "I overtook him just as dusk fell on the forest. In only a few minutes I had convinced him to tell me everything."

He looked forward again to where Michael rode with the troops. "Michael has a level head, and he knew what was at stake. It was clear to both of us that you had not gone anywhere willingly with the wolf's head. So we raced, as if the Devil himself were chasing us, back to the keep."

Mary's head swam with confusion. "To the keep?"

Erik gave a wry smile. "Lynessa is a master manipulator. I knew that she would have her fingers in everything that went on regarding your fate. There is no way that Bronson would have acted alone in this." He gave a soft shrug. "So my two choices were to scour the entire countryside trying to find you myself – or to ensure Lynessa brought me straight to you."

His brow creased. "By the time Michael and I returned to the keep, Lynessa was gone, as was Sander. We had every man out looking for you, and I nearly went out myself, but Michael cautioned patience. He pointed out that Lynessa would never abandon her chance to win me when she was so close to achieving her goal. And the key to finding you was Lynessa. So I waited, pacing the courtyard until I'm sure I wore a trench through the stone." He gave a small smile. "But, of course, Michael was right. Soon enough Lynessa came trotting back in, as pleased as punch, saying she had gone by her family home to summon her guards to join in the hunt."

The pieces were settling into place in Mary's mind. "So that is when you told her the story of needing my signature?"

He twined his fingers into hers. "I cannot tell you how hard it was to look into her eyes, to know all she had done, and to still play the besotted beau. But yes, I pledged my love to her, and explained the situation we were in. We could only have the keep and lands if you were still alive."

He chuckled. "You should have seen the change that came over her. Suddenly she wanted to ride out to talk with her guards. Apparently an idea had come to her. And by the next evening we were heading out to Caradoc's tower."

Mary's mind went back to the dungeon, to her acceptance of death. To her feeling of being reborn when she saw Erik's eyes.

Her voice was a mere whisper.

"You came for me."

His breath sighed out of him, and he reached his hand up to gently caress her cheek.

There was a pop, and a whistle, and Erik was diving at her, throwing both of them from their horses. He spun their bodies in the air so that she would land on top of him; his breath blew out at the hard impact. It came at the same time as the solid *thunk* of a crossbow bolt slammed into an oak tree beside them.

Michael's cry rang along the wooded path. "Attack!"

The soldiers spread out in all directions, swords high, slashing at the underbrush. Erik rolled from beneath Mary, his own blade out, his eyes searching through the dappled woods for any sign of the assailant.

Michael was by them in an instant. "Are you hurt?"

Erik's eyes flashed to her, and Mary shook her head. Erik called back to Michael, "We're fine. Go after him."

In a moment Michael was lost, racing into the shadows of the forest.

The hue and cry of the men faded into the distance as they spread out in all directions. Erik stood alertly over Mary, and it was several long moments before he eased his ready stance, before he reached a hand down and drew her up to stand alongside him. Still, his sword remained prepared, and he kept Mary behind him, carefully tucked between him and the steeds.

Mary's voice was a low whisper. "Sander?"

He nodded without speaking. His gaze swept the shadowed forest around them.

Mary shook her head. "But surely –"

There was a creak, and a footstep, and she froze. Erik took a half-step back, sandwiching her between him and the steeds, shielding her with his body.

Out of the dappled browns and greens stepped Sander, his flaxen hair askew, his face set with determination. The crossbow in his hand was fully cranked back, the bolt aimed for Erik's heart.

Erik settled into a steady stance, but Mary noticed in a stray corner of her mind that he did not crouch as he might if he were preparing to spring. She realized that he was not risking the lower profile – was not opening up the opportunity for Sander to shoot her. She dropped to one knee behind him, to give him more freedom to act.

Sander laughed at that, a harsh, barking sound. "Think you can dodge a bolt?" he challenged. "I've seen these things go straight through metal." He scoffed dismissively at Erik. "Your body is feeble protection for your Lady Fair. This missile will plow straight through your gut – and lodge deep within her heart. I will take out two troublesome pests with one shot."

Erik shifted his feet in the soft ground, finding purchase. "I am the one you want," he reminded Sander. "Let her go. I am the one who killed Bronson."

Sander's face mottled. "You killed him," he snarled. "Bronson had been my best friend since we were born. He was the brother I never had; the man I could depend on no matter what happened." His voice grew rough. "You stole him from me."

Erik's gaze held steady. "I am the one who should pay," he insisted. "You want to face me."

Sander's eyes turned into hard marbles. "I want you to die knowing you failed," he growled. "You will know you died unable to protect what was most precious to you." He shifted his aim lower down Erik's chest, to point to his stomach. "I will ensure you live an hour or two in agony, clutching the lifeless body of the only person you have ever truly loved. That might begin to show you just what I will face for the rest of my life."

Mary's heart thudded in her chest. If she could just dodge out of the way, she could draw Sander's fire – and it would take the man a full thirty seconds to reload. By that time Erik could cross the distance and overpower him. If she could just figure out –

Erik's left hand grabbed her hard by her arm, holding her in place.

His voice rumbled out of his depths. "Sander, there is one thing you have not accounted for."

Sander raised his brow in amusement. "And what might that be?"

The bright silver of a sword burst through the center of his chest, followed by a crimson bubbling. Michael's head appeared over Sander's shoulder, and he eased the man to the ground. Michael lifted the crossbow from Sander's lifeless hand and tossed it far into the bushes.

His voice was rich with relief. "That would be me."

Chapter 19

The sun was just arching to its highest point in a glistening azure sky as Mary and Erik rode side by side through the gates of their keep. The courtyard was filled with every inhabitant, and the walls rang with the sounds of cheering and applause. Erik was beneath her to help her from her saddle, and then he swept her up in his arms, causing the cheers to grow even louder.

Mary knew he was as exhausted as she was, but she couldn't tell it by the firm steps he took to carry her through the main hall, up the spiral staircase, and into their room.

A warm fire blazed in the hearth, candles flickered on the tables and sills, and a large, half-barrel tub waited to one side, filled with steaming water. Mary's body ached, and she didn't resist as Erik stripped her down before helping her to ease into the deliciously warm water.

A long moan wrenched out of her as she settled down into the rose-scented liquid, sinking lower until only her chin floated on the surface.

He gave a low chuckle, settling down on the floor next to her, taking a bowl of dried figs from the nearby table. "Like that, do you?"

She closed her eyes in bliss. "Oh, do I."

There was something sweet at her lips, and she parted them, letting him feed her a fig. In a moment she was washing it down with some warm mead. It was a long while before she opened her eyes again, taking in the familiar surroundings.

Erik rested a hand against her cheek. His eyes grew serious. "Oh, Mary, could you not just have told me the truth from the start?"

She gave a wry smile. "If Michael has told you the whole of it, then you know I could not. I gave your mother my vow."

He gave a short shake of his head. "So many ills have been caused by her stubborn nature and the influence she had over others," he murmured. "I thank God we are finally free of it." He turned to face her fully. "I want us to swear, from this day forward, that we will be honest and true to each other. My mother and her machinations are now behind us."

She took his hand in hers and brought it to her lips. "I swear it."

His tension eased at that, and he sat back against the bed, closing his eyes in weary exhaustion. For a long while they remained in drifting silence. Eventually she took up the wood ash soap and worked over her limbs one by one, gently removing what seemed to be archeological layers of dirt and sweat. An eternity passed before she felt truly clean.

At long last she was ready to emerge. He was at her side by the time she had gained her feet, wrapping her in a soft towel. Then he lifted her effortlessly in his arms, walking the few steps to gently lay her in the bed.

When she crawled beneath the heavy blankets, she felt as if she could sleep for weeks.

He gently stroked her hair. "I will be right down the hall if you –"

She sat up in a panic. "Down the hall?"

His brow creased. "I thought, after all you had gone through, that –"

Her voice hardened. "You thought wrong! You were going to leave me?"

Erik waved a hand at her clothes laying by the tub, still coated with blood and dirt. "I only thought with all you had –"

Mary crossed her arms before her chest. "If you think I want to be alone, without you, after everything I have endured, then you were absolutely wrong!"

He held her eyes for a long moment, and there was a glimmer of hope within them - an easing which melted her heart to see. Then he nodded and moved to the tub.

"In that case, I, too, am in need of some cleansing."

Mary piled the pillows behind her so she could sit up while he carefully stripped down past the many wounds and injuries on his body, until he stood before her in the firelight.

God's teeth, the man was magnificent.

It seemed only seconds before he had removed the caked blood, eased off the layers of sweat, and was again approaching their bed.

He drew to the opposite side and looked at her for a long moment. "To think of all you have endured, to honor your vow."

Her eyes held his, shining. "For the vow – and for love."

His breath left him, and then they were one.

Chapter 20

Mary blinked awake to streaming sunshine, and it was a long moment before she could sort out just where she was. The room, both familiar and new, felt more like home than anywhere she had known before. At her side Erik still slept, an ease in his face that she had not seen before.

And she was free.

It was almost too momentous to take in. For so long, for ten long years, her sole mission in life had been to train for two tasks: the tasks of making sure Erik was detached from Lynessa's influence, and then turning the keep over to him.

That day was now here.

Mary knew she should be thrilled. She should be grateful that she had done what she had been ordered to do. She had fulfilled her mission to Lady Cartwright. She had safely seen the keep into hands well worthy of its care.

Yet, for some reason she could not name, she felt hollow within. It was as if she had lost her purpose in life; as if the quest had been what had kept her going.

Erik blinked his eyes open, focused on her face, and a smokiness eased into his gaze. His voice was low and pleased. "I could get used to waking up like this," he murmured. His hand drew up to stroke her cheek.

She smiled, the gloom fading. "Oh, could you?"

Then he was pulling her down to him, and all else was lost.

* * *

She found herself going from room to room throughout the keep, the feeling growing within her that this might be the last time she saw it all; that soon her time here would draw to an end. After all, she had fulfilled her promise. Her feet took her into the kitchen buildings, where a stew bubbled merrily in the cauldron over the hearth fire. She spent time in the stables, drawing a fond hand down her steed's mane, breathing in the familiar scents.

Eventually her feet took her out to the cemetery, to the elaborately carved grave. The sun shimmered through the clouds, sending waves of tangerine and crimson toward Avoca's Folly. She knelt before the headstone, drawing stray grasses away from the crocuses that now bloomed there in lavender, sapphire, and pearlescent white.

She sat back on her heels, looking at the streaked granite. Her voice was a mere whisper. "I hope you are proud of me," she murmured. "I hope my actions were worthy of all the time you spent; all the care you invested in me. I wish –"

Her throat closed up, and she looked down. She didn't know what she dared wish. She had already been granted so much, when everyone else in her village had perished in those flames. It would be ungrateful to ask for anything more.

There was a shuffling noise behind her, and she glanced up. Erik stood there, his blond hair glistening in the setting sun, and her heart caught. His green and silver tunic fit his rippling muscles with just the right caress, and when he put his hand out to her it was all she could do not to fold fully into his arms. Instead she gave it a squeeze before walking with him back in to the main hall.

Something was off as she approached the head table, but it took her a long moment to realize what it was.

The elegantly carved wooden throne was gone.

She looked up at Erik in confusion.

"My mother is now at peace," he stated, "and it is time for us to relegate her to the past. The chair is in the guest room, beside the bed it matches. Let it serve as an honored seat for visitors there. You and I, we have our chairs, and they suit us well."

He held a hand out to her, and she could feel the strength in his fingers as he guided her to her seat. Michael sat at her other side, and it was almost too much to take in.

Zelda came by with roast pork, Tina's red ringlets bounced as she poured them fresh mead, but all of Mary's thoughts were on the end of the meal. It seemed only seconds before their apple tart was being cleared away.

She turned to Michael.

He patted her hand, giving her a supportive nod.

Mary stood, holding out both hands, and the room fell into an attentive silence. Erik sat back in his chair, his eyes on her with curiosity.

Mary looked out over the familiar room, over the people she had known for over a decade. She looked at the large fireplace with its ring of chairs and couches, and thought how many nights she had sat there, dreaming of the future.

"My dearest friends. I want to offer my deepest gratitude to everyone who helped rescue me and bring an end to the bandit menace. I do not exaggerate when I say my life was at risk. It is only due to Erik, Michael, Lord Paul, and many of the soldiers here that I was brought safely home."

Her throat closed up at the thought of that word – *home*. She truly had come to think of this keep as her home.

What did the future hold for her now?

She forced herself to smile, and pushed on. "You have been gracious to me during my time as Lady Cartwright. But clearly there was always one man intended to be Lord of this keep, and that is the man sitting at my side. Lady Cartwright, his mother, invested me with the solemn duty of caring for his birthright until he was fully home."

Tina scurried up before her, handing her the large ring of keys, before blushing and returning to her place. Mary held the iron ring high for all to see, before turning to Erik, who was now sitting forward, pale.

Mary held the keys out on both hands. "Erik, the keep is yours."

Erik blinked as if he could not quite grasp it all. He rose to his feet, looking first at her, and then at the room. A hush held the gathered people.

His hand came down to hers, and for a long moment it lingered there, his fingers caressing hers. Then he smiled. He looped his hand through the keys and held them high.

The room burst into applause and cheers, with the clinking of mugs and shouts of approval.

At long last the room quieted and he looked out over the faces. "I could not have asked for a more able or valiant regent to watch over the keep while I was away," he stated, his voice hoarse. "I will never be able to repay Mary for all she has done. She deserves, at last, her freedom. Her freedom to do whatever she wishes, unburdened by any restrictions."

The cheers were even louder this time, and Mary was moved by the smiles. It warmed her to know that her efforts had been appreciated. Her cheeks flushed crimson, and she took a long drink of mead.

Michael stood and moved to Erik's other side. "I have something for you as well."

Erik raised an eyebrow, turning to look at the older man.

Michael reached into the leather pouch at his pocket. "I was with your father, the day he was gored by the stag. He gave this to me, and asked me to present you with it when you grew of age and became Lord of this keep." His eyes misted. "I have waited long for this day."

He drew out a signet ring, holding it toward Erik.

Erik drew in a long breath, and there was a pause before he reached out his hand to take up the gold ring. He turned it in his hand, as if he did not quite believe it was real, before at last slipping it onto his finger.

Another burst of cheers and applause sounded, and Erik drew Michael into a warm hug, holding him for a long moment. Then the musicians were playing a country song, the room was filled with music, and a heartfelt celebration began.

Mary heard the lyrics, she felt the beat of the drum in the soft vibrations of the table, but somehow a distance was forming between her and the room around her. The feeling of loss, of emptiness, steadily grew. The transition was now complete. She had lost her place in the world. Her goal, her life's purpose, was gone. The future loomed before her, black, empty, and directionless.

She pushed herself away from the table and headed out of the hall, across the quiet courtyard, and up the thin steps to the top of the curtain wall. As she had so many times before, she moved around its edge to the far side, where only a whistling wind kept her company. She leaned against the crenelated stone, looking out over the trees. The bitterness of winter was fading, and the fragrant hint of spring was laced in the breeze. Stars twinkled overhead in a cacophony of silver and white, and she wondered if she could make out Avoca's Folly in the glistening moonlight.

The thought of the doomed woman sent an echo through her own heart. Just how had Avoca felt, to have her sister pushing her, driving her, telling her what path to take in life? Avoca had chosen to escape by leaping out a window, to bring a brutal end to an all-too-brief existence.

Mary had been driven by that same whip; had known the same harsh taskmaster in life. She had done everything asked of her. She had trained in sword and knife, in stealth and horsemanship. She had struggled vainly for approval. Even now, with the task done and behind her, she felt as if it was not quite enough. A chasm yawned before her, and it was pulling her in.

There was a noise behind her, and she turned in surprise.

Erik stood there, his face edged with concern, his shoulders tight with tension.

He gave a wry smile. "I thought I might find you up here. It is where I used to come, when I needed to think."

She ran a hand along the rippled stone, thinking of all the years he had stood in this same place, perhaps filled with the same chaotic issues with his domineering mother.

He took a hesitant step forward. "Mary, I know something has been troubling you. What is it?"

She shook her head, looking back out into the distance. "I feel lost," she admitted. "For so long my life has held one focus. Now that is gone."

He came up to stand beside her. "You did far more than my mother could ever have expected," he murmured. "You are free of that burden now. You can go anywhere. You can do anything you wish."

Her face flushed with heat, and she turned to look at the keep, at the torches shining around it, sending a gentle glow along its walls. Her throat closed up, and she could barely get the words out. "Where else could I possibly want to be?"

Erik groaned, then pulled her in hard against his chest. Suddenly the emptiness was filled, was overflowing, and all she wanted was to be with him, to be a part of his world. The chasm behind her vanished in the mists, and a future spread out before her, dream-like in its unreality, in a fantastic nature that she never could have imagined possible.

Then he was lowering himself onto one knee, holding her hand, and looking up at her with glistening eyes.

"Choose to stay with me, of your own free will, and let me love you. Let us care for this keep together and raise children to run laughing through its hallways. Let us dance and ride and watch the night stars side by side until the final light fades from our eyes."

Mary blinked, overwhelmed, and she shook her head in bewilderment. "But I am just a village girl," she protested. "Your mother never meant —"

He stood at that, staring down at her with focus. "My mother is dead," he reminded her forcefully, "and from this day forward you are free to do what you want to do. To follow your heart." It was a moment before he spoke again, his voice tight. "Do you love me?"

Her breath sighed out in disbelief. "Do I love you? I adore you, I treasure you, and I would wake up each morning grateful beyond measure to have you as my husband."

He smiled at that, running a hand tenderly down her hair. "Then you will be my wife?"

Mary threw herself into his arms, pressing herself against his broad chest. When his arms came around her, her world was complete.

"Yes," she whispered. "Yes, yes, yes."

Chapter 21

Mary nervously brushed down the length of her embroidered green dress, then checked herself in the mirror for the fortieth time. She could still not believe the day had arrived at last. The week had been beyond busy with preparations and arrangements, and Mary wondered if she had even slept. But the moment had at last arrived, and the seamstress had proven herself a miracle worker. Mary knew she had never seen a dress as beautiful as this, with its stitchery of the crossed swords along the hem and neckline.

There was a knock at the door, and Michael's voice eased around the corner. "Are you ready?"

Mary smiled. "Come."

Michael pushed open the door, then stopped, gazing at her with a distant look. "You are stunning."

Mary blushed. "Is everything ready?"

He nodded, his face growing serious. "Between our men and Lord Paul's, the place is watched on all sides. But it's not an assault of that nature that I'm worried about."

Mary tucked her arm into his, giving him a warm squeeze. "If Lynessa were going to harm us, she would not want to martyr me through an anonymous attack at my wedding," she stated calmly, forcing herself to believe it. "I don't think that's her style. She would want to do it in a personal way, where I would suffer long, knowing what was done to me."

Michael's brow creased. "I'm not sure that makes me feel much better," he muttered.

She smiled up at him. "It means, for today, we should relax and enjoy the celebration."

He sighed and nodded. "Of course. I just worry about you, lass."

She gave him a nudge. "Soon that will be my husband's job," she teased him.

His face eased at that. "I think Erik has considered that his task since he first laid eyes on you in that dungeon cell," he pointed out.

The walk down the stairs and across the hall seemed to glisten with supernatural beauty, every banner and candle flame taking on new significance. Then they came out the keep's front doors, and Mary's heart sang.

The entire staff was dressed in their Sunday best, looking up at her. Spring flowers decked every available surface, and banners drifted in the late afternoon sunshine. But all the beauty shimmered out of her awareness as her eyes drew to the chapel.

Erik was standing at the steps, his eyes steady on her, his face glowing with pride and love. She knew with absolute certainty that he was everything she could want in a husband. It was almost too much to take in, that he was to be hers.

Michael was moving at her side, guiding her, but all she could see was Erik growing closer, and the feel of his sturdy hand taking hers. The priest stood above them, reciting his sacraments, but it was only Erik that mattered, only his gaze on hers, the knowledge that they would be bound together and none could ever take them away from each other again.

There was cheering, he drew her in to him, and the world fell away.

* * *

The celebration was at its height, Erik was spinning her around to a rousing dance, and at last she collapsed back into her chair, laughing in delight. Tina bobbled by with yet another mugful of mead, and Mary took a sip, wondering if she could burst from pleasure. Surely she had eaten enough figs, dried pears, candied apples, and other treats to last a lifetime. And it seemed more food was arriving!

A pair of ginger-haired teenage boys was coming forward with an elaborately engraved silver flask. One of them gave a flourishing bow. "And now, the traditional wedding drink!"

Erik gave a low laugh. "Ah yes, the special mead. Old Gemma is something of a goddess in this area. Legend has it that every woman who drinks the mead has her fertility multiplied."

One of the boys nudged the other one. "We're proof of that!"

Mary looked between them, laughing, realizing that they seemed to be twins. She put a hand on her abdomen, turning to Erik. "I'm not sure I'm quite ready for twins," she teased him.

His eyes shone, and he gave her a long kiss. She was breathless when he released her. His eyes held hers as he murmured, "I think you are ready for just about anything."

A flush ran through her body, and suddenly she wanted to finish with the celebrations, take her new husband up to their room, and close the doors.

Husband.

A thrill ran through her, and she saw the answering heat in his eyes.

The boys held up the flask, shouting out, "Drink!"

The room took up the chant, and she smiled, reaching out her hand. The flask was cold, slick, and she removed the stopper. She tilted up the container, drinking down the liquid, noting the curiously lumpy texture to it. When she was done she stoppered the flask and handed it back to the pair.

One of them patted the other on the back, smiling. "Ding, dong, done."

Mary's world spiraled to a halt. Visions and sceneries spun in her head, sorting and resorting. Erik was staring at her in concern, asking her something, but she shook her head, grasping at the images.

Mary turned to Michael, and her voice ground out of her. "Get Tina to my room with a pail and the bark of elder. Quickly." Then she was turning to the crowd with a bright smile on her face, waving. Her voice was full of mirth when she called out to them. "And now, it's time for me to spend some time alone with my new husband." The calls, cheers, and applause that followed them up the stairs was all she could have hoped for, but she barely registered them. She half-ran to the door, and Erik was by her side at every step.

His voice was taut with concern. "Mary, what is it?"

Tina raced into the room, a bucket looped under one arm, a pottery jar clutched in the other. Mary tossed the bucket into the center of the room, grabbed the jar, and started ingesting the bitter, dry bark, forcing it down her throat.

Michael was in the doorway. "Elder bark?"

Erik was kneeling at her side in a heartbeat, drawing the pail before her. "Poison?"

Her stomach was heaving, and it was all she could do to nod before the purgative did its work and she was retching out everything she had consumed throughout the long evening. Thank all that was Holy that she had stuffed herself thoroughly and created a dense mixture for the poisoned mead to settle onto. If she were fortunate, she would force it all out before any had begun to take effect.

Only time would tell.

At long last her stomach had fully emptied itself. She wearily sat back against the bed. Erik drew a wet cloth across her forehead, looking at her in worry.

"Did you think it was the mead?"

She nodded, brushing back a stray hair. "The two boys. They were the ones who took the cart from Bronson," she explained. "I didn't recognize them until it was too late."

Tina was peering into the pail, poking into the liquid with a stick. "Holly berries," she reported. "Quite a number of them."

Erik's eyes darkened with rage. "I will grab the boys and –"

Mary put a hand on his arm. "No, wait," she insisted. "I remember now the last time I heard of Gemma. It was three years ago, when your mother was celebrating your birthday."

Erik's face paled. "And Gemma sent her mead?"

Mary nodded. "We had so many things to eat and drink that night that I scarcely remembered it, but the engraved flask does seem familiar now. When your mother became sick, we hardly knew what of the many dishes to blame. Nobody else was sick, after all."

Erik's face was stone now. "All the more reason to –"

Mary shook her head. "Gemma came to your mother, just before she died."

Erik sat back in shock. "What?"

Mary thought to that desolate evening. "Gemma was huddled in a shawl, and the room was dark, so I could barely see her. Your mother was beyond speaking by that point; she lay motionless in her great bed. But Gemma knelt by her ear and talked with her for a long while. We were beyond hope by that point, willing to try any remedy. Gemma had sent word that she had a tea that might bring some relief to Lady Cartwright. But, of course, nothing could be done."

"And you think that was Lynessa?"

Mary held his gaze. "I think Lynessa wanted to look into your Mother's eyes as she was near death, and to let her know just who had taken her life." She gave a wry smile. "Just as she will want to do with me."

Michael stepped forward. "Absolutely not. We will *not* use you as human bait to draw that monster in."

Mary put her hand on Erik's arm. "I am surrounded by our troops," she pointed out. "I got the poison out of me before it could get absorbed – I will be at full strength. Once we get her into the keep, the threat will finally be over."

Erik was shaking his head, and she clutched at his arm. "It will never be done with until we get her in our grasp," she insisted. "She will always slither away to hide. The boys would probably rather die than give her up. We need her to come to us. And we know she will."

Erik stroked her hair, and at last he let out a breath. "We do this my way," he stated, brooking no opposition. "No going behind my back. No keeping me out of the loop."

Relief rippled down her spine, and she eased against him. "We do this together."

He pressed his lips to her forehead, then her cheek, then her lips. She slid against him, and behind her she heard Tina and

Michael slip from the room, closing the door firmly behind them.

And then the world fell away.

Chapter 22

It was March third, St. Owen's Day, usually one of Mary's favorite holidays of the year. The craftsmen of the keep would all be celebrating their works, showing off deftly inlaid ring-boxes and delicately crafted leather necklaces. And yet here she lay, sequestered in the guest bedroom, the curtains pulled tight across the windows and the room settled in deep shadows.

Mary nestled herself deeper into the heavy blankets. There would be plenty of feast days in the coming years. Every hour she acted this part brought her one step closer to Lynessa's final capture.

Mary knew in intimate detail just how Lady Cartwright's illness had progressed; just what symptoms to share with Tina and Zelda at each visit. The two servants then passed the tragic news on to the rest of the staff. Mary hated to worry the people she had grown up with, but it was necessary to make the deception complete. Lynessa would sniff out any hint of duplicitous behavior.

Erik poked his head through the door. Seeing none else were in sight, he came in with a smile, closing the door firmly behind him. "And how is my favorite patient?"

Mary chuckled, bringing herself up to a seated position. "Biding well enough," she offered. "We're on the third day now. Another two days and -" Her face shadowed and she looked down at her hands. Her voice quieted. "Another two days was when your mother lost the ability to speak. She could only moan. That is when Lynessa arrived, in the guise of the elderly healer."

Erik nodded, settling himself into the ornate chair by her side. "Lynessa would want to be perfectly safe before she came to gloat," he agreed. "No chance of her deed being revealed by her victim."

She twined her hand into his. "Still, it is hard being apart from you, when we had only just been joined."

He lowered his head down to tenderly kiss her hand. "This was your idea," he reminded her. "The more alone and isolated Lynessa feels you are, the more she will be drawn in to talk with you. The story is that we don't yet know if your illness is contagious or not, so you insisted on sleeping separately from me."

Her eyes darkened with passion. "But now that you're here …"

* * *

Another long day, and then Wednesday dawned with grey skies and distant rumbles of thunder. Butterflies of trepidation circled in Mary's stomach. This would be the day that the staff was told she had lost the ability to talk. Lady Cartwright had died an agonizing two days after that point. Mary knew that Lynessa would not want to miss her window of opportunity.

Her heart rose when Erik came in to settle by her side. He gently kissed her forehead, his brow creased with worry. "Michael has doubled the patrols, just in case we can catch her unawares" he murmured. "Lord Paul has done the same. She must be out there somewhere nearby, watching and waiting."

Mary looked up at him. "We don't want to scare her off," she reminded him.

He nodded in agreement. "We have let it be known that Caradoc's distant cousin is in the area, seeking revenge for his family's slaughter. Our patrols are said to be precautions against that threat."

Mary shook her head. "It won't help," she murmured. "Lynessa won't be found. She will sneak in, like a tendril of ivy, and poke into existence where least expected."

A thought sprang to her mind, and she gave his hand a squeeze. "When Lynessa was discussing her new plans for the great hall, she said she wanted ivy and holly there. She claimed that it would be fitting."

He drew a hand along her brow. "Soon it will all be over," he promised her. "Just another day or two."

The twisting intensified in Mary's stomach as she thought of Lynessa returning to the keep, coming dangerously close to Erik. For so many years she had trained to keep Lynessa away from him, to ensure Erik was safe.

She knew now why she had felt hollow these past days. Her mission was not yet over.

There was a rapping on the door, and both glanced up in concern. Michael poked his head around the door. When he saw they were alone he strode in with a smile, waving a scroll. "We have good news from the sheriff."

Erik stood, taking the scroll with a sigh of relief. "Lynessa?"

Michael nodded. "They have her, down by the Folly. She was skulking around the tower when they came across her. She was disguised as an elderly woman."

Erik unrolled the curl of parchment. "And the message is from the sheriff himself?"

Michael leant against the closed door. "The messenger swears he saw the sheriff write the note personally."

Erik had the scroll open in his hands and sat down to read it. Mary leant over to take a look – and stopped.

Smudge marks smeared the letters – ever so slightly – to the right.

Mary kept still. She had been Lady Cartwright's assistant for ten long years, and the Lady had been left-handed. Mary knew the challenges the Lady had with writing with an ink-dipped quill. Moving the quill to the right created a trail of wet ink behind it, and just the slightest tip of the left wrist or sleeve would drag through that ink, smearing it. It was a challenge that right-handed writers did not have to contend with.

Mary had seen the sheriff fighting in the courtyard when the men came to her rescue. He was most definitely right handed.

Mary dropped her eyes. If Erik left on this quest he would be safe from harm. Lynessa was luring him away from the keep so she could come face Mary one on one. The further Erik was from that, the less chance he could be hurt.

There was silence, and Mary glanced up. Erik was still staring at the scroll, and then his eyes turned to hold Mary's. She could not read the emotion held within them.

His voice was even. "What do you think, Mary?"

Mary wet her lips. It was one thing to want to keep him safe. It was another to directly lie in order to do it.

"I think if the sheriff sent this, and he has Lynessa, that you should go ensure justice is done."

He held her gaze. "And do you think the sheriff sent this?"

She could hear her own heart beating in the silence. She opened her mouth – and then closed it again. At last she dropped her eyes and shook her head.

Erik looked at the writing on the scroll. "No, this is not from the sheriff."

Michael stepped forward, looking between them in confusion. "The sheriff didn't send the note?"

Erik ran a finger across the lines of words, his lips pressed together in a line. "I would know this writing anywhere," he murmured. "Lynessa couldn't read or write, so she had a young priest do her messages for her." He gave a low snort. "I imagine he did other tasks for her as well." He looked up to Michael. "The priest tried to disguise his handwriting here, but clearly this was done by him."

He drew his eyes back to Mary. "Besides, the priest is left handed, which is clear from this letter. You and I both know that the sheriff wields his sword with his right."

Mary flushed. "Erik, I just wanted –"

He crumpled the parchment in his fist. His voice was hoarse. "Mary, I am your husband now, and you are my wife. If we do not have full, complete honesty between us -"

She put her hand over his. "I know," she ground out. "I swear, I know. It's just been so long that I've been set on this task." Her voice caught. "If you were hurt –"

He sighed, dropping to a knee at her side. "And I would do anything to keep you safe," he countered. "We must trust in each other, and handle this as a team. Together we will get through this."

She nodded, looking up at him. "So what do you want to do?"

He glanced again at the crumped paper in his fist. "She has taken the bait. She feels it would be safe to come in, as long as she gets me a distance away. So we give her what she wants."

Mary's heart leapt with hope. "So you will go down to the Folly?"

He pressed his lips into a line. "I will head in that direction, at least," he amended. "When Michael sees she is approaching the gates, he can light the torches on the back side of the curtain wall. That will be my signal to come about and return. Once she gets within the gates, we can have the men grab her and hold her."

Mary sharply shook her head. "No."

Erik and Michael stared at her with shock. Their voices came in unison. "No?"

Mary knew how she felt with growing certainty. "I was by your mother every day since you left her," she pointed out, "and I know how much harm Lynessa caused her. I know what the woman has tried to do to you and me. I want to hear what she has to say when she feels she has nothing to lose. I want to make sure we know the full extent of her schemes. There may be yet more traps we have to be wary of."

Erik's brow shadowed. "Surely we can question her at length once we have her in chains."

Mary gave a short laugh. "You know Lynessa better than anyone," she pointed out. "The woman is a master manipulator. Once she is captured, will we be able to trust anything she says?"

Erik was silent for a long moment, and at last his shoulders dropped. "She would say anything in order to get loose."

Mary leaned forward. "This is my one chance for getting any sense of what she has done – and if any other threats remain. Once this chance is gone, I know it will never come again."

Erik ran a hand through his hair. "But to let her in here with you? Alone? Unguarded?"

Michael stepped forward. "I would be happy to be in here as a guard."

Mary shook her head. "Lynessa would never talk with you in the room," she pointed out. "She wants to ensure her deeds go with me to the grave."

Erik's brow creased. "When she came to visit my mother, what did she do then?"

"She never looked at me," explained Mary. "She shambled around in a heavy cloak and kept her eyes on the floor. Probably so nobody could identify her. Then she asked for me to fetch some mint leaves for her potion. Of course, I ran off immediately for them."

Erik nodded. "All right, then. We can have Tina in the room with you, and it seems likely she'll send Tina off on some quest. Once she does, then Tina can fetch Michael and me from where we are hiding in my room, and the three of us can wait right by your door, listening in. That way, the moment she stops speaking, we can come in and grab her." His voice became somber. "And if she tries anything else, we can stop her in time."

Mary gave his hand a tender squeeze. "Lynessa would not want to martyr herself," she promised. "She wants me to die in slow agony, knowing all along that she has won. She will probably want to tell me how she will be there to pick up the pieces, once you are a lonely widower."

He gave a low chuckle at that, then kissed her forehead. "Well then, I should be off soon." He turned to Michael. "And you –"

Michael nodded. "I will ensure everything is ready."

Erik held Mary's hand for a long moment, and she was caught in his gaze. He seemed as if he were soaking her in, as if he were heading out on a long journey and did not know when he might return.

Then he stood, and they were both gone.

Chapter 23

Tina turned from the curtains with a pale face, her ringlets bobbing with the motion. "The torches have been lit," she nervously whispered. "She must be here, in the courtyard."

Mary's heart was drumming, but she fought to remain calm. "Pull the curtains," she advised the woman, "and take up your mending in the far corner. Remember, I have been sick for many days now. Your watch over me is now a tragic routine. I am not even talking now – just laying on this bed, waiting for death to take me. This is a room of somber silence."

Tina nodded, returning to the small wooden stool and working on the frayed tunic. Mary could see the tense sharpness in her stitches, but she imagined Lynessa would not think twice about it. That could be attributed to the maid being upset at her mistress being ill.

The minutes dragged on, and Mary was sure that every quiet thump, every ragged creak was news of Lynessa approaching the door. She began to wonder if something had gone wrong. Perhaps Lynessa had been spooked by Michael's behavior and had fled.

A soft rapping came, and she froze.

After a moment Tina got up and slowly approached the door. When she drew near she called out, "Who is it?"

Zelda's rich voice came through the wood. "It's Zelda, Tina. I have a visitor for the Lady – it's a local healer. She says she might have a cure that will save her."

Tina hesitated for a moment, looking back at Mary, and then she pulled open the door. "Of course, we will try anything we can, and with thanks."

Mary blinked through the bed's curtains at the figure by the door. Surely this could not be Lynessa? The woman was elderly beyond all reckoning, with deep, carved furrows in her face and a twisted nose. Her hair, which stood out from the edges of a ratty grey cloak, was spindly and brown. She was hunched over and walked with the help of a gnarled oak cane.

Tina ushered her in, then closed the door behind her. The maid helped the woman over to the carved chair by the bed. "I'm afraid she won't be able to tell you her symptoms any more," she sighed. "The poor Lady lost her ability to talk a full day ago. Now all we hear are inarticulate moans."

The woman patted her hand. "Not to worry, dearie. I shall soon make everything right as rain."

Tina returned to her chair at the other corner of the room, returning her gaze to her mending. "I am resigned to praying that she will be out of her misery soon," she admitted. "That seems to be the only path left to her."

The old woman's eye twinkled, and for a moment Lynessa was staring out from within the wizened face, her avarice sharp and primed. The look vanished as quickly as it had come. Once again it was simply an elderly crone, worn down by life, offering to do what she could for a fellow human being.

Lynessa stared calmly at Tina for a long moment, considering, then turned her full attention on Mary.

Lynessa's voice came as the creak of a wagon wheel long in need of a good oiling. "Now, then, dearie, let's see just what state you are in." She leant forward, drawing back the curtain. "My name is Gemma, and I am here to help you. You just leave everything to Gemma."

Mary had done her best to mimic the symptoms that Lady Cartwright had presented. She had spent the time since Erik left wrapped in cool, wet cloths, and only removed them a short while ago. Her skin was clammy. She gave low moans as Lynessa turned her head to and fro, lifted her left arm, and gently pressed in at her lower abdomen. Lynessa gave clucks of disappointment at each stage. Finally she turned to Mary.

"She is near the end, quite near. It is sheer luck that I made it here before she passed altogether."

Tina's face fell, and her eyes welled with tears. "Is there no hope then?"

Mary held back a smile. She would have to give the woman ample praise later on for such a fine performance.

Lynessa began to shake her head, then paused as if considering. "Well, now, I'd heard … but one never knows …" Her look brightened. "Yes, I think it's worth a try. Do you have any sage in the pantry?"

Tina perked up. "Absolutely we do," she agreed, nodding her head. "Shall I bring you some?"

Lynessa tapped her finger on her chin. "Yes, a handful of sage and a small bowl of charcoal. Make sure you steep the charcoal in the bowl with hot water for five minutes before bringing it up. That will help to activate it."

Tina leapt to her feet, nodding. "Five minutes. I promise, it will be done exactly as you have asked."

She gave one last long look to Mary, then she turned and moved through the door, closing it softly behind her.

Mary took in a long, steadying breath. She could not give away, in the slightest manner, her true state of health. Lynessa had to believe she was completely incapable of speech or controlled movement for this to work.

Lynessa waited a long moment, watching the door, and then her face split into a contented smile. She stood, stretching, her hunch easing as she did so. She moved to stand at the door and pressed her ear against it. Then she slipped off her cloak and gave it a kick with her heel to ensure it lay firmly along the base.

A thin tremor of nervousness ran through Mary. Could the others hear what she said now? She dismissed the worry. Lynessa would have her say, and then she would leave. As soon as Lynessa opened that door to depart, the men would take Lynessa into custody.

It would all be over.

Lynessa returned to sit by the bed, grabbing onto Mary's wrist with strong fingers. "Mary. Mary – are you in there?"

Mary feebly blinked her eyes, slowly turning her head as if trying to focus on the sound. She gave a low moan.

There was a sharp pain at her wrist as Lynessa dragged a thumbnail along her delicate flesh.

Mary's moan was sharper now and no longer feigned.

Lynessa's eyes brightened with delight. "There you are. Come up out of those fogs, if only for a moment. I have something to tell you."

Mary allowed her eyes to draw into focus - to settle onto the hard marbles in Lynessa's face.

Lynessa's mouth was curved into a satisfied smile. "It is me, Lynessa," she announced in triumph. "For ten long years, Lady Cartwright has set you after me, training you to foil my plans. But you failed, Mary. You and your vaulted Lady have both failed. First I killed the Lady, right in her own hall. She died without ever being able to set eyes on her beloved son again. And now you will die in the same bed, after having given him back the keep I wanted him to have."

She gave Mary's wrist a sharp twist, and Mary shuddered in pain. Lynessa leant forward. "So everything has worked out perfectly for me, just as I knew it would. The meddlesome Lady is dead. You lived just long enough to turn everything over to Erik, and now he will be right back in my clutches again, with no protection at all." She gave a short bark. "You even arranged to remove Caradoc and his crew from the picture, so I no longer have to share any of my plunder with him. The entire keep and all it entails is completely my own. I could not have planned for a more perfect ending if I had tried."

She glanced at the curtained window. "Did you know that fool Caradoc tried to cut me out of my share, years ago? When he realized my mother and I were angling to have me marry Erik, he immediately started in on Avoca. Almost had her too, from what I saw." Her mouth twisted into a grin. "Until I let the Lady know what Avoca was up to, of course. That was back when the Lady trusted me. I might have exaggerated some of the details, but you know how high strung the Lady was. She would have laid into Avoca even without my prodding."

Mary's blood ran cold, but she focused on her breath. *In, out.* Soon the vixen would be in custody and this all would be behind them.

Lynessa gave her a patronizing pat on the cheek. "Ah, my dear girl, you don't know how satisfying this is. I'm still not quite sure how you escaped my little trap at your village."

Mary's body chilled into shimmering ice. It took her a moment before the words coalesced into meaning.

Lynessa's eyes sparkled with amusement. "It seemed that every time Erik returned from overseeing one of those village dances that he could not say enough about a rural girl with ebony hair who played the tambourine and watched over the little ones." She rolled her eyes. "Your compassion, your patience, your caring …"

Mary could barely believe what Lynessa was saying. She had not thought anyone paid attention to her at the dances. She had been shy, so she had always volunteered to take care of the younger children while her mother sang and her father played the bodhran. She had no idea she had been noticed.

Lynessa smoothed back Mary's hair. "I knew in another year or two you would cross into womanhood, and that Erik might seek to draw you out of your shyness. His attachment to me, for all my mother and I had done to nurse it along, could easily dissipate once he spent more time with you." The corners of her mouth turned up. "And so I went to Caradoc and hatched a little plan."

It was all Mary could do to hold still. She had to force her breathing into an even pattern; to let the woman speak unimpeded.

Lynessa leant forward to put her mouth by Mary's ear. "I was perfectly safe, of course, that long, dark night. I was with a priest friend, eating minced lamb with fresh mint. We toasted with the finest cyser. But for your friends …"

Her eyes sparkled with pleasure. "I made sure Caradoc knew to grab your father and mother first, but not to kill them. Your parents were to be tied to that ancient oak by the church. And then you were to be dragged before him."

Her lips were brushing against Mary's ear now. "Caradoc was to strip you naked. And then he would use you, and his lieutenant would use you, and so on, until every man in his entire bandit clan had experienced the taste of your flesh."

Lynessa shook her head in mock sorrow. "They searched high and low for you, but you could not be found. So Caradoc simply decided that your mother –"

Mary rolled up off the bed, leading with her left fist, and landed a hard blow on Lynessa's temple. The woman let out a hoarse yell of surprise, which morphed into a howl of fury as awareness lit her face. Then she sprang at Mary, her clawed hands aiming for Mary's throat.

Mary drove her hands up from her center, flinging them outward, breaking Lynessa's hold on her. Lynessa's hand darted to her hip, then she swiped out, and Mary felt a stinging pain follow the movement, searing across her chest. A line of red darkened her chemise.

There was a heavy thunk at the door, but to her surprise it stayed steadily shut. The bolt's channel was clear – Lynessa had not touched that in any way. Only her cloak lay at the base. Mary backed up into the center of the room, putting it out of her mind. If Lynessa had kicked a wedge or other device into the door, Mary would be hard pressed to figure it out while Lynessa was trying to take her life. She had to take care of the threat first.

The door shuddered again, and hoarse cries sounded from behind it. Mary's focus remained on the woman before her - the eyes of Lynessa in the weathered face of a crone. The steady knife hand poking out from a tattered tunic.

Lynessa's voice was a deep growl. "So you thought you'd draw me in, eh? A lamb to the slaughter? We'll see just who gets sent to their final repose tonight."

Mary inched cautiously back toward Tina's mending pile. The woman had a pair of bronze spring scissors in with the cloth, and the double blades would be exactly what Mary needed right now.

The door gave a resounding echo, Lynessa half-turned, and Mary lunged for the pile of fabric. She tossed aside the tunic and wrapped her hand around the base of the scissors. Lynessa screamed with fury and slashed high with her knife, the blade making a glittering arc toward Mary's shoulder. Mary dodged back, dove in, and impaled Lynessa in the left arm.

Lynessa cried out in pain, barreling full force into Mary, driving her hard into the curtained window.

The world flickered in slow motion. There was the delicate, almost beautiful music of the window shattering into a thousand little crystals. Mary could imagine each one spinning and floating into the evening air, the tinkling of a brook over a gentle waterfall. The dense curtains billowed out next, the wings of a large, forest-green butterfly stretching high over the mossy ground.

And then she and Lynessa were sailing in the air, turning beneath a cloudless sky. Lynessa's face gleamed bright with fully realized satisfaction. Her voice carried high into the firmament.

"He'll never be yours!"

Mary flung out her arms, her entire being focused on her desperate will to live.

A strong, steady grasp clamped down on her right wrist, held her, and as all her weight slammed down against the outside of the keep's walls, the grip did not let go.

Beneath her, there was a wail, a heavy thud, and then silence.

Mary's heart threatened to beat clear out of her chest, and it was a moment before she could turn her head to gaze up the length of her arm and into Erik's eyes. His face was a melding of relief, pride, and love.

He lifted her steadily up into the room. He set her down on her feet and drew her in against his sturdy chest. Mary knew that there were others moving around the room, asking questions, checking on her, but nothing else mattered. Nothing mattered but that Erik was safe, and that she was finally at peace.

Chapter 24

Three years later.

Mary smiled in fond amusement as Cecily toddled after her big brother Ralf, older than her by only a scant five minutes. The girl's long, raven hair swept over his blond locks as she grabbed a hold of his waist and they both tumbled into a giggling pile before the fireplace. Erik swept them both up, one under each arm, grinning at his wife as he brought them over to their chairs at the head table.

A cheer resounded across the hall, and Mary turned to see Ygraine entering, a large tray in her arms holding an elaborately decorated apple tart. The twins stopped squirming in their father's arms, their eyes round at the massive pastry. Their usual mischievous energy was temporarily reined in by their fascination.

Erik shook his head as he settled the twins into their places. Tina and Zelda took up stations by the pair to ensure they, for the moment, remained safely in their chairs.

Erik tucked Cecily's locks back from her face, then turned to look at Lord Paul. "You'll have your hands full as their godfather," he warned the older man. "They already get into more mischief than I can possibly imagine. In a few years …" He sighed at the thought. "We'll be lucky to keep them from breaking all their limbs. Twice."

Lord Paul reached over to give a fond tweak to Ralf's cheek. "Ah, but where Cecily dashes head-strong into danger, Ralf is always there to see her through to the other side," he pointed out. "They adore each other. As long as they are together, they will be fine."

Michael nodded in agreement. "The lad has quick reflexes," he praised. "He will make a fine swordsman." At Mary's amused look he quickly added, "And Cecily too, of course."

Mary gave a proud pat to her daughter's head, causing the lass to squirm. The girl's eyes were fixed determinedly on the tart that lay before them on the table.

Ygraine finished cutting the first square of tart, and, before Mary could take the plate, the cook had placed it proudly in front of Ralf.

Mary could have predicted what would happen next with her eyes closed.

Cecily, outraged that Ralf had something she did not, lunged a pudgy fist toward the fragrant dessert. Ralf, quick as an owl pouncing on prey, had her wrist pinioned to the table, keeping his treasure for himself. The two pulled and grunted, each determined not to give one inch.

Erik moved to stand behind Mary, fondly running a hand along her neck. "They are a treasure," he murmured.

Mary chuckled. "And feisty, too."

Erik lowered his head to tenderly kiss her cheek. "I always did value a bit of feistiness," he teased.

Cecily had managed to move her hand forward and cradle half of the tart, but Ralf's determined grasp meant she could not move any further. Then the lad's eyes lit up. With his free hand, he cupped the other half of the apple dessert. Carefully, attentively, both twins lifted the tart up off the table, and brought their heads in. Their noses touched as they nibbled at the sides of their birthday treat, contented sighs emerging from the depths of their small bodies.

Erik ran a hand fondly through Mary's hair, drawing her against him. "I pity the man or woman who tries to come between those two," he murmured. "I see a lifetime of adventures in their future."

Lord Paul stood and moved over to the fireplace. A large sheet of fabric hung above the mantle, with a long, green ribbon attached to it. "Are we ready?"

Mary looked up at Erik with curiosity. He had taken full control of the painting project, and she promised not to look until he was done with it. She was eager to see the results. Would it just be his first born son featured in the image? Or would he have included the younger sister as well?

Erik wrapped his arm tighter around her waist, and then gave a nod to Lord Paul.

The ribbon was freed, the fabric fluttered to the ground, and Mary stared at the image in open-mouthed surprise.

All four of them stood represented in the painting, standing on the front steps of the keep. Erik's blond hair shone in the sun, the leather of his tunic fitting him like a second skin. In his arms he cradled Cecily. Her small hand was wrapped around his wrist, and she looked up at her father in absolute adoration. Her other hand held a small tambourine.

At Erik's side stood Mary, her embroidered green dress elegant in the morning light. She held Ralf in her arms. Ralf was looking across at his sister, gazing at her with protective attention. A small wooden sword hung at his hip.

A forest-green banner fluttered from the keep above them, bearing the house standard. But, as Mary looked more closely, she realized it was not the standard she had known for over ten years. There were the crossed swords, yes, but integrated with them was a shimmering tambourine bearing a celtic knotwork design. The effect was stunning.

Her eyes misted with tears, and she leant against Erik. Her throat closed up with emotion.

His voice whispered low in her ear. "So, do you like it?"

Mary could barely get the words out. "*Like* it?"

She slid an arm around his waist, looking up, and their gaze caught for a long, time-suspending moment. Mary felt his love to her very core, and there was nothing else she could possibly want out of life.

Her voice was a mere whisper. "Thank you. Thank you for saving me."

His voice was hoarse. "We have saved each other."

He leant down, his lips pressed to hers, and the world became brilliant with infinite possibilities.

There was a sound from the doors, and they looked up.

A guard was standing there with a slim young woman, about Mary's age, dust-covered from long travel. Her long, ebony hair was braided down her back and her eyes shone in determination.

The guard's face was creased with concern. "My Lord, I wouldn't have interrupted you, but this woman has traveled all the way from Somerset. She's seeking out …" His voice faded low. "She's looking for Gemma."

Erik stepped protectively nearer his two young children. His voice had a rough edge to it. "What do you want with Gemma?"

The woman gaze was set. "I've spent everything I have on this trip. Please, you must let me see Gemma. She's my father's last hope. She's the only one who can cure him."

Mary's heart went out to the woman. "Please, come sit with us. You must have been on the road a long time. I am Mary, and this is Erik. What is your name?"

"I am Jessame," the woman said. She took a few steps forward, clearly exhausted, but then she pulled herself to a halt. "Please, is Gemma here? If I could see her, and get some of her medicine, then maybe my father could finally be cured –"

She broke off, tears coming to her eyes.

Mary looked to Erik with sadness in her gaze. It would break her heart to tell the poor woman the truth. She asked, "Do you know what the cure was supposed to be?"

"Something about white lilies naturally growing from anthills. They can't be artificially planted them. It must be spontaneous." Her eyes shadowed. "Please, it is my only hope left. I heard that Gemma knew of some …"

Mary's brow creased. She guessed that it was let another ruse Lynessa had devised, but she didn't want to let the poor woman down. "We do have white lilies growing in our cemetery, and they do sprout from anthills. If you think they might help –"

Jessame's face shone in relief. "I knew it! I knew in my heart that I had to come here! Something has called in me for months.

That I absolutely had to come up here. That I would find the solution which would make everything all right."

Her throat tightened. "Whatever you want, I'll give it to you. I'll do free labor. I'll give you everything I still own." She looked down, her face wrenching. "I even had to sell my sword. My father had given that to me ..."

Mary's hip buzzed.

She looked down to the sword there. To the sword which she had been given six long years ago, at the funeral of Lady Cartwright, by the newly wed Storm and her husband, Falcon.

What had Storm said to her?

Do not become too fond of Andetnes. When you have at last found contentment, there will be another whose fate balances on the point of a pin. You will know when it is right. And the sword will have a new mistress.

Mary had not believed it at the time – that there was any hope for contentment. She thought the most she could possibly find was the knowledge that she had done her best to fulfill her vow.

And now, looking across her beloved family, she knew.

She brought her eyes to Jessame, her gaze shimmering with joy.

"Come, Jessame. Come sit with us and tell us everything. I am sure we will be able to help you find what you seek."

* * *

The Sword of Glastonbury series continues with Book 7, *Lady in Red*–

If you enjoyed *Sworn Loyalty*, please leave feedback on Amazon, Goodreads, and any other systems you use. Together we can help make a difference!

https://www.amazon.com/review/create-review?ie=UTF8&asin=B00FBE82O6#

Be sure to sign up for my free newsletter! You'll get alerts of free books, discounts, and new releases. I run my own newsletter server – nobody else will ever see your email address. I promise!

http://www.lisashea.com/lisabase/subscribe.html

Join my online groups to get news of free giveaways, upcoming stories, and fascinating trivia!

Facebook
https://www.facebook.com/LisaSheaAuthor

Twitter
https://twitter.com/LisaSheaAuthor

Google+
https://plus.google.com/+LisaSheaAuthor/posts

GoodReads
https://www.goodreads.com/lisashea/

Blog
http://www.lisashea.com/lisabase/blog/

Free Ebooks

Be sure to download all of my FREE books! Each of these is completely free and available on Kindle.

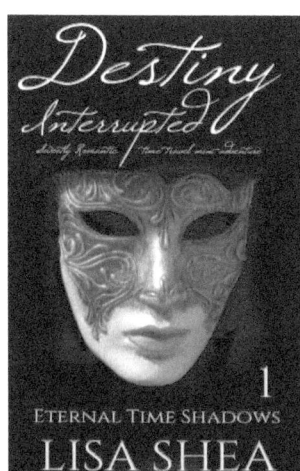

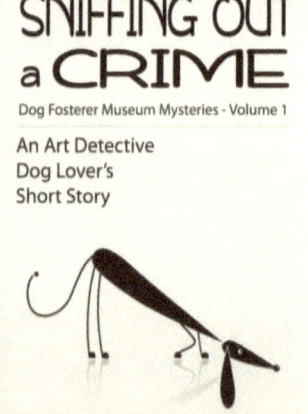

About the Songs

Medieval life was rich in songs and stories. Most people could not read or write, so the way they preserved tales was to put them to music. People did not have television or radio. To entertain themselves, they would sing and play songs together.

The first song Mary sings, about the cherry with no stone, comes from "Songs and Carols: Printed from a Manuscript in the Sloane Collection in the British Museum" edited by Thomas Wright. The book was published in 1836 and is now out of copyright so you can find it for free on the web. This song is song number eight (viii). The Sloane manuscript itself is thought to be from the mid-1400s, but the songs undoubtedly had been sung for centuries before finally being written down.

The second song, about a love being far away, is based on the song "My Lief is Faren in Londe" – i.e. my love has gone away to the country. This song is mentioned in The Nun's Priest's Tale in the Canterbury Tales, written by Chaucer at the end of the 1300s. The song was already well known by then. A documented source for the full song is Secular Lyrics of the Fourteenth and Fifteenth Centuries by Rossell H. Robbins.

The third song is part of the famous Corpus Christi Carol, first written down (as far as we know, of course) in 1504. It is thought by many to represent the suffering of Christ. The woman by his side is supposed to represent Mary. For example, the word "pall" in the song refers to a funeral cloth.

Medieval Dialogue

I've been fascinated by medieval languages since I was quite young. I grew up studying Spanish, English, and Latin, and loved the sound of reading Beowulf and the Canterbury Tales in their original languages. I adore the richness of medieval languages. How did medieval English people speak?

There are three aspects to this. The first is the difference between written records and spoken language. The second is the rich, multi-cultural aspect of medieval life. And the third is how to convey this to a modern-language audience.

Let's take the first. Sometimes modern people equate the way medieval folk would talk, hanging around a rustic tavern, with the way Chaucer wrote his famous *Canterbury Tales*. Something along the lines of this (note this is a modern translation, not the original Middle English version):

> *"Of weeping and wailing, care and other sorrow*
> *I know enough, at eventide and morrow,"*
> *The merchant said, "and so do many more*
> *Of married folk, I think, who this deplore,*
> *For well I know that it is so with me.*
> *I have a wife, the worst one that can be;*
> *For though the foul Fiend to her wedded were,*
> *She'd overmatch him, this I dare to swear."*

Sure, it seems elegant and rich. But did worn-down farmers sitting around a fireplace with mugs of ale really talk like this?

Do we think the London street-dwellers in the 1600s skulked down the dark alleys emoting like Shakespeare –

Two households, both alike in dignity
In fair Verona, where we lay our scene
From ancient grudge break to new mutiny
Where civil blood makes civil hands unclean.

And, in the 1920s in Vermont, did farmers really wander down their snowy lanes murmuring to their farming friends, a la Robert Frost:

Whose woods these are I think I know.
His house is in the village though;
He will not see me stopping here
To watch his woods fill up with snow.

As someone who lives in New England, I can pretty resolutely say "no" to that last one. And, given my research, I'm equally content saying "no" to the previous two. There is a big difference between poetry written with deliberate effort and the way "normal people" talked, flirted, cajoled, and laughed day in and day out. People simply did not talk in iambic pentameter. I'm a poet and even I don't talk in iambic pentameter :).

Modern people sometimes think of the medieval period in terms of the plays we see. We imagine actors on a stage, speaking in formal, stilted language, carefully moving from scene to scene. But medieval life wasn't like that. It was a rich cacophony of people struggling hard to survive amongst plagues and crusades, with strong pagan influences and the church trying to instill order. People fought off robbers and drove away wolves. They laughed and loved in multi-generational homes. It was a time of great flux.

England - A Melting Pot
England wasn't an isolated, walled-off island. It was continually experiencing influxes of new words and sounds. The Romans came and went. The Vikings came and went. The French invaded. Nearly all of the English men headed off to the Crusades, leaving behind women to gain strength and position.

The men returned with even more languages. Pilgrims went to Jerusalem. Merchants arrived from all over. This was a true melting pot.

So, in part because of this, Middle English was a rich, fascinating language. People in this time period had a wealth of contractions, nicknames, abbreviations, and combinations of words they used. Often people could speak multiple languages - their old English, the incoming Norman language, Latin from church, and random other words from tinkers, merchants, and pilgrims they encountered. Medieval people had all sorts of words for drinking, for fighting, for prostitutes, you name it. They had slang and shortcuts just like any other language does. After all, these are the people who turned "forecastle" (on a ship) to "foc's'le" and who pronounce the word "Worcester" as "Woostah."

But, here's the trick. With the medieval language being so rich, varied, intricate, and full of fascinating words, how can we bring that to life for a modern audience?

Centuries of Change

Let's start with a basic issue - most modern readers simply cannot understand authentic medieval dialogue. They don't have the grounding in Middle English, French, and Latin that would be required. Even the fairly straightforward, basic Chaucer works look like this:

And Saluces this noble contree highte.

Modern readers generally wouldn't know that "highte" meant "was called" as in "And Saluces this noble country was called."

This happens over and over again. Words change meaning. In the Middle Ages, if you *abandoned* your wife it means you subjugated her. You got her under your thumb. It didn't mean you left her - quite the opposite. Awful meant *awe-ful* - as in stunning and wonderful. It had a positive connotation. Fantastic wasn't great - it was a fantasy; something that didn't exist.

Nervous didn't mean worried or agitated - it meant strong and full of energy. Nice meant silly, and so on.

If a book was written with proper medieval words and meanings, first, even if the words are reasonably close to what we use now, modern readers would have to struggle with the spelling -

By that the Maunciple hadde his tale al ended,
The sonne fro the south lyne was descended
So lowe, that he nas nat to my sighte
Degrees nyne and twenty as in highte.

But, again, that is just the tip of the issue with medieval language. The word "bracelet" didn't exist until the 1400s. Necklace wasn't a word until 1590. The word "hug" wasn't around until the mid-1500s. We also didn't have the words tragedy, crisis, area, explain, fact, illicit, rogue, or even disagree! Shakespeare invented the words "baseless" and "dwindle" in the 1600s. Staircase is from 1620. A story written solely with words that existed in the year 1200 - and that still retain their modern meaning so modern readers could understand them - would be fairly basic.

(Speaking of which, the word "basic" didn't exist until the mid 1800s.)

Conversely, some words we might think of as thoroughly modern, like "puke", were also used in Shakespeare's time. "Booze" traces back to the 1500s. And these are just the proofs we have. While "shiner" for a black eye can be traced definitively to the 1700s, it could easily have been used for centuries before then and we just don't happen to have a letter or newspaper article which mentions it.

It's fair to say that people in medieval days did get black eyes and had a wealth of interesting terms for that situation. After all, it could be a rough life back then. Was one of the terms used "shiner"? Maybe, maybe not. Out of the ten fun phrases they used, probably nine of them would make zero sense to a modern reading audience. So authors strive to find phrases that provide meaning to a modern audience without being too *l33t* and techno-speak. It doesn't make sense to completely avoid the word "bracelet" simply because it technically didn't exist in the 1200s. Surely people in the 1200s had several words for "bracelet" and we are simply using the word modern readers understand. Similarly, people in medieval times hugged! They just called that action something else.

Medieval people loved playing with words. They called their kids "dillydowns" and "mitings" (little mites). They called sweethearts "my sweeting" and "my honey. They loved snapping out insults, from "dunce" to "idiot" to "pig filth" and "maggot pie." And, again, these are just the ones that happened to get recorded.

Medieval people loved contractions. There's a phrase "ne woot," meaning *knows not*. They'd simply say "noot". They did this with all sorts of words.

So writing in modern English should have this same sort of loose, fun sense to the writing. It's important to remember that even the kings, in this era, were rough fighters. They were out with soldiers, crossing multiple countries, and experiencing a range of languages. They weren't necessarily concerned about speaking in iambic pentameter. They were more concerned about breaking down their enemy's walls to plunder what lay within and then drinking themselves under the table to celebrate.

So, certainly, treasure the poetry and prose of the time. As a poet, I appreciate that immensely. But also keep in mind that people did not talk in poetry. They did not speak in fantasy-speak of *Lord of the Rings* or *Game of Thrones*. They talked and laughed, flirted and cursed, gossiped and cajoled in a rich, multi-lingual, contraction-filled, sobriquet-laden dialogue which mirrors how we talk in modern times.

About Medieval Life

When many of us think of medieval times, we bring to mind a drab reality-documentary image. We imagine people scrounging around in the mud, eating dirt. The people were under five feet tall and barely survived to age thirty. These poor, unfortunate souls had rotted teeth and never bathed.

Then you have the opposite, Hollywood Technicolor extreme. In the romantic version of medieval times, men were always strong and chivalrous. Women were dainty and sat around staring out the window all day, waiting for their knight to come riding in. Everybody wore purple robes or green tights.

The truth, of course, lies somewhere in the middle.

Living in Medieval Times

The years in the early medieval ages held a warm, pleasant climate. Crops grew exceedingly well, and there was plenty of food. As a result, their average height was on par with modern times. It's amazing how much nutrition influences our health!

The abundance of food also had an effect on the longevity of people. Chaucer (born 1340) lived to be 60. Petrarch (born 1304) died a day shy of 70. Eleanor of Aquitaine (born 1122) was 82 when she died. People could and did lead long lives. The average age of someone who survived childhood was 65.

What about their living conditions? The Romans adored baths and set up many in Britain. When they left, the natives could not keep them going, and it is true they then bathed less. However, by the Middle Ages, with the crusades and interaction with the Muslims, there was a renewed interest both in hygiene and medicine. Returning soldiers and those who took pilgrimages brought back with them an interest in regular bathing and cleanliness. This spread across the culture.

While people during other periods of English history ate poorly, often due to war conditions or climatic changes, the middle ages were a time of relative bounty. Villagers would grow fresh fruit and vegetables behind their homes, and had an array of herbs for seasoning. The local baker would bake bread for the village - most homes did not hold an oven, only an open fire. Villagers had easy access to fish, chicken, geese, and eggs. Pork was enjoyed at special meals like Easter.

Upper classes of course had a much wider range of foods - all game animals (rabbits, deer, and so on) belonged to them. The wealthy ate peacocks, veal, lamb, and even bear. Meals for all classes could be flavorful and well enjoyed.

Medieval Relationships

Some movies present a skewed version of life in the Middle Ages. They make it seem that women were meek, mild, and obediently did whatever their father or husband commanded.

This was *far* from the truth!

Medieval times were times of immense change. Men were off at the Crusades, leaving the women to run things. Christianity was trying to get a foothold, but many areas of Britain were still primarily pagan, with all the Goddess worship and female empowerment which had been tradition for centuries. The vast majority of brewers were female. Most innkeepers were female. Women's knowledge about herbs, health, and food was respected. Healthy women were treasured as the key to a child-rich partnership.

Medieval life was heavily focused on fertility. Farm animals had to be fertile in order to create meat to feed the family. Women had to be fertile to create helpers for the farm and household. Celebration after celebration in medieval times focused on fertility. These people weren't shy about the topic. They watched their horses, cows, and dogs continually engage in these activities. Their festivals focused on the topic with bawdy delight. Their songs lusted about it.

The church tried, again and again, to squelch this behavior so that all aspects of relationships could be regulated by the church. However, half of all medieval couples were together outside of a church marriage and, for those sanctified by the church, a large proportion were "sealing the deal" for a couple already pregnant.

This was the way the medieval people looked at it: they needed to know their partner could create children. This was a key consideration for a relationship.

The Medieval period was far from an era of Victorian prudity. Quite the opposite. People of this era celebrated fertility, felt it was wholly natural, and even felt it was unhealthy for a man or woman to go for too long without sex. The celibacy would block critical flows of the body.

It was considered natural that a male noble might take on mistresses and that unmarried couples might seek out partners. It was the same as someone needing food if they were hungry. It was a bodily function which had to be tended to for the health of the person.

So where does marriage fit in with this mindset?

Medieval Marriage

In medieval times, marriage was primarily about inheritance. It was almost separate from sexuality. Sexuality was an important part of bodily health, like eating well and getting enough exercise. Marriage, on the other hand, was about ensuring one's lands and chattel were cared for from generation to generation. Sex, within a marriage, was focused on creating family-line children to then tend to that wealth.

For this reason, wealthy families would put immense energy into arranging optimal marriages for their children. This was about the transfer of land far more than a love match. Parents wanted to ensure their land went to a family worthy of ownership - one with the resources to defend it from attack. It was not only their own family members they were concerned with. Each block of land had on it both free men and serfs. These people all depended on the nobles – with their skill, connections, and soldiers – to keep them safe from bandits and harm.

That being said, both the woman and man would be consulted about the match. Their input was a critical aspect of the decision. Choices were often made with intricate selection processes. Keep in mind that the woman and her suitors would have been raised from birth to think of this process as natural. They would participate in that choice-making with an eye as to how it would secure the stability of their future family.

Yes, villagers sometimes married for love. Even a few nobles would run off and follow their hearts. Even so, they would have first seriously considered the potentially catastrophic risks which could result from their actions.

Here is a modern example. Imagine you took over the family business which employed a hundred loyal workers. Those workers depend on your careful guidance of the company to ensure the income for their families. You might dream about running off to Bermuda and drinking martinis. But would you just sell your company to any random investor who came along? Would you risk all of those peoples' lives, people who had served you loyally for decades, to satisfy a whim of pleasure? It is more likely that you would research your options, map out a plan, and made a choice with suited both you and your responsibilities.

Medieval Women

In pagan days women held many rights and responsibilities. During the crusades, especially, with many men off at war, women ran the taverns, made the ale, and ran the government. In later years, as men returned home and Christianity rose in power, women were relegated to a more subservient role.

Still, women in medieval times were not meek and mild. That stereotype came in with the Victorian era, many centuries later. Back in medieval days, women had to be hearty and hard working. There were fields to tend, homes to maintain, and children to raise!

Women strove to be as healthy as they could because they faced a serious threat - a fifth of all women died during or just after childbirth. The church said that childbirth was the "pain of Eve" and instructed women to bear it without medicine or follow-up care. Of course, midwives did their best to skirt these rules, but childbirth still took an immense toll.

Childhood was rough in the Middle Ages – only forty percent of children survived the gauntlet of illnesses to adulthood. A woman who reached her marriageable years was a sturdy woman indeed.

You can see why fertility was so important to medieval people!

To summarize, in medieval days a woman could live a long, happy life, even into her eighties – as long as she was of the sturdy stock that made it through the challenges of childhood. She would be expected to be fertile and to have multiple children, which again weeded out the weaker ones. This was very much a time of 'survival of the fittest.' Medieval life quickly separated out the weak and frail. Those women who ran that gauntlet and survived were respected for that strength and for their wisdom in many areas of life.

So medieval women were strong - very strong. They had to be. They were respected. Still, would they fight?

Women and Weapons

Queen Boudicia, from Norwalk, was born around AD60. She personally – and successfully - led her troops against the Roman Empire. She had been flogged - and her daughters raped - spurring her to revenge. She was extremely intelligent and quite strategic. Her daughters rode in her chariot at her side.

Eleanor of Aquitaine, born in 1122, was brilliant and married first to a King of France and then to a King of England. She went on the Second Crusades as the leader of her troops - reportedly riding bare-breasted as an Amazon. At times she marched with her troops far ahead of her husband. When she divorced the King of France, she immediately married Henry II, who she passionately adored. He was eleven years her junior. When things went sour, Eleanor separated from him and actively led revolts against him.

Many historical accounts talk of women taking up arms to defend their villages and towns. Women would not passively let their children be slain or their homes burned. They were able and strong bodied from their daily work. They were well skilled with farm implements and knives, and used them with great talent against invaders.

Many of these defenses were successful, and the victories were celebrated as brave and proper, rather than dismissed as an unusual act for a woman. A mother was expected to defend her brood and to keep her home safe, just as a wolf mother protects her cubs.

Numerous women took their martial skills to a higher level. In 1301 a group of Italian women joined up to fight the crusade against the Turks. In 1348 at a tournament there were at least thirty women who participated, dressed as men.

This is not as unusual as you might think. In medieval times, all adults carried a knife at their belt for daily use in eating, chores, and defense. All knew how to use it. Being strong and safe was a necessary part of daily life.

Here is an interesting comparison. In modern times most women know how to drive, but few choose to invest themselves in the time and training to become race car drivers. In medieval times, most women knew how to defend themselves with a weapon. They had to. Few, though, actively sought the training to be swordswomen. Still, these women did exist, and did thrive as valued members of their communities.

So women in medieval times were far from shrinking violets. They were not mud-encrusted wretches huddling in straw huts. They were not pale damsels locked away in towers. They were strong, sturdy, and well versed in the use of knives. Many ran taverns, and most handled the brewing of ale. Those who made it through childhood and childbirth could expect to enjoy long, rich lives.

I hope you enjoy my tales of authentic, inspiring heroines!

Glossary

Ale - A style of beer which is made from barley and does not use hops. Ale was the common drink in medieval days. In the 1300s, 92% of brewers were female, and the women were known as "alewives". It was common for a tavern to be run by a widow and her children.

Blade - The metal slicing part of the sword.

Chemise - In medieval days, most people had only a few outfits. They would not want to wash their heavy main dress every time they wore it, just as in modern times we don't wash our jackets after each wearing. In order to keep the sweaty skin away from the dress, women wore a light, white under-dress which could then be washed more regularly. This was often slept in as well.

Drinking - In general, medieval sanitation was not great. People who drank milk had to drink it "raw" - pasteurization was not well known before the 1700s. Water was often unsafe to drink. For these reasons, all ages of medieval folk drank liquid with alcohol in it. The alcohol served as a natural sanitizer. This was even true as recently as colonial American times.

God's Teeth / God's Blood – Common oaths in the middle ages.

Grip - The part of the sword one holds, usually wrapped in leather or another substance to keep it firmly in the wielder's hand.

Guard - The crossed top of the sword's hilt which keeps the enemy's sword from sliding down and chopping off the wielder's fingers.

Hilt - The entire handle part of the sword; everything that is not blade.

Mead - A fermented beverage made from honey. Mead has been enjoyed for thousands of years and is mentioned in Beowulf.

Pommel - The bottom end of the sword, where the hilt ends.

Tip - The very end of the sword

Wolf's Head – a term for a bandit. The Latin legal term *caput gerat lupinum* meant they could be hunted and killed as legally as any dangerous wolf or wild animal that threatened the area.

Parts of a Sword

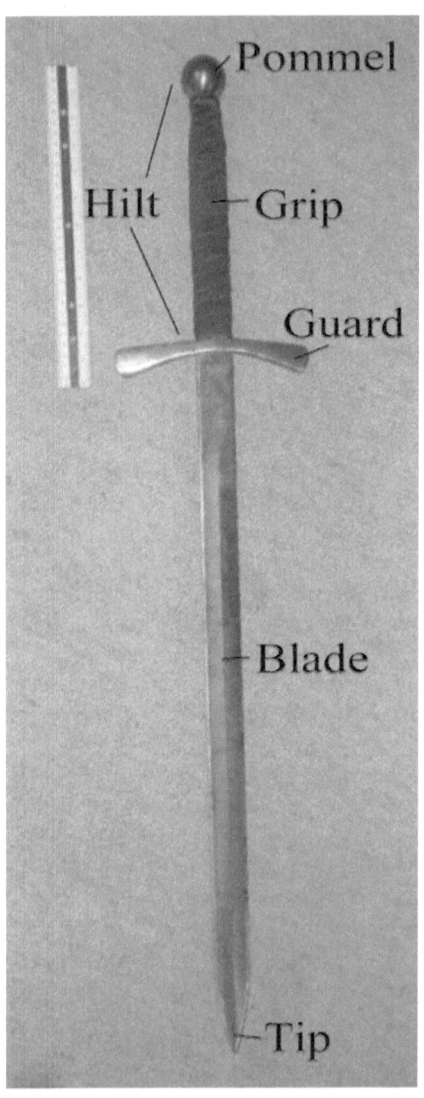

Medieval Clothing

Medieval people - despite modern stereotypes - did have noses and did like to stay clean. Public baths were popular, and people liked to swim as well. However, they did not have the luxury of bathing daily. Also, in medieval times people were often cold. Castles were damp and drafty. Fireplaces were not kept blazingly hot all night long. There is a reason that people wore many heavy layers including cloaks. That way they could add or remove layers as necessary to keep warm.

The basic under-layer was a chemise. This thin nightgown would be worn at night as well as during the day. Because it was against the body it kept the actual clothes clean from sweat. That way you could wash the chemise regularly and not have to wash your actual dress every day. Think of it like when you wear a turtleneck and a wool sweater. At the end of the day you would wash the turtleneck, but you would not wash the wool sweater after every wearing. If you wear a t-shirt under a jacket, you would toss the t-shirt into the washing machine but just hang the jacket on a hook again. The same is true for medieval outfits. The inner layer would be washed, while the other layer would be reused multiple days before it had to be washed.

The chemise was generally not meant to be seen, especially in colder months. It was underwear. There would always be an over-dress with a floor-length hem on top of that. Perhaps a glimpse of the chemise would show at the neckline or at the end-of-sleeve area. In hotter months the chemise might be more visible as the outer dress had short sleeves or no sleeves.

Men would typically wear a tunic over leggings. Men working in summer heat would sometimes wear simple linen "shorts" without anything else. Their chest and lower legs would be bare. This is a stark difference from how covered up women would be.

Both sexes would wear boots or shoes. There was no "left" or "right" - both halves would be made in the same oval shape.

Cloaks would be worn when going out into poor weather, to help keep you warm. These cloaks could be quite heavy if they were full circle cloaks, and incredibly warm.

Monks would wear similar clothing to non-religious men, but the monk's hair would be cut short and have a "tonsure" - or bald spot - shaved out of its center. The tonsure was a sign of their humility. This illuminated image is from a 12th century manuscript at the library at Cambridge University.

Women's Clothing

A number of readers had specific questions about women's medieval clothing so I created this page with those specific details. To illustrate it, I have included a drawing done by Andreas Muller, a famous German artist known for his work restoring ancient paintings. This drawing was published back in 1861, so it's now out of copyright. As you might expect the drawing shows German people, not English, but the fashions are from the 1200s and are quite similar in style.

So, the basics. Women wore at least two layers of long dress. The bottom layer, or "chemise," was often plain white but could be fancier with nobles. This was what was against the skin, got sweaty, and would be washed. The chemise was often slept in, again especially if the person was poor.

The outer layer, what we would call the "dress," was the prettier layer. This would have the nicer stitching and designs. It could have embroidery or different fabrics stitched together to create designs. The outer dress could have long sleeves, short sleeves, or no sleeves, depending on how hot the weather was. In general, though, a woman's arms and legs were covered by the inner chemise and perhaps also by the outer dress as well. Women in medieval times did not tend to show skin from those parts of the body.

You might see images on the web with medieval women wearing long "trumpet" sleeves which made housework impractical. These were sometimes worn by French nobles who were showing off that they did not have to do menial labor. They were not a normal fashion in England or most other areas.

By the same token, women who had to work hard would wear shorter dresses - ending above the ankle rather than dragging on the floor. That was so their dresses did not catch or drag while they went about their work. Noblewomen who had a quiet day planned or a formal event would wear longer, floor-dragging dresses. These subtle differences helped to show off their status.

If it got even colder women would wear cloaks. These range from light, like the woman in the middle is wearing here, to heavy and full-circle, which could be amazingly warm. I have one of those.

Here is an illuminated image done between 1285 and 1292 which shows the famous poet Marie de France. Marie primarily wrote between 1160 to 1190 and was well known by nobility in France and England. Again, you can see how her outer long dress goes to the floor and the inner dress is visible at the arms. This copyright-free image comes via the National Library of France.

Women had an immense array of colorful dyes to choose from, some more expensive, some less expensive. So clothing could be quite bright and cheery. Just as in modern times, practicality had an aspect here. If someone was going to work in the pig pen all day long they'd probably wear something brown and old. If they were going to church they'd wear their best outfit they had.

In modern times we can sometimes think of dresses as "fancy" items we wear to "dress up" that are hard to move in. In medieval times, a dress was normal and natural! These were the outfits they wore every single day. Women made their dresses so they could do all their normal activities in them. To them a dress was like our modern t-shirt and sweatpants. So they're no question about "could they do chores in a dress" or "could they ride a horse in a dress." Of course they could - that's what the clothing was made for. Medieval women didn't generally hide out in tower rooms. Noblewomen would do archery and horseback riding for fun. Working women would scythe hay, ride to the market, and do a myriad of other chores in their dresses. It was what one wore. So those outfits absolutely were made to easily let them do those tasks. Dresses were loose to allow all of that. Women didn't ride side-saddle in medieval days - they simply put their legs on either side for stability. And their clothing was made for that. To ride, a woman could either tuck the skirt beneath her, like when one sits on a chair, or let it flow behind her. Either way works!

In terms of underclothes, most medieval women did not wear a bra. Their simple, straight dresses were meant to keep the body hidden rather than emphasized. A large breasted woman might wear a "binder" to keep the breasts from jiggling around while they tried to work. Current thought is that women didn't wear "underwear" (underpants) either. With their long multi-layer dresses it would be a challenge for underwear-wearing women to go to the bathroom. Instead, they would just move to a section of the field, fluff out their dresses, and go. Then they could get back to work. The same in the outhouses.

Even during the time of their periods, many researchers feel that the philosophy of the time was that binding or constricting a woman's flow would damage her fertility. So she simply bled into her underdress and that was washed. This free-flow practice continued long after medieval times. It was mentioned in doctors' journals in the 1800s. Even as recent as the 1900s there were cotton mills in the United States that had straw-strewn floors to absorb female workers' blood, so again this was not a short-term trend. And given that tampons can cause toxic shock syndrome, maybe those medieval women knew what they were doing :).

Let me know if you have any other questions about medieval women's clothing! I have a library of books here to help with research.

Dedication

To my mom, dad, siblings, and family members who encouraged me to indulge myself in medieval fantasies. I spent many long car rides creating epic tales of sword-wielding heroines and the strong men who stood by their sides. Jenn, Uncle Blake, and Dad were awesome proofers.

To Peter and Elizabeth May, who patiently toured me around England, Scotland, and France on three separate occasions. Elizabeth offered valuable tips on creating authentic scenes. Visiting the Berkhamsted motte and bailey was priceless.

To Jody, Leslie, Liz, Sarah, and Jenny, my friends who enjoy my eclectic ways and provide great suggestions. Becky was my first ever web-fan and her enthusiasm kept me going!

To the editors at BellaOnline, who inspire me daily to reach for my dreams and to aim for the stars. Lisa, Cheryll, Jeanne, Lizzie, Moe, Terrie, Ian, and Jilly provided insightful feedback to help my polishing efforts.

To the Massachusetts Mensa Writing Group for their feedback and enthusiastic support. Lynn, Tom, Ruth, Carmen, Al, and Dean all offered detailed, helpful advice!

To the Geek Girls, with their unflagging support for my expanding list of projects and enterprises. Debi's design talents are amazing. I simply adore the covers she created for me.

To the Academy of Knightly Arts for several years of in-depth training and combat experience with medieval swords and knives. I loved sparring with Nikki and Jo-Ann!

To B&R Stables who renewed my love of horseback riding and quiet forest trails.

To my son, James, whose insights into psychology help ground my characters in authentic behavior.

To Bob See, my partner in love for over 19 years and counting. He enthusiastically supports all of my new projects.

About the Author

Lisa Shea is a fervent fan of honor, loyalty, and chivalry. She brings to life worlds where men and women stand shoulder to shoulder, steady in their desire to make the world a better place for all. While her medieval heroines often wield a sword, they equally value the skilled use of their intelligence, wisdom, courage, and compassion.

Lisa has studied the Middle Ages since she was quite young. She has trained in medieval swordfighting for several years. She studied medieval dance and music with the SCA. She has been to England numerous times and loves exploring old castles and churches.

Please visit Lisa at LisaShea.com to learn more about her background and interests. Feedback is always appreciated!

As a special treat, as a warm thank-you for reading this book and supporting the cause of battered women, here's a sneak peek at the first chapter of *Lady in Red*.

Lady in Red - Chapter 1

England, 1198

"Time discovers truth."
-- Seneca, Roman philosopher

Jessame sauntered into the boisterous hubbub of the evening party with a wide smile. Instantly all eyes turned to her, drawing in her riotous, uncovered curls of ebony hair, her shocking exposure of décolletage, the clingingly tight cut of her hellfire-red dress, and the outright indecent exposure of her ankles above the matching red silk slippers. A trio of jack-a-dandy teenage boys nudged one another with open-mouthed delight, a young girl with blonde ringlets had eyes as wide as pound coins, and an elderly woman in widow's garb nearly swooned, supported by a pair of scowling matrons whose eyes shot poniards.

Jessame grinned with delight and curtseyed to the crowd. The night's festivities were beginning exactly as planned.

The noise rose around her as she strolled across the polished plank floor toward the refreshment table. Now the voices held a sharper, hushed tone, and shocked outrage rang from all sides.

She chuckled in satisfaction as she looked down the heavy oak table, perusing her options. A collection of pewter cups to her left were grouped as neatly as schoolchildren on their first day of class. A large wooden bowl held a red wine punch, apple pieces floating merrily on top. Further to the right were a juicy roast duck, a fragrant apple pie, a lush bowl of fresh raspberries, a pungent platter of minced onion, and several other treats.

Her mouth watered. It had been a long while since she had eaten this well. She would make the most of the night's offering, at least for as long as she was allowed to stay.

Her hand was just reaching for an elegant, wide-brimmed cup when a sharp, hissing voice drilled into her ear.

"Are you sure you are in the right place, woman? This party is for *proper* members of our village."

Ah, the welcoming committee had arrived.

Jessame turned with a bright smile on her lips. Standing before her was a woman in her mid-twenties who, she had to admit, was stunningly beautiful. Her honey-gold hair cascaded around her face, and the richly woven fabrics which embraced her curvaceous figure spoke of a life of luxury.

Jessame's eyes danced with delight. "Ah, Lady Cavendish," she purred. "I was not aware this was *your* home."

The woman's alabaster skin pinkened and she drew her lips into a tight line, drawing herself up haughtily. "You well know that it is not," she retorted. "However, I am sure I represent the thoughts of the entire village when I state you are not welcome here."

Jessame's eyes twinkled. "What, only a brief two months since you deigned to descend from London to wed our wealthiest citizen, and already you speak for our community?" Her voice dropped into a murmur of teasing reproach. "And here you call *me* a fast woman."

Lady Cavendish's mouth opened into a round O of shock, but, before she could formulate a response, her eyes shifted to look behind Jessame. Her features froze in place.

A low rumble of a voice came from behind Jessame, calm, pleasant, and openly curious.

"My dear Lady Cavendish, would you please introduce me to my newest guest?"

Every inch of Jessame's skin tingled; time slowed down to the gentle dripping of water from a leaf after a rainstorm. She knew that voice, at least knew the echo of it from its greener days. She and Berenger had played together in the fields of her home, had fished in her trout pond on lazy spring days, and had

stretched side by side on those long summer nights gazing at the
stars and watching for comets. From the moment she could
toddle on two feet she had chased after him, raced with him,
dug for earthworms, twined reeds into chains, and carved
branches into whistles. She could almost feel his eyebrow arch
as he looked her over, wondering at this strange new addition to
his homecoming celebration.

Ten long years. She would have known him in an instant;
known the rich sound of his voice and the steady set of his dark
brown eyes. But it was critical for her task, absolutely core to
what she was doing, that he not recognize her. She hoped that
his decade in the Crusades, amongst Saracen and Italian and
Arabic cultures, had made him long since forget their simple
childhood times together.

To make sure, she would do everything in her power to
make a strong impression on him. She had to convince him that
this wild woman before him was nothing like the sensible girl
he had grown up with.

She turned slowly and gave an elaborate curtsey, head
lowered, making sure his first vision was of the low cut of her
body-hugging crimson dress - of the tousled curls of hair which
had grown far darker since her youth. She kept her eyes lowered
as Lady Cavendish was reluctantly drawn into the role
demanded by custom.

"Yes, certainly Berenger," the blonde stiffly agreed. "This
woman is a relative newcomer to our cozy village; a visitor, you
might almost say. I get the sense she might be moving along
any time now. She is temporarily lodging at the old Sawyer
house down by the stream. Her name is Besame."

Jessame focused on the strongest London gutter accent she
could draw into her mind. She'd picked it up from a traveling
merchant who came through once a season with tin lanterns and
boxes. She barely made any effort for most of the villagers –
there was little need to try to throw them off her true identity.
They rarely gave her a kind word in her Besame role and saw no
further than her bright red clothes and flouncy manner. She had
been isolated from village life for so many years that it never

occurred to them that Besame the prostitute and Jessame of the Dwinnel family might be the same person.

But Berenger ... he was no fool. He could see through people, gaze into their inner soul ...

She shook off the notion. She could not falter now. His return home had been quite unexpected, but she would deal with it as she had dealt with so many other hurdles. She would see her task through.

Resolved, she drew herself up, speaking with a heavy, deep accent. She made sure he was distracted by the dress, the movements, and the voice before he saw her face.

"Ot's fine, just fine, Sir. Oi'm settlin' in good like a pig in fine mud," she resounded heartily, graveling her voice. "Sure's mighty good to meetsya."

She steadied herself, then raised her eyes up to meet his.

Her heart thundered against her chest, and she sucked in a deep breath, willing herself to stay steady.

He was exactly as she remembered him.

The gold flecks in his tawny brown eyes; the right eyebrow nudged up in surprise and curiosity as he took in the woman before him. He was the same. The same full, dark head of hair, falling in waves to his shoulder. The same strong set to his jaw.

And yet he was changed. When he had left that abrupt July morning, he was just turning eighteen. He had been verging on thin, still more boy than man, even to her untutored young eyes. Now he was a week shy of twenty-eight and life had filled him in. His muscles were strong and supple beneath his leather jerkin. He wore a sword at his hip and its well-worn scabbard indicated he was proficient in its use. He smelled not of the fresh fields and clean waters, but a more heady mixture of leather, sweet sweat, and some exotic spice she could not name.

God's teeth, how she had missed him.

His eyes narrowed; she turned quickly to the table, giving herself a moment to recover. On impulse she grabbed a handful of raspberries. She'd regret this in the morning, when the rash spread across her chest and drove her into an itching frenzy. But for now it would serve to drive home the idea that she was not Jessame but an entirely different creature altogether.

She turned back to face him, popping a plump berry into her mouth with a bright smile, then gushing with rumbling pleasure, "God's blood, but your tables are groanin', M'Lord. Margr food. Lots, I mean. Kind o' you to open yours doors to mes." She tossed another raspberry into her mouth, adding, "Mmm, godr!"

The door opened at the far end of the room, and Lady Cavendish had her hand on Berenger's shoulder as quickly as a hawk pounces on a field mouse. "Ah, it is Father Stockman," she advised Berenger with enthusiasm. "We must go and greet him at once." In a moment the two had moved into the general throng and Jessame was left alone.

She let out a long, deep breath.

She had done it.

The worst was over. He had not seen through her disguise, and now he would get more and more used to her in this new persona as the days went on. Hopefully her deception would only have to last a few weeks longer.

She sighed, turning back to the table and ladling out some of the fruited wine into a pewter cup. She drank down the punch in one long draw. She followed it up with another raspberry, giving a wry smile. She did enjoy their flavor, and if she was going to develop a rash anyway, she might as well enjoy herself while she could. Soon she would have to return to her normal life.

Normal life. Despite the dangers of her current position, Jessame was enjoying herself immensely and did not want her masquerade to end too quickly. As much as she loved her father, remaining cooped up in the house with him for these six long years had worn down her soul. She would do anything to have him cured from his illness - to have their routine return to its former, happy times.

She let out a resigned sigh. It was but a dream to think any hope of a remedy still existed. She would have her few weeks of freedom. She would cherish her days of enjoying the pleasures of the community – what few were afforded to her in the guise she wore – before she returned to the virtual nunnery of her childhood home.

She poured herself another large helping of red wine, then glanced around the room. Most of the townspeople were ignoring her now, talking amongst themselves or examining the room's décor with hushed conversation. Jessame found herself gazing around as well. She had visited Berenger's home only a few times during their childhood; he had come to her doorstep every morning, and in her youthful innocence she had never thought to question it. She had only been allowed to visit him the times he had encountered accidents at his home. Strange, he had always been surefooted and agile when he was with her, but somehow at home he had ended up with broken arms, twisted ankles, even a burned leg one time.

During those few visits she would play with Berenger here in the main receiving room, or sometimes in his father's library. Those were the only two rooms she had been granted access to. She remembered them as being sumptuous, almost garish, stocked with golden knick-knacks and embroidered tapestries. She recalled a beautiful desk with inlaid wood and carved legs that she and Berenger would play beneath.

Now the son had returned home after his father's death and the room had been redone in a much more elegant fashion. Dark burgundy tapestries hung on the walls, and the solid oak furniture had been pushed to the sides to make room for the guests. Candles shone on all walls to hold back the falling darkness.

All except one corner, which remained steadfastly tucked in shadows.

Jessame gently smiled; she knew who would be hidden away there. She walked forward to stand before him. His once handsome face was now creased by a jagged scar which began just over his left ear, zigged its way across his closed left eye, then crossed his brow to vanish into his greying sandy-blonde hair. His look was distant and haunted, deepening the wrinkles which lined his face. Even his clothing was somber grey, blending him further into the gloom.

She curtsied before him. "Roger. How did I know I would find you here?" she offered tenderly. "It looks like we are both the ignored ones tonight. You at least have a profession the townsfolk respect. For me, whether it is my look or my actions, the little ones are hurried off lest they be tainted by my breath."

Roger's eyes shadowed. "You can at least take off your dress, while I cannot undo my damaged face."

Jessame's laugh bubbled out of her rich and full. "You think things would go better for me if I removed my dress, then?"

Roger's mouth quirked, and then a smile spread across it as well. "I imagine not," he conceded with a chuckle.

"That's better," teased Jessame. "You are the only one who has been kind to me since I arrived; well, you and Mary, the seamstress who helped me with this new dress. I appreciate your welcome."

"I know what it is like to feel the displeasure of these townsfolk," he noted, nodding. "They are happy to have me make barrels for them or fix their shelves. However, when it comes to social events, they act as if my scar is catching."

"They are just jealous of your skills," she responded soothingly. She was fond of Roger; he was like the kindly uncle she never had. He smelled of sawdust and wood oils and, when she could get him talking, had shown a gentle, understanding nature.

"Well, apparently they want me to turn coal into gold," he grumbled, his gaze dimming again. "Just last week Lord Cavendish waltzed into my shop and instructed me to create him a new dining table made of his favorite elm tree, which had come down in those wild rain storms we had last month. I had it pulled in to my shop – and the bug damage is immense. There's no way to create the table that Lord Cavendish wants."

He sighed, his shoulders dropping. "He is adamant; he thinks I am simply holding out for additional money. He thinks more gold will fix any malady. But I am not a miracle worker."

Jessame's eyes lit up with delight. "Come with me for a moment, and I will show you a miracle," she promised.

Roger's gaze was wary, but he followed behind her as they left the noise and brightness of the main hall for the secluded quiet of the library. It was just as Jessame had remembered it. Shelves holding codices and scrolls lined the back wall, and windows, with thick curtains drawn, faced them. A large desk stood before the shelves, its fine inlay and imposing carved legs making an impressive sight in the flickering candlelight.

Roger's look became morose. "Oh, yes, the famous desk of Aldric. Is this supposed to make me feel any better?"

Jessame gave him a pat on the arm. "Bring over that candle from the shelf, will you?"

Roger retrieved the beeswax candle in its pewter holder, carrying it to the desk. In the light the desk almost glowed with its oak, elm, and birch inlays.

Jessame nodded her head at the ground. "Now sit on the rug with me."

Roger's lips pursed. "Besame," he ground out hesitantly, "it is not that I do not appreciate your offer, but -"

Jessame shook her head. "I am not suggesting a tryst," she countered with a chuckle. "I just want to show you something. Something about the desk. However, you must swear to me that you will never mention this to another living soul."

Roger blinked, but nodded. "Yes, certainly. I promise."

He paused a moment, then eased himself to sit on the thick brown rug which the desk rested on. Jessame sat alongside him, then leant back and looked up at the underneath of the desk.

She waved a hand to him. "Bring the candle over and take a look."

Roger leaned over on one arm and held up the candle with the other. Then he stopped, took in a long breath, and raised the flame higher for a better view.

Twisted folds of intertwining layered wood shimmered in candle light. The burl of a tree could be discerned, sawn length-wise. The result shimmered in the light, almost moving before their eyes, resembling an oceanscape with curling waves and receding foam.

Roger's voice was quiet awe. "Beautiful, simply beautiful."

Jessame smiled. "I thought, of all people, that you would appreciate this," she murmured.

Roger's eyes drank in the grain of the wood. "I never would have thought it. Thank you for sharing that with me; it has changed my outlook on what I can do."

Jessame's eyes drifted to the heavy wood leg which was closest to her, and she froze. There, carved into the oak in a hand she knew intimately, was a fish. The elegant, curved shape drew a half a circle with its body. She put a finger hesitantly to the figure, tracing its lines, feeling a connection through time to the boy who had made it. It seemed like yesterday …

There was a loud voice-clearing sound from the doorway, and Jessame scrambled to her feet, with Roger close beside her.

Berenger stepped around the corner of the doorway, his eyes moving from Roger's rumpled clothes to Jessame's quick smoothing down of her dress.

His eyes were unreadable in the dark. "I was just checking that everything was all right in here," he offered in a smooth voice.

Jessame's throat drew tight; she was unable to make a sound. It was all so sudden, still, to see him before her, to see her dreams brought to life.

After a long moment Roger stepped in to the silence. "We were just discussing the nature of beauty," he explained with a half-smile. "Nothing more."

Berenger pursed his lips. "Nothing more, and yet the most meaningful of topics," he returned, half to himself. "*Beauty lies in the depths of one's soul.*"

Jessame found herself echoing the proper Latin version of the phrase without thinking. "*In imo animo stat pulchritude.*"

Both men turned to stare at her, and she hoped the darkened room hid her furious blushing. She leaned heavily on her accent. "'Ot's what my priest made me repeat – God's Teeth, must've been a 'undred times a night - to repent for my sins."

"Yes, of course," returned Berenger evenly. "Well then, I must return to my other guests. They must wonder what is going on in here." He turned and was gone before she could say another word.

Roger looked after him. "He is right, of course," he mused. "The moment we step out of here together, the talk will begin. If you wish, I can do my best to set them straight."

Jessame chuckled. "Certainly, if you wish to help protect your reputation, I will do all I can." Her eyes twinkled. "However, I fear my own is beyond salvation."

Roger put out an arm to her. "In that case, let us face the callous town together and show them we are not afraid of their petty babble."

Jessame smiled, taking his arm, and together they strode out into the brightly lit hall, once again bringing all conversation to a stuttering, mouth-opened halt.

Roger did not falter; he guided Jessame over to the food table and selected raspberries for her, gathering them on a plate. In a moment a middle-aged woman, slim, wearing a simple but expertly crafted dress of pale blue, came over to join them.

"Ah, Roger, Besame, there you are," she greeted them with a smile. "I am so glad you both are here. I was beginning to feel quite alone."

Jessame smiled tenderly at Mary. "You have clothed most of the visitors here," she countered easily. "Of anybody, you should be the most welcome."

Mary blushed and looked down for a moment. "You are very sweet to say that, Besame," she whispered.

Roger handed the small plate of berries to Jessame, then assembled one for Mary. "You are well deserving of the praise," he murmured.

At the other end of the table, Lady Cavendish strolled up, a portly matron close at her side. The blonde gazed over the offerings with an approving eye. "Berenger knows quality when he sees it," she praised, "but no feast in London would be complete without a centerpiece of an elegant swan."

The matron's mouth went round with appreciation. "I have never tried such a dish," she gushed. "What does it taste like?"

Lady Cavendish gave a vague wave. "Oh, I really am not sure," she offered dismissively. "I hear they are a bit gamey. Their corpses are there for the display, for the show of extravagance." Her eyes lit up. "I shall show you on Sunday, when we have our soirée. And you must come in that fine new coach of yours, so I can show it to my husband. I am sure he will want to have one just like it." Her eyes turned to search the crowd. "Where is that man? Never around when money needs to be spent." She turned and strode into the group, the matron hard on her heels.

Jessame put her cup of wine down hard onto the table, staring after the woman. "She would slay a swan, just to have its dead body lie on a table?" she muttered, reining in her anger with effort. "Surely she knows they mate for life. What poor partner was left behind, bereft, all to stoke her vanity?"

Roger shook his head, then turned to look at Mary. "And you spent the past week in the company of her and her vain sister? You deserve the highest honors indeed for what you put up with," he suggested with a bit of heat. "Lady Cavendish's younger sister is beyond extravagant. Three dresses finished in the past two days? Just so she could be sure to have backups on hand in case she changed her mind?" He let out a snort. "The girl is spoiled rotten."

Jessame glanced around. "Is Cassandra here? I did not think I saw her."

Roger rolled his eyes. "The woman is undoubtedly waiting outside for her opportunity to make a grand entrance. One that nobody could miss."

Jessame bit her tongue. She had, in fact, done that very thing only a half hour earlier, although she gave herself dispensation for the cause in which she took the action. Cassandra's sole focus was her own ego.

There was a flurry of noise by the front of the room. Roger looked up, a wry grin creasing his face. "Speak of the …"

It was indeed the blonde beauty, a stunning younger version of Lady Cavendish, her dark violet dress exceedingly proper and still exuding almost a scent of luxury and beauty. Her hair was the color of liquid honey, cascading down her shoulders and rippling against the velvet of her clothing. Her mouth artfully pouted into a smile as she drew her older sister into an embrace, and then …

Jessame's heart pounded furiously in her chest, as if it were a trapped cat seeking to escape a cage sliding into a pond. Berenger had been brought forward. He was taking Cassandra's hand in his own, bowing to her, drawing closer to hear her greetings, and Jessame could not watch any further. She poured herself a fresh glass of wine punch, downed it all in one long draw, and closed her eyes.

It was going to be a long night.

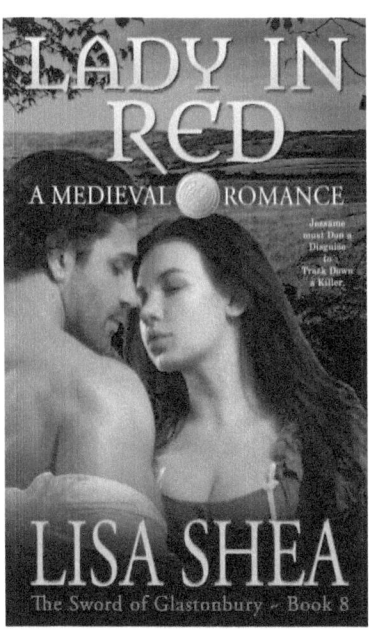

http://www.amazon.com/Lady-Red-Medieval-Romance-Glastonbury-ebook/dp/B0084S7X14/